ATONEMENT

a Novel

by

Paul F. Schmit

This book is a work of fiction. Names, characters, places, and incidents are the product of the author's imagination or are used fictitiously. Any resemblance to actual events, locales, or persons, living or dead, is coincidental

ISBN: 143927648X
ISBN-13: 9781439276488
Library of Congress Control Number: 2010909619
Cover design by David Denhart

DEDICATION

This novel is dedicated to My parents,
Fred and Eva Schmit. Thanks for the genes.

To my wife, Janet for standing beside
me and putting up with me.

Acknowledgements

I believe Hilary Clinton phrased it first, "It takes a village to raise a child." I'd like to paraphrase that sentiment. "It takes a village to write a book." From the many folks at Coffee and Critique—Lou, Donna, Claudia, Judy, Nick, Doyle, Alice, and a host of others your contributions, large and small, are greatly appreciated.

To Gary Walton and Eldon Ukestad of the Minnesota Bureau of Criminal Apprehension, BCA, for answering all my questions about nearly everything under the sun relating to fingerprints and firearms.

To my fellow "Sisters" at the Greater St. Louis Chapter of Sisters in Crime for all their support. Special thanks to Jo Hiestand for her excellent editing efforts. Goodness knows I needed that.

To the fine folks at the St. Peters Barnes and Noble for putting up with my corny jokes and your words of encouragement and the many friends I've made while hammering away at my computer. Fellow customers and employees

Fred, Lloyd, Victor, Bill, Lynn, Dave, Nate, Cynthia, Anne, Shelly, Melissa, Melanie, Stephanie No. 1 and 2, and all other fine folks at B and N.

Special thanks to Darlene Gardner for spending a morning taking my picture, given what she had to work with, she did good.

There is one person in particular to whom I owe a huge debt, Mr. Noah Webster Every word in *Atonement,* except one, is lifted from him.

Last of all, but not least, any technical or grammatical errors are wholly owned by me.

ATONEMENT

a Novel

Chapter 1

I'm heading to the shower when the phone rings. Caller ID says it's that pesky Ruth Ann Boyer.

I ignore it.

No doubt she's near tears, aching to apologize for last night when she said, "I never, ever, want to see you again, Archie Schultz."

She probably wants to make up by fixing my breakfast. Hah! Let her stew. After all, a man can only take so many, 'I never, ever's. Right? Although if I had a dime every time she's said that to me, I'd've collected close to thirty bucks in the past few months.

By the time I'm finished, my specially brewed coffee has dropped about twenty degrees and barely raises blisters on the roof of my mouth.

There's a pounding on the front door. My butler is temporarily away from the country, so I answer it myself.

The woman of my affections is standing there. The first words out of Ruth Ann's mouth are: "Sometimes, Archie, I can not fathom how you do your job."

Her statement takes me aback. Yet, her love and kindness so eloquently expressed are almost more than I can bear this early in the morning.

She's wearing her typical look of humbleness.

Her eyebrows look like furrows in Farmer Jones' field. Straight and dark. Her mouth looks pretty much the same. Her right foot is slightly forward and she's tapping her toe.

"And just why didn't you answer the phone?"

My shoulders droop, my eyes look like a lost puppy dog's, and I respond somewhat less than forcibly. "Busy?"

Obviously satisfied with my answer, she rushes into my arms to beg forgiveness, misses by at least six feet, and continues to the kitchen.

"Where the hell are your cups today?"

I marvel how she overcomes her *faux pas*.

She recovers, finds a cup, fills it, takes a sip and makes a face.

"Yuck." Then Ruth Ann adds cream. Lots and lots and lots of cream. Good thing I wasn't planning on making a strawberry/whipped cream dessert tonight. After she wrecks my ambrosia, she says, "I'll lay it out for you. Mayor Jackman was found this morning."

"I wasn't aware he was lost. He told me himself, he and Helen were taking a week's vacation to get some sun in Florida. Did Rupert take a wrong turn and head for Wisconsin?"

"No, he didn't do anything of the sort. Let me take that back. He must have. He was found floating in Clover Bottom Lake. A rather large hole between his eyes."

Chapter 2

It takes me a minute to decide how this particular event is apparently my fault and why it means I'm not doing my job. I am after all, Chief of Police in West Clover Bottom, Minnesota. Now, it appears, I no longer have a boss.

"Why do you know this bit of information and I don't?" I ask from my six foot two height and lord it over my five foot four adversary.

"My Uncle George—you know, our city pier's caretaker?—found him. Rather, his body, banging up against the dock. Since he trusts the competence of his intelligent newspaper-editor-and-crack-reporter-niece over, say, an incompetent law enforcement officer, it was only natural he called me first."

I immediately think of my favorite writer, Sir Arthur Conan Doyle.

This dastardly dead likely means this lovely lady is *not* going to be making my breakfast.

✧ ✧ ✧

I tell Ruth Ann I'll drive. We head the short distance to the town dock.

Over the years, as folks from the Cities sought *The Best Fishing in the Whole Upper Midwest*—by the way, West Clover Bottom's official motto—our humble lakeside has mushroomed in size. The dock has been expanded and the city erected a full-fledged, full service marina. Ruth Ann's uncle is on the city payroll as caretaker.

Our town of nine hundred and twenty-one is quite prosperous with its wide, well maintained streets, manicured lawns, and a city-owned designer marina. All of this thanks to my ancestors, great, great grandfather John A. and his son, my great grandfather, John B. They built WCB from the profit of their lumbering business. Then they damned Clover Bottom creek. The result is the lake where our beloved mayor was found.

Did I mention it's my family's tradition to name the first male in the generation 'John'? I'm the fifth John, hence my real name is, John E. Schultz. That is until Ruth Ann decided to change it to Archie, when we were on a fifth grade field trip to St. Louis where I fell in love with the Arch.

Uncle George is waiting for us, puffing a big fat cigar, and sipping a cup of coffee. I've known him since I was a tad. I also know his coffee will raise your blood alcohol off the charts.

Add to that he's somehow related to the Schultz clan, and therefore Ruth Ann is, in all likelihood, some distant cousin.

Being nimble minded, I ask, "Where's his wife, Helen? Why didn't she report Rupert missing?"

I see Ruth Ann's head shake and shrugs. That tells me she has no idea either.

Questions to be answered later.

Her uncle's holding a pike-pole and stabbing at Rupert. Through a dense cloud of smoke I make out George's face.

Cough, cough. "Gimme that coffee, boy."

I hate it when he calls me 'boy.' I pick up his oversized cup and make the mistake of getting it close to my nose, inhaling some vapors. One more whiff and I'll have to arrest myself for public drunkenness.

I *trip* over a dock plank and spill his coffee. Disaster is adverted as I direct it away from his smoldering cigar.

"Why're you poking our mayor with that damn pike, George?"

"'Fraid the wind'll blow the old coot away. Scare off biness."

"Sure you are. It looks to me like you're trying to bury his corpse."

I dig out my cell phone and page through my contact list which, I swear, holds every citizen in town. I scroll to Doc Swenson, our aged coroner, and hit the call button.

"Doc," I say, "best get out to the dock."

His crude response wouldn't be permitted on cable TV.

When he's done speaking, I exhale and say, "Look, if I wanted the FBI, the CIA, and NSA to know, I'd call them directly. Just come over here. K?"

Ruth Ann pipes up. "That's no way to talk to Uncle Pete. He's a sweet, elderly gentleman. I want you to apologize."

God, is every male in this town, besides me, her uncle?

I'm sure if I respond, I'll collect another dime, so I keep quiet. Perhaps, if I'm remorseful, I can con her into making breakfast after we're done here. I mull over the alternatives. A frozen TV breakfast with green tinged sausage that was fresh right after the Civil War or humbling myself to Uncle Pete.

Doc finally shows up and immediately steps over to George. "Got any yer coffee?"

"Damn cop over there"—he's pointing somewhere way off to my right—"spilt it."

Since there's only four of us around, I figure George had a few cups earlier and he really means me.

"Can't do whatever in Hades I'm supposed to be doing until I get my coffee, boy."

"Any left in your five gallon thermos, George?"

"Might be a cup or two."

Duty calls and I head for George's office at the end on the pier.

When I return, the uncles smile and pat me on the back. Almost in unison they say, "Mighty nice of you, son."

I glance over to Ruth Ann, making sure she's caught my thoughtfulness. She rolls her eyes as if to say, "Should have done it sooner."

Pete slurps down his drink, belches, and speaks. "So what in Sam Hill did you call me out here for?"

I walk over to the side of the dock and stare at the water. No Rupert. Maybe the wind blew him under the dock. I lie down and dangle my head over the edge. Nope. Still no Rupert.

George staggers over and lets one rip. Fortunately his cigar has gone out or we would have the first documented human flame thrower.

I stumble, trying to get above the fumes, and end up falling into the lake.

Lady Luck is with me as the water is only up to my chin. Sputtering, I splash around trying to make it to the shallows. I bang my toes on something solid, and fall completely under the waves. When I finally surface, Ruth Ann is mumbling. Faint noises reach my water-logged ears. Sounds like she wants to see me soon, or something like that.

The uncles are guffawing and tossing back more coffee.

I look around and see a few bubbles rising. Apparently one of George's jabs at Rupert punched a small hole.

"Give me that pike, George. I think I know where our mayor is."

Chapter 3

Fortunately, Uncle George didn't poke Rupert too badly or he would've skittered off like a punctured balloon. I'm waist deep, surrounded by rising decomposition gases. I grab at George's pole. Inadvertently, of course, I jerk the handle, hoping to have some company.

Maybe I should've paid more attention in high school physics class. Too late I recall that for every action there's an equal and opposite reaction. Trying to pull a two hundred and fifty pound man off balance when floundering in water tends to be counterproductive.

I think the lake must have lowered three inches based on the amount of water I swallowed while righting myself.

When I surface again, Ruth Ann is rolling on the dock. No doubt concerned for my safety.

I glower at George. "Gimme that pole, damnit."

While I was conducting my geologic survey of the bottom, I spotted some ropes. I hook them with the pike and tug. Almost the same reaction I had with George. I flop down, butt first, in the water.

From my sitting position, I attempt to bark an order. The lake level drops another inch as I manage to tell Ruth Ann to call Dutch.

Dutch Schultz is my cousin. He's twenty three, which pretty much matches his IQ. He came by his moniker because of his insatiable appetite for anything dealing with the New York gangs of the Thirties. The original Dutch Schultz was his hero. I sometimes wonder about reincarnation.

One major difference between the two of them is my cousin is pretty much harmless. At four feet six and one half inches no one gives him any lip.

Oh, did I mention that's the distance between his shoulders?

From head to ground, Dutch measures six-eight. He also weighs two hundred and ninety pounds. I'm betting a full gram of that is fat.

Our prosperous town has the best behaved teen-aged boys in the State of Minnesota thanks to Dutch. If anyone tries to mess with a townsfolk or a business, Dutch just picks the offender up, and tosses him into the lake. He makes sure he goes in head first.

Five minutes after he's summoned, the dock shakes as he strides right up to Ruth Ann.

"You're lookin' mighty purty today, Ruth Ann. Purtyest ever."

"Thank you, Dutch. Must say you're probably the most handsomest Schultz in the county."

He turns red and nearly dissolves.

She obviously wants to stay in his good graces and gives him a peck on his cheek. I know she really wanted to say Dutch was the second most handsomest Schultz. He sees me up to my waist in the water and starts to laugh.

"What the hell you doin' there, cousin? 'Resting some walleye?"

Ruth Ann finds this hilarious and slaps her knee.

"Grab this pole, cuz, and walk to shore."

He has an easier time pulling what's got to be close to four hundred pounds than I do getting to solid ground.

Twelve feet from the water's edge, the lake shallows quickly. The question of where the mayors wife, Helen, is, is answered.

The reason Rupert bobbed to the surface is his killer failed to understand the concept of decomposing body buoyancy. Helen was well weighed down and was a frail person to start with. The three concrete blocks attached to her legs were enough to keep her on the bottom.

When I say Helen was frail I don't mean ninety year-old-lady-frail. I mean blonde-bimbo-twenty-five-year-old-trophy-wife-frail.

Sixty one year-old Rupert's first wife died three winters ago in a car crash on a icy turn. Head on.

A year later, down in the Cities attending a mayor's conference, he hooked up with Helen, aka, *Stormie Knight,* at some exotic dance club. After a whirlwind three-week courtship he proposed, and a month later, married.

Anyhow, Rupert was on the surface because of the lack of weight. Hell, he'd need at least three times as many blocks to keep him down. Done properly, we might never have known he was sleeping with the fishes, as my cousin would say.

I keep Doc, George, Dutch, and Ruth Ann several feet away while I start my investigation.

There is no 'large' hole between their eyes. I figure the size of the wound grew every time Uncle George swilled a cup of his coffee.

Both Jackmans were shot execution style. One bullet to the head. An entrance wound, but no exit. That tells me their killer used a 22. Rupert's back pocket contains his billfold, six hundred in cash, three credit cards, along with a host of other plastic.

Helen, aka *Stormie*, is wearing a ruby necklace. Her fingers are adorned with expensive looking jewelry, capped off with a diamond that nearly makes the use of concrete blocks unnecessary.

My highly trained eye concludes robbery wasn't the motive. That, however, raises the question of why? Did someone have it in for the mayor, or his bimbo wife? I've never heard anyone bad-mouthing Rupert. I'm not so sure about Helen, though. I better find some time to beat it down to the Cities and pay a visit to The Gentlemen's Lounge. The bar where Helen performed.

Chapter 4

I know the Jackmans left for Florida Saturday. Today is Thursday. Based on their state of decomposition, they've probably been in the water at least five days. We've had an unusually warm spell for the first week of May, and I need to test the water temperature.

There's a thermometer in my evidence kit. It's a gen-u-wine imported, hand tooled, imitation vinyl bag I picked up for a song on e-Bay. I hurry to the end of the dock. I know the water's twenty feet deep here and it'll give me a decent reading. Providing I can keep from falling in.

Two minutes later, it registers sixty-one. Thinking back to *The Effects of Water On Human Decomposition*, a class that had me on the edge of my seat. Partially due to interest, but mostly trying to keep my lunch down. Hell of a thing to have right after eating, especially cafeteria food, which I generally had problems keeping down anyway.

At one time, the prof said, "Decomp begins when the water temperature reaches forty degrees." He had a high pitched, grating voice. Kinda like the howl when your power steering unit is out.

"The warmer, the faster. As the bugs begin their insipid process, the body fills with gasses and it becomes buoyant. In all likelihood, you'll hear people call them floaters. A term I find almost as abhorrent as the reason they're in the water to start with. Terrible, just terrible."

In this case, Rupert was very buoyant, until Uncle George deflated his ego, so to speak. Three hunks of concrete were hardly enough to keep him with his new friends, the fishes.

I squat down to look at Rupert's fingers. They remind me of Clover Bottom Bratwursts. I'm definitely switching brands on my next cook-out.

Maybe, if one of the Jackmans struggled, there might be some evidence under their fingernails. I don't see anything, but bag their hands just in case.

"Hey, Doc. I make the murders to be Sunday. Your thoughts?"

Doc has trouble walking. It takes some effort on my part to keep him from wading to the drop-off. I wonder how many cups of George's coffee he's had.

"Sunny, you zay, boy?" Followed by a belch that rolls across the lake.

"Right. Given his state of decomposition . . ." I might as well be talking to Dutch. I stop in mid-sentence to pull Doc back out of the water.

He hiccups, belches again, and looks at the bodies. "Why you got them tied to them concrete blocks? 'Fraid they're gonna run off?"

He finds this very funny and staggers back into the lake. I'm tempted to let him go. Instead I motion for Dutch and tell him to put our inebriated coroner in my car.

"Ugg," Dutch's way of acknowledging my request. Doc is unceremoniously tossed into my back seat. Head first.

Next, I call Ruth Ann over to tell her she can do her competent-editor-crack-reporter thing for her Saturday paper.

"Do me a favor though, don't mention *where* the Jackmans were shot. Just say they were victims of a random shooting. K?"

She's making notes and nods. After she fills up another page, she gives me the most loving smile and whispers in my ear.

"I've been here over an hour watching you flop around in the water and I'm getting hungry. You have to go home to change clothes. Tell ya what. Take me along and I'll fix your favorite."

My legs turn to jelly. "Really?"

"Uh huh. Cream cheese stuffed French toast. And *I'll* make coffee."

Ha! The secret's finally revealed. Spend an hour in Lake Clover Bottom wrestling with dead bodies is all it takes to get her to fix breakfast.

Wonder what I'll have to do tomorrow?

Chapter 5

Before I can indulge my breakfast fantasy—because the incapacitated coroner is in the back seat of my cruiser—I call my deputy, Jerome Dixon.

"Howdy, boss. What's up?"

"We got our hands full. Need you out at the pier, ASAP."

"What's goin' on? Can I use my *sireen*? Can I run the light if it's red?"

"NO! Just drop whatever you're doing and get out here. I'll explain when you arrive."

"Ten-four. Roger. All clear—"

I hang up knowing he's going to reel off a dozen sign offs.

Next I call the ambulance and request its presence.

"What for, Archie?"

Getting tired of this. I want people to do what I ask without all these damn questions.

My frustration slips out. "Listen, Newberry. Just get out to the town dock. No sirens, no lights, no running the stop light. Just come on out."

Doc moans in the back seat. I'm starving, drenched to the skin, and freezing my butt off. Ruth Ann and everyone wants a detailed explanation.

She senses my frustrations and kisses me, a long, warm passionate kiss.

I'm speechless. That's twice this morning. Since I already know what it takes to get her to make breakfast, I simply have to add working with a bunch of characters to get a kiss.

Not a bad deal, all-in-all.

The ambulance arrives first, Newbury Jones sees the bodies, and loses his last dozen meals.

After he cleans off his shoes, I ask, "Where's your partner?"

He's turned away from the scene so I have to walk around him to speak face-to-face. His countenance looks like an old barn painted white, sometime before the turn of the century, the Twenty Century, and hasn't seen a painter's brush since.

"She's sick today. I'll need some help from ya."

Gad. Ruth Ann wants to make my delayed breakfast and Newbury needs help. But, being a service-first cop, I set aside my gastronomical needs, as well as my romantic feelings, and volunteer to assist.

"That's nice of ya, Chief, I really do appreciate that."

Newbury opens the rear doors and points to a locker. "Body bags in there."

My aforementioned razor sharp mind grasps the situation. He is not about to fulfill his job description. I open the damn locker and wrest out two bags.

This is NOT going to be the highlight of my day. No, make that week. On second thought, year.

I struggle to put on a pair of latex gloves, tear one, put on another and carefully cut away the ropes on Rupert's and Helen's legs, taking precautions not to disturb the knots. There's nothing I like better, other than several sharp sticks in my eyes, than working on bloated, decomposing bodies.

I manage to stuff the former mayor and West Clover Bottom's First Lady into their bags. "How about a little help here, buddy? Rupert weighs a ton," I grunt, trying to lift Rupert.

"Yeah, sure."

Newbury sits on the rear fender and lowers the vehicle two inches. Wow! What cooperation.

Fortunately, Helen is easy and I slam the doors shut.

"Anytime you need some assistance, Newbury, just call my deputy. K?"

"Well, thanks fer the offer, Chief. I surely will do that."

As the ambulance leaves, Jerome's cruiser coasts into the parking lot. He gets out, yawns, scratches, and slowly looks around before ambling over.

He is the embodiment of every eccentric deputy ever seen on TV. Although he leans towards Barney Fife. He even has most of Barney's mannerisms. I inherited him when I took over the WCB Police Department.

I don't bother asking why a five minute drive, even if our single stoplight was red, took nearly an hour. He more than likely figured we had a dangerous situation and needed to go home to hunt for his pistol.

And bullets.

"What's the problem, Chief? Other than somebody's been littering the reserved parking space with some damn old blocks."

I take him aside and explain about the mayor and his wife.

As he tries to comprehend the news, I say, "Put on some gloves and bag the ropes and blocks. Haul 'em to the station and unload them into the back room. Can you do that by noon?"

Catching sarcasm never was Barney's, uh, Jerome's strong point.

I can finally turn my attention to Ruth Ann and breakfast. As soon as I step into my cruiser, she bolts out.

Running away, she yells out, "You absolutely stink, Archie. Until you bathe in something like AXE, I never want to see you again."

I suggest she ride on the hood. "That way you'll always be upwind."

She stomps off to Dutch and says something.

Whenever she speaks to him, like earlier on the dock, my cuz becomes dumb-struck and mortified. He turns as red as a big, fat beet. I can imagine that she wants him to drive her to my place to get her car. So, I get into my cruiser and start heading home. Twenty feet later, I can't stand myself, stop, and step out for some fresh air.

Apparently my *eau de cologne* has miraculous powers of penetration. Both of them are *pretending* to gag. Dutch punches the gas and burns rubber. I wonder if I can drive while sitting on the hood.

I power down all the car windows, turn the A/C to max, and drive with my head out of the window. Allowing myself to breathe every two minutes, I pull up to Doc's house. Uncle George's coffee is pretty well worn off . He's fighting to get out. I guess my delicate aroma has gotten to him as well. Maybe if I can bottle the smell, it'd make a best selling hangover drug. I manage to jerk him out and toss him onto the lawn and race off for home.

As expected, Ruth Ann waits for me. A sopping wet towel wrapped around her face with only her green eyes visible. A can of Febreze in each hand. I'm enveloped in a cloud so thick I can't see. 'Course, if my eyes were open, that might help.

I immediately head for the shower. Every step of the way I'm followed by, fzzzzzzt, fzzzzzzt, fzzzzzzt.

I slam the bathroom door, but she's right outside, fzzzzzz-ting through the keyhole and under the door.

After two hot showers, I wrap a towel around me and make a break for my closet. I expect to be sprayed, but I'm rewarded with the sounds of rattling pots and pans.

Ah, a Ruth Ann breakfast.

There's a note on my bedroom door along with a garbage bag.

"Put your clothes in here and don't even think they can be worn a second time. If I ever see you in them again, I'll never speak to you."

I wonder if I can chalk up another dime.

It's signed: RA.

I add a T, then quickly crumble the note and toss it into the bag.

For the second time this morning, I graciously descend the grand staircase. Funny, no music is playing and no one is around to see my arrival. Some other time.

In the kitchen, Ruth Ann holds an arm out. "Not one more step, mister."

Her cute, perky, up-turned nose in working overtime. She reminds me of a rabbit with sinus problems.

Grinning, "Is that Calvin Klein's *CK ONE* I smell?"

I bow in agreement.

More nose twitching. "And *Old Spice*?"

I smile, with hooded eyes, conveying my *haute couture*.

Cough, cough. Followed by a sneezing fit that would have buried ECB in a foot of dust, had I been making coffee.

"Tell me that isn't Liz Claiborne's *Eternity*. Where is your sense of smell? Back on the dock?"

Fzzzzzzt, fzzzzzzt, fzzzzzzt.

I manage to get through four pieces of stuffed French toast, a glass of OJ, and what Ruth Ann jokingly calls coffee.

Hoping for another kiss before she leaves, I close my eyes, pucker up, and feel a piece of paper being stuck to my maple syrup coated lips.

The banging of the screen door, along with the growl of her souped up sports car tells me she left.

I peel off the note.

'Kiss, kiss'.

I look around. God, that woman creates a mess.

While doing the dishes, I realize I'm stuck with a messy kitchen, two murders and zero clues.

Chapter 6

The part about no clues is not entirely true. I know the Jack-mans aren't victims of a robbery gone wrong. There's the ropes and concrete blocks, and I'm pretty sure they were killed Sunday. One thing was drummed into our skulls at the U by Prof Joel.

"There's always a transfer of evidence between the perp and the vic."

Doc Joel made his point abundantly clear as he thumped on our skulls. Then we have to find his skin cells.

This was a difficult task for one of our colleagues. He was maybe ten years our senior. 'Ol Morgenthau, we called him. He had the worst case of dandruff I've ever seen.

If, a real big if, the Jackmans' killer wasn't gloved, there might be DNA stuck in the twists of the rope.

I'll call one of my other profs to see if DNA might survive five days under water. Doc Schugal is the guy who wrote the paper *The Effects of Water On Human Decomposition*.

My first task, though, is to call Rupert's son before he reads about his dad in the Minneapolis paper.

I make sure Maggie has food in her dish and refill her water pitcher. For some unknown reason, my cat's brain cell tells her water in her Garfield bowl isn't nearly as good as out of an old creamer. I guess it keeps the water wetter.

In payment for being pampered, she occasionally catches a mouse. Cats!

After drying the last pan, I drive to the two-storey Municipal Building, home of my office. It and the jail are located on the lower level. In the bull pen of the station is, Barn, uh, Jerome's desk. He shares it with Alexia Johnson, my night-shift deputy, although she's on vacation this week. Towards the back is our luxurious six-cell jail. There's the normal buzz as I enter the upper level, home of the city offices. The lack of noise tells me Jerome hasn't made it back yet. If he had, I'd be pummeled with questions.

I motion to Jacqueline Mortenson, Rupert's secretary, and usher her into his office, suggest she sit, and break the news. I'm pretty sure her scream alerts the entire office staff something's wrong. They must think I'm attacking her.

I steal a quick glance at Rupert's window that overlooks the lake to ensure her Beverly Sills-like soprano exclamation didn't crack it.

She's acting like people you sometimes see who wail, tear at their hair, and roll around on the ground in their grief. In this case, though, she rolls on Rupert's carpeted floor.

Jackie, as we all call her, switches gears and goes into denial. "Are you sure? It must be a mistake. I don't believe you. You're wrong, wrong, wrong."

A crowd is gathering. I see them peeking though our former mayor's office window. Ignoring them, I offer Jackie what comfort I can. They are becoming vocal so I give her a hug and leave her to her grief.

With the entire staff assembled, I give them the bad news. Fifteen minutes later, I've answered all questions I can. Not surprisingly, nothing will get done today. Probably for the next few days.

Back in Rupert's office, I tell the distraught secretary I have to call his son. She nods and through her tears shows me his Rolodex. There are two listings for Hank Jackman. One for 'HM' and the other, 'WK'. Figuring he's at WK, I try that first.

I've known about Hank all my life. He was quite a star pitcher for the U baseball team. Came close to making it to the Bigs with the Minnesota Twins. But blew out his arm first year on their Triple A team.

The conversation is tough. How do you tell someone his dad and step-mom were murdered? It takes a lot out of me and I head to the offices of *The West Clover Bottom Clarion* to see if I can commiserate with Ruth Ann.

Before I leave, I take a minute to look at Rupert's desk. The usual stuff: a blotter, and a gold pen and pencil set. He also has a day calendar. One of those reminders ones? One you enter activities for the day. I flip through it and nearly miss something. I go back to last Saturday and see the following week is blanked out. In bold letters he spelled out FLORIDA.

What is strange is the page for the preceding Friday is missing. I file this info away and start to leave for Ruth Ann's.

Before I can get up from Rupert's desk, Jackie enters and plops down in the chair across from me. She's dry eyed now. I gather the puddle scoping under the door came from her.

"Yes?"

"I'm sorry to bother you, Archie, but I still can't believe he's dead. I told him many times. Yes sir, many times."

"What did you tell the mayor?"

"I told him she was all wrong for him. She'd do him in one of these days. I told him. I really did."

I'm getting a picture here. I'm not ready to declare it yet, but almost. Apparently, his secretary had a few words with Rupert about Helen.

"What led you to this conclusion, Jackie?"

"Well, first of all, look at the age difference. Rupert was thirty-six years her senior. Can any marriage take that? I told him she was all wrong for him. That's what I told him. Yes siree. I didn't mince any words. Not one."

"You worked for him for some time, didn't you?"

"Forty years, I did. I saw it all. His first wife. Now she was better than that hussy, Helen, ever thought of being. Then, their kids. I was there for him when he had his problems with Joyce. I helped him get through it all. Then Joyce died in that awful accident. I hear her brakes failed; that's why she died in that crash."

She's been talking faster than a machine gun can spit out lead. I catch a breath for Jackie. Someone's gotta breathe.

Fortunately, she stops to cry some more. I say, "I'm sorry for your loss, Jackie. I'll leave you with your memories."

Before she can regale me with more, I bolt out of the office and rush to Ruth Ann's business.

I enter her office. She's bent over what looks like a draft of Saturday's front page. She doesn't see me so I use the time to enjoy the view.

If you look at her quickly, you'd think she was Audrey Hepburn. Sweet, innocent, the girl next door. Her dark auburn hair is cut pixie style. She's got that cute button nose and there's a pencil behind her ear. Her shredded-knee jeans fit her verrry nicely. As does her beige blouse. Oh, there's one minor difference.

Ruth Ann is Audrey with an attitude.

"A-hem," I say to attract her attention.

No doubt she's thrilled to see me. So thrilled, she fails to look up.

"Stop pestering me, K?"

I wasn't aware walking into her office was considered pestering. Second. She's taunting me with *my* use of the abbreviated 'Okay.'

Right now, I don't need this and turn to walk out.

"Oh, come on back. I was just—"

I assume the look on my face is what stops her.

She rushes around the counter and into my arms. This time she nearly knocks me down.

"What's the matter? You…you look awful."

I go for the max of sympathy and exaggerate the time I spent talking to the office staff and Hank.

"I just spent an excruciating forty-five minutes telling everyone in City Hall about Rupert and Helen. Then another twenty minutes on the phone with Hank. He fell apart."

It works and I get a hug and a peck on the cheek.

Really, though, I hate this part of my job. I became a detached professional recovering the bodies. But there's nothing detached about telling the next of kin and friends about the death of a loved one. Now I have to face who did this, and why?

Rupert had been our mayor for nigh on to forty years. Through his leadership, we have the best schools and teachers in the state. Ninety-eight percent of our kids graduate from high school and seventy percent of those attend college. They become doctors, lawyers, scientists.

He wisely used the legacy my ancestors left. A shrewd investor and pinched pennies were necessary. Our town's bank account is in the eight figures.

Now that he's gone, I feel the burden.

I telegraph my despair. Ruth Ann holds me closer. There's no attitude now. All I want this instant is to leave town with her and never return.

We silently communicate our feeling for each other as she breaks the embrace. The brief interval recharges my batteries.

Not willing to let go, I pull her back and whisper, "The Clover Bottom Inn opens tomorrow night. Be my date?"

I figure she accepts, based on the kiss I get.

I try to keep that feeling as I head for the hospital.

In the morgue there are two murdered people who need me to be a cop, not some blubbering idiot that can't face up to the task. I know I'm only thirty, but I can handle the investigation. I suck it up and put on my cop face.

Chapter 7

Before continuing to the hospital, I detour by my office. I want to give the ropes a quick once over. Sometimes, Barn...ah, Jerome, surprises me. He's in the office, working on paperwork. Hopefully writing up the crime scene report.

"Hey, Archie."

"Hey Bar ...Jerome." I have got to break this habit. 'What's up?"

"Got the evidence logged in. Even put the bags in the back like you wanted."

"Good. I'm debating whether or not to take everything to the BCA or examine it here."

"Don't doubt your abilities, Chief, but them boys in St. Paul, they're pretty good, too." He pauses and adds, "Figure we got our hands full up here. Hate to have you tied up."

Apparently the irony of his statement finally sinks in as he nearly falls off his chair laughing.

"That there was a good one, right, Archie?"

For once my mouth waits for my brain. "Yes, Jerome, a real good one. Makes sense." Like I said, sometimes Jerome surprises me.

"I'm going to call the Bureau and see if they can fit us in. Want to drive down there tomorrow? Maybe escort the deceased as well."

His face loses its color. So do his arms. Probably his whole body. I expect to hear drip, drip, drip as blood leaks into the basement.

"Would I have to ride with dead people?"

"No, just give the ambulance an escort."

There is one thing my deputy loves about being a cop. Using, in his words, the *sireen*.

His blood makes a rapid return from the basement and his eyes glow. He has the happiest look on his face as he appears to contemplate four hours of using the *sireen*.

I'm sure he and Newberry'll decide they'll need it on the way home, too.

"Sure thing, Archie. Anything to help out."

I nod and disappear into my office to call the BCA— Minnesota Bureau of Criminal Apprehension

"BCA," a pleasant sounding woman says.

"This is Chief Archie Schultz from West Clover Bottom."

I swear I hear muffled laughter.

The gal, her voice choking, responds, "Yes, Chief?"

"I'm afraid we're in need of your services. We had a double murder up here. Got two autopsies and some evidence for you folks to look over."

There was no hint of laughter now. "Yes, sir. Let me connect you with the right people."

I'm connected and make arrangements for Jerome to travel to St. Paul.

I holler out, "Jerome, come in for a moment."

I relay my conversation with the BCA. I swear his feet never touch the floor as he leaves.

I suspect he missed one or two minor details so I call him back in.

"Review for me what you're doing tomorrow."

A huge grin splits his face. It extends further than the old 'ear-to-ear'. His mouth probably meets behind his neck.

"Me and Newberry gonna take the ev-i-dense and bodies to the BCA."

"You got it half right. The bodies go to Ramsey Hospital. K?"

"I don't know where that is."

"One. Drop off the ropes and blocks with the BCA. They're on Maryland Avenue in St. Paul. Take the department's GPS, and to make sure you program it right I'll draw you a map."

"That'll help, Archie."

"Two. Take the mayor's and Helen's bodies to Ramsey. It's now called Regions, but a lot of people still call it Ramsey. You only have to go a couple of miles from the BCA building. Ask them for directions. By the way, go easy on the *sireen*. You don't need to use it going through towns, especially St. Paul. K?"

"Can I at least use the lights?"

"No."

I watch Jerome deflate.

He drags himself out of my office.

I deflate as well. I've put off going to the morgue long enough.

Chapter 8

A thought strikes me as I leave for the hospital. This'd be a great time to do a little digging into Helen's past. Besides, who wants to spend time in some old morgue? With dead bodies?

I figure if I leave in about thirty minutes, I'll be in St. Paul right about noon. From my college years, I know that was a good time to catch the lunch-time crowd. The gals would put on a great display. Not that I ever visited a place like that. Just what some of my chums in school told me.

My trip is without event and at twelve-thirty I park across the street from the club. There's a steady stream of suited males entering. Not all folks are obvious businessmen, some are in old shabby army fatigues. Others look like they were bikers—long hair, lots of leather outer clothes, and a ton of chains. Someday, I suspect, they'll be hanging from their noses.

Rather than flashing my badge and getting in free, I pay the entrance fee. That way I'll get a better idea of what's going on.

My entrance is in the middle of an act. The lights are dim and, from where I'm standing, the performer looks pretty good. I move closer to the stage and see she's a gyrating ad for that TV evangelist's wife's line of cosmetics. Probably could use the woman's make-up applicator to mud drywall joints. Three minutes is all I can stomach and I wave a waitress over. Oh my, what a set of charms she's supporting. Whomever manufactures silicone gel probably signed her up to be their spokeswoman. What advertising for them.

"Hi, ya, honey. Can little ol' me get you a drink? Maybe champagne?"

She ought to be in sales. I debate her offer, but resist. I remove my badge and dangle it in front of her.

"Officer, I'm over twenty-one. I can prove it, I just look eighteen."

"I'll take your word for it. The owner around? I need to speak to him."

"It's a her. I'll get her. You're not going to hassle me, are you? You believe me, don't you? I really am twenty-one."

"No problem. Just need to see the owner."

The youngster dashes off and disappears through a door flanking the stage. A few minutes later, my waitress is accompanied by an older woman. I guess she's the boss. Her employee is gesturing in my direction and from her body language, she's convinced I'm here to arrest her.

I gather I'm not the first cop to make the assumption about the suitability of the girl, as the owner is striding my way like a steam locomotive building up speed. Chug, chug, chug.

"Let me see your badge, copper."

I don't want to get into a spitting contest, so I hand it over. She scrutinizes it and then states the obvious. "You're not from around here. Where the hell is this West Clover Bottom, anyhow?"

Using my patentable smile, I flash it at her, knowing she'll apologize for her rudeness and beg forgiveness faster than Ruth Ann ever thought of.

She starts with, "So you don't believe Misty's twenty-one, huh?"

"Who's Misty?"

"Misty Skyes. Your waitress."

"I assure you, ma'am. I have no interest in Misty's age, or for that matter, her real name. I'm here to talk about Helen, ah, Stormie Knight."

"What about her. She in trouble again? Some sugar daddy get upset and bust her chops?"

This paints an entirely new picture of our former mayor's wife. Rest her soul. "Actually, I didn't catch your name."

"That makes two of us, I don't know yours either."

"I'm Archie Schultz, Chief of Police in WCB."

"What the hell is WCB stand for. Oh, I get it. It's that Bottom place, right?"

"Yes. That place."

"You're not shittin' me about Misty, are you?"

"No, I'm not. Ms—"

"Thelma Dankirk. If you're not here about Misty, what then?"

"Stormie?"

"Oh, right. What about her?"

"She used to work here, correct?"

"Right as rain."

"You probably haven't heard. She was murdered. Along with her husband, the Mayor of West Clover Bottom."

My news is a shock to Thelma, as she sits down. If I look closely, I can just make out the tiniest tear forming. Or, she has something in her eye. "Can you tell me something about her? You mentioned a sugar daddy."

"Oh yeah. Stormie has a real sweet tooth, if you catch my drift. Loved to satisfy her craving. Seems she had a new man every couple of weeks. Some were a little on the rough side. I caught hell from several men after she left. They were quite upset she wasn't around so they could feed her some sugar, if you know what I mean."

"I believe so. Tell me, were any of them upset enough to kill?"

"I'd say not more that six or seven."

"Names?"

Chapter 9

With a list of gentlemen, I head back home. The closer I get, the more I dread my pending visit to the hospital. After parking, I resume my interrupted trip to the morgue, walking as slowly as possible. I tell myself I need time to think. Then it dawns on me, where the hell are the city council members? I call Jackie on my cell.

"Mayor Jackman's office."

Her voice cracks like a dead tree in a wind storm.

"Jackie, it's me, Archie."

She begins sobbing. After a minute, she composes herself. "Yes, Chief?"

"Where are the council members? Has anyone told them about . . . ."

More wails. "Didn't you know?"

Actually, I know quite a few things. But, the answer to her question was beyond the capacity of my brain cells.

"Know what?"

"They went to Florida, too. The mayor hosts bi-annual off-site strategy meetings, don'tcha know." Her conversation is interrupted by sniffles and a loud honking as she blows her nose.

While she attends to her nose, an acronym for their gatherings enters my mind. B.A.S.S. Bet a lot of *planning* is done on a fishing boat.

Keeping the skepticism out of my voice, I reply, "They do?"

More honking. "Yeah. To plan for the next five. They do this every other year, to make any necessary adjustments, you see."

What I did see is the mystery just grew in scope. It takes a full micro-second to postpone my visit to the hospital, at least for a while longer. After all, it's not like there are strict visiting hours for dead bodies.

I thank Jackie and head for the Clover Bottom Coffee and Tea Shoppe. I hate it when people try to be clever and add a superfluous, unnecessary, and a useless letter to a word. Point becomes *Pointe* or Shop becomes *Shoppe*.

Nonetheless, I'm not about to suggest a change in the spelling since Betty brews coffee that's seventy-five percent as good as mine. Well, maybe fifty. I wonder if East Clover Bottom has ever been buried in a dust storm caused by the *Shoppe* grinding *their* coffee. As I walk in, the aroma of Betty's home-made pies tantalizes my olfactories. The clock over the counter informs me it's way past the lunch hour, which goes a long way to explain my hunger pains.

Ruth Ann's French toast was wonderful, but it is four in the afternoon. There's plenty of time for the morgue. Besides, I need to contemplate just what the hell is going on in town.

Betty is in her sixties, a buxom woman who's not about to take any twaddle from anyone. I'm pretty sure she wrestles our county's resident black bears in her free time.

I'm betting they loose.

The townsfolk know this, but occasionally a tourist ventures over the line and harasses her. Betty picks up a slice of pie, blueberry is the preferred choice, and slams it into his face.

If he complains about his treatment, I inform him, her justice has never been successfully challenged in court. The pie recipient is free to file a complaint, but ten times out of nine, *he* ends up spending a night in cell two.

Betty knows my tastes and fixes my rare 'burger, translucent fried onions, and French fries. She adds three dill pickle wedges, saying, "You're just too sweet, Buster. When you gonna make an honest woman out of Ruth Ann?"

"Hell, Betty. First, I got to get her off that straight and narrow path."

Betty places my meal on the counter and squeezes my shoulder. The deep bone bruise should recover within a week. It has before. When the immediate pain subsides, I relish her gesture which means almost as much as my hug from Ruth Ann.

Betty's *Shoppe* is not equivalent to the solitude of our public library. Getting any quiet time is as likely to happen here as in the middle of a concert given by the latest tween heart throb.

I avoid most of the questions about Rupert and Helen with the time honored dodge, "We're in the middle of a criminal investigation. Can't go into details."

This is interspersed with, "We've got several promising leads."

Wolfing down my food, in my hurry to get out of the din, my cheeks must look like a chipmunk that realizes winter's going to strike tomorrow and he doesn't have a thing in his larder.

I mutter to Betty, "Puf mi tob."

She understands me and makes a note on a slip of paper.

To avoid more questions, I slip down an alley, through a yard, and into the hospital's back door where I run into our newest MD, Doctor Joyce. His parents must have been sadistic. They tagged him with James as his first name.

It takes all my resolve not to ask him if he's seen any poems or trees lately.

"Doc, I need to examine Rupert and Helen. Okay with you?"

"Your Deputy Dixon was here thirty minutes ago. He seemed, ah, how do I say this?"

"Happy?"

"Yeah. Said he was going to escort the bodies to the Cities. Acted like—"

"I know. Jerome likes his job. Mind if I check them for any evidence I might have missed earlier?"

"Right this way, Chief."

He escorts me down dark, concrete steps to the morgue. I sign in and check to see Rupert and his wife are still in their body bags. Actually, there's no desire on my part to check for evidence. This is the only place that came to mind for some quiet time without going home.

Jackie's comment earlier about our council members joining the mayor and Helen in Florida comes to mind.

Why didn't they call home when hiz Honor didn't show? Where's Rupert's pickup? Where'd the murders take place? Certainly not in Florida, if I'm right about the time of death. 'Course, I could be off. But, not more than a day. Decomposition leading to bloating takes longer than two days in water. Hum, could they have been murdered, put in some hot box to accelerate decomp and then dumped in the lake?

Why would someone go to that kind of trouble? To throw us off the track? Even though I asked Jerome to get out an APB on Rupert's vehicle—it's a beautifully restored '65 Chevy pickup—I suspect it's pushing up daisies, or whatever a chunk of Detroit iron does when it departs this world. It's probably already been through some chop shop and its parts scattered.

No answers here; maybe the BCA will find some. That hope brings to mind another point. I'll call them tomorrow after Jerome gets back.

I head out, having successfully avoided pawing around two dead bodies. Besides, I did a pretty thorough exam at the lake while bagging them.

And, after all, isn't a real close exam what autopsies are for?

Chapter 10

Hurrying out of the morgue to avoid running into more people and their questions, I take all the back yards around. Even have to go two blocks out of my way to find one. Deep in thought, I realize I'm heading out of town. Whistling, as though this was a carefully planned maneuver all along, I doff my cap to Mrs. Pederson and bound over her flower beds, hardly leaving a print. Well, not more than six and only a few flattened sprouts.

"They'll be just fine in a week or two, Mrs. Pederson."

I expect to feel her trowel weeding my back. In mid-leap, an idea strikes. Racing through her yard to the street, I reverse my direction and trot downtown. I wave at Ruth Ann through the newspaper's plate glass window, she spots me and motions for me to enter. The look on her face resembles the Cheshire Cat's grin. That should have been a warning.

Pretending nothing happened, although keeping my eye open for Mrs. Pederson and her trowel, I nonchalantly ask, "How's Saturday's paper coming along?"

"Wait and see. This intrepid reporter had coffee with someone. Someone I can't mention. Have to keep my sources confidential, you know. There's been a development with one of the missing council members. Take me out to supper and I'll fill you in."

Damn! I fell right into her trap.

"Give me a clue," I plead.

"Un uh, mister. I do that and you'll weasel out of paying."

I muster a wounded look. "Would I do that?"

"Let me count the times. Last week, two weeks before that, then . . ."

"K. You win. Just for that, I'm withholding what Betty said earlier. So there."

"Tell me."

"Sorry, got to see your Uncle George. Pick you up around six?"

"Oh, you poop."

Could've taken her to my office and sweated the info out, but memories of grade school came back. *I'd* probably end up being water boarded if I used any harsh methods on that woman. Long ago, it became clear that a medium-rare steak, a few glasses of wine, some soft music, I'd be eating out of her hand. No. *She'd* be eating out of mine.

Knowing who won that round of one up-manship, I head to the dock.

George is doing touch-up painting. His coffee cup within arm's reach. Good thing the dock only has a single color scheme—white. Otherwise with a color-blind, tipsy old coot dauber in charge of illumination, it'd probably look like the paint job on a hippie, psychedelic van straight out of the '60's. As it was, some parts of the pier that were never meant to be painted came under his brush today.

Like the lake end decking and the sign stating this is a city owned and operated facility.

Or the bronze plaque dedicated to John B. Schultz, my great-grandfather, commemorating his efforts to build the marina and pier. I could overlook a lot of things Uncle George did. This one really pisses me off.

I *accidentally* kick his coffee cup. It ends up twenty feet away in the lake. Moments later, two fish go belly-up.

Looks like a couple keeper-walleyes.

"Wa the hell you do that fer?"

"George, you clean off that plaque or you're gonna spend twenty-four hours in the poky. And stop painting the decking."

"No call to kick my favorite cup."

"Just be thankful I need you for some work, or you'd be on your way to jail. Now, get busy 'cause I got a paying job for ya."

George staggers to his office. A few minutes later, returns with a can of solvent.

I stand upwind as he starts scrubbing. Not because of the paint remover fumes, but to avoid those emanating from George.

When the bronze shines, I tell him what needs to be done.

"All's I gotta do is drive Dutch around?"

"Dragging the lake is slightly more complicated, George. You drive the boat in a straight line. Dutch'll help you. Just do what he tells ya."

"And if I don't?"

"You know Dutch. If you screw up, you're going in the lake head first. Another thing. You better sober up 'cause Dutch'll be here first light. You don't want him to wake ya and find you're still drunk."

A quick glance at my watch reveals there's still time to get to *Louie's Repair and Auto Wrecking* before they close. Cousin Dutch is Louie's chief mechanic and chief disassembler. Dutch may be slightly low in the IQ department, but give him a challenging auto repair task, or a set of hydraulic nippers, and watch out.

Although on two recent occasions, he got the jobs confused.

Louie and I have a comfortable relationship: I never question where he gets all the cars Dutch renders into parts and he lets me borrow my cousin anytime he's needed.

Entering Louie's establishment I'm immediately assaulted by a god-awful noise. Now it becomes clear why Dutch is a man of few words. He's got to have hardly any hearing left.

You know those tiny hairs inside the ear canal that help send sounds to the auditory nerve? I figure in my cousin's case most of them long since migrated into the quiet spaciousness of his brain.

I lean close to Louie and ask if a red Chevy pickup has come his way. Doubt anyone would be dumb enough to have a local chop Rupert's car. I take that back, Dutch would.

Talk about hard of hearing, I have to yell my question three times before he answers. I drag him down the block and he confirms my hunch. No cherry-red, to say nothing about a black, yellow, or blue pickups have come in this month.

"Need Dutch tomorrow from six in the morning till at least noon. Maybe part of the afternoon as well."

"Sure thing, Archie. I'll tell Dutch."

Dutch comes up, a big grin on his face. "Need me tomorrow?"

"Yeah. George is going to drive you around the lake. Got to see if Rupert's truck was dumped there."

Moments later, I can hardly breathe, I'm being crushed in a Dutch Schultz hug. Stomping on his toes gets his attention and he releases me.

"Not so hard, Dutch."

His face falls. "Just happy to help, Archie."

Now my cousin is on the verge of crying. After I reassure him it's okay, he brightens. Dutch may be slow, but he follows directions to a T. I give him a sketch of the pattern George is to follow.

"You know where the last house is on the east side of the lake, right?"

"Yup."

"Start there and go to the south shore. Keep going slowly back and forth. But, listen closely, each pass has to be four feet from the last. I'll set some stakes on the shore for George to shoot for. He drives the boat and you hold the drag line. Can you do that?"

"Does a bear hunt ants in a tree?"

He may have his metaphors slightly out of whack, but he understands.

If the mayor's vehicle *is* in the lake, there's no way it can be more than twenty yards from shore. By night fall I've set out three dozen stakes. Just to make sure George and Dutch cover every possible inch.

With the last stake driven, I head to the center of town. Hope Ruth Ann's still at work. It's a safe bet I can take her to Betty's for supper where she'll be spilling the beans about the break in the case faster than water comes out of a primed well-pump.

Her office is dark. So much for an intimate, secret spilling meal. I'm only an hour and ten minutes late. Still, that's no reason for her not to wait.

After resigning myself to a lonely and clueless meal, I walk across the street to the *Shoppe*.

The special tonight is hot roast beef sandwich. I'm pretty sure Betty's beef is a lot fresher than the Civil War era stuff in my TV dinners. Her's got to be at least WW I vintage. I order the special.

The sandwich comes with a half dozen strips of meat on white bread, a heap of slightly soggy mashed potatoes, and canned green beans. The beans look to be straight out of Tom Jefferson's garden. He probably served part of the harvest to Ben Franklin and the boys when they were arguing over the wording of the Constitution.

Betty smothers the entire plate with gravy. No way to tell how green the meat is.

With another slice of bread, I sop up the grease, ah, gravy. As an afterthought, I order a piece of blueberry pie.

Actually, it wasn't an afterthought. Dessert was planned all along. Just didn't want it drowned in gravy.

Heading on home to watch a little TV and dream of what could have been on my dinner date with Ruth Ann. Betty's question, about making Ruth Ann an honest woman, keeps floating in and out of my brain cell. I'd ask Ruth Ann to become Mrs. John E. Schultz in a New York minute. Well, maybe a Minnesota minute. But, being of German extraction and living in a state heavily influenced by cautious Scandinavians, and even more cautious Germans, a Minnesota minute typically lasts a couple decades.

I pour a drink—good ol' Kane-tuck bourbon—give up trying to find anything of interest on TV to anyone older than ten, and go to bed.

My alarm is set for five.

Probably should have set George's as well

Chapter 11

I wake before the alarm goes off. Good thing. Its warble is akin to opera singer Beverly Sills' high note. If it sounds too long, the fillings in my teeth'll shatter. I shut it off and hurry through my morning routine, take a quick shower, shave my chin a tad too close—a few sheets of toilet paper staunch the flow—skip coffee making, and out of the house by five-thirty. Betty's *Shoppe* is open and I stop for coffee to go. She's recently switched brands and I swear it's made from reused asphalt instead of beans. Two sips and I'm wide awake. Doubt my eyes will even blink before ten.

Dutch is already on the dock, and much to my surprise, so is George. Although he looks a little wet and stands in an ever-widening puddle.

Probably should've warned George. My cousin thinks going for a boat ride is a tenth of a point lower in his fun rating system than tossing people in the lake. George appears wide awake and sober. Probably visions of continued dunking by Dutch contributed to his current state.

To my way of thinking, George's wake up call pretty much makes up for his painting John B.'s plaque.

After going over the instructions one more time, I show George the route he's to follow.

"George, get a bunch of buoys. Line them up with the stakes I drove last night. Follow me?"

"Yeah. Guess so."

"It's really simple. Just drop one every four feet. Tell ya what. Go to the south end and see my stakes. Repeat that pattern like it shows on your chart."

A 25 watt bulb seems to light up over his head and he nods.

"Good. I'll check back in an hour, guys. Head on out and get going."

Dutch sits in the front and George fires up the inboard—he owns a classic ChrisCraft—and they start off. I shake my head in frustration. With Dutch in the bow and George driving from mid-boat, all the weight is forward. The boat just circles. A blast from the whistle I use to direct traffic, an Acme Little Thunderer, not only gets their attention, but all the neighborhood dogs start yowling.

I wave them back.

"Dutch, you need to get in the stern. George, you're okay where you are."

This time they travel more or less in a straight line.

I return to my cruiser. Surprisingly, Betty's coffee has worn off and I grab some sleep.

An hour later, the growl of the ChrisCraft's V-8 Chevy engine rouses me. Somewhat groggy, to say nothing about being stiff, I clamber out of my attractively painted blue and white cruiser. George is idling alongside the pier; he and Dutch are engaged in an animated conversation. He better watch it as Dutch's heated arguments generally end in the same fashion. Someone goes into the water, head first. My money's on Dutch doing the tossing.

"Whoa, boys. Take it easy. You make three dozen passes already?"

My cousin's mouth far exceeds his brain's capacity to keep up. Most of what comes out is gibberish, although I make out several cuss words. Since his sausage-sized finger is pounding on George's chest, I gather the driver didn't follow directions.

"Speak—slower—cuz," drawing out the words so he can hear what I mean.

I'll tone down what followed. "This @2#$%@ fella wouldn't &*$# slow down."

George's turning red. I'm not sure if it's embarrassment or a reaction from Dutch beating his chest.

Squatting down, waving my hands in front of cuz's face to get his attention, he stops hammering.

When a semblance of order is restored, I turn to George. "Just how fast were you going?"

He pauses for several counts. "Maybe I used a little too much throttle."

Dutch chips in. "A little? The damn drag line couldn't sink. Just skipped along on the surface."

"Not paying you for this hour, George. Now get back out and do it right. Go as damn fast as you want getting to the other side of the lake, but from then on, trolling speed. You hear me?"

Dutch adds emphasis by cutting George's head. His hat sails off and ends up on shore. "Tol' ya."

I retrieve the baseball hat. Couldn't tell if it was a Minnesota Twins or a Moscow Midgets cap. Looks like George uses it to wipe off dip sticks.

So, that explains his hair.

He guns the motor and roars away, a huge rooster tail following.

The last thing I see is Dutch grinning from ear to ear, bellowing with joy.

A feeling of despair comes over me. Perhaps it's only symptoms of withdrawal from Betty's coffee.

Yet, I sense Dutch and George are on a wild goose chase.

Chapter 1 2

As the ChrisCraft fades to a smudge against the rising sun, I attempt to shake off my feeling that this is all for naught. The lake has to be dragged, but I've spent enough time on this folly. The frustration never leaves.

From the sound, or lack thereof, George obviously took my message to heart and has apparently slowed his boat to a crawl.

At a snail's pace, I return to my cruiser and head for the office. Jerome should be about ready to strike out for the Twin Cities. Turning the corner onto Main, I spot the two-unit parade racing for Highway 2. Both the ambulance and cruiser's sirens going full blast. I better prepare myself for the inevitable complaint calls. Old Lady Carlstrom is probably dialing the station now. Her scratchy voice will go something like this:

"Them damn *sireens* woke me and my cats. Now Fluffy's yowling like she's in heat. You damn cops got to wake the dead ever time ya go out of town? Believe you me, the mayor's gonna hear about this one."

I'll be mighty surprised if she does reach old Rupert.

The boys are on their way, playing with their toys, plainly forgetting what they were told earlier. I get on the radio and tell Jerome to cool it with the sirens. The line becomes quiet.

Probably won't last.

On to Betty's *Shoppe* for breakfast.

Apparently she spotted me coming and has a cup of her asphalt ready.

"What's with Jerome and that lazy, good-for-nothing Newberry Jones that got them all het up ? Them and their *sireens* and all."

To ponder my response, I pause before answering. So far, I've kept a lid on the murders. No special reason why, except I hoped to let the townsfolk know in a more subtle and caring way. On the other hand, everyone's going to know about them sooner or later. If I tell Betty, it'll damn well be sooner.

She staggers back, catching herself on the counter. Someone's easy-over eggs, sausage, and wheat toast crash to the floor. In an attempt to catch the plate, two more orders join the mess.

Betty's moving like she's in a trance, no doubt wondering whom to tell first. Moments later, my usual breakfast of blueberry pancakes, one scrambled egg, two sausage links, and OJ comes sailing down the fake marble Formica. The dishes seemingly float and stop six inches from me. I wonder, did she get her training at some bar?

Her ample rear end disappears though the swinging kitchen doors. There's a phone back there. In less than three minutes, my food is in my stomach. I no more than step outside when I'm beseeched by theories of whodunit and requests for the *latest*.

By the time I wade through a mass of people and reach City Hall's front door, it seems the entire population of West Clover Bottom has approached me. There are so many unrelated questions, I half expect someone to ask, "How many angels can dance on the head of a pin?"

Too bad someone doesn't ask. I know the answer, providing the angels are Schultz's.

None.

In the remote case there are Schultz angels, the clan is not known for their ability to 'trip the light fantastic.'

Seeing Jackie is my main task. The missing city councilmen's families have to be contacted. But, since none live in WCB, it'll have to be by impersonal phone calls.

It was bad enough having to inform the Jackman family their father and step-mother were murdered, now I have to tell the councilmen's families their parents are missing.

Jackie's still beside herself with grief. At least her disheveled looks say so. Her hair is awry, her clothes wrinkled, and her make-up smeared and streaked.

The councilmen's office is next to the mayor's, but it's divided into three gray walled cubes.

Silently, she goes from unit-to-unit and finds their phone indexes. She asks in the smallest voice, "Want to use Rupert's office? Probably more privacy."

An hour later, I've managed to reach their sons or daughters and give them the bad news. I wonder, are all three families estranged? Instead of being pummeled with questions like:

"Any leads?"

"Any clues?"

"Any reasons?"

No one is even a little bit interested. Strange.

There are no answers to my questions ,either.

"Any enemies you know of?"

"Any personal problems?"

"Any financial problems?"

"Any idea why they disappeared?"

I thank Jackie for her assistance and head down to my office. With Jerome away, there'll be some quiet time to ponder the situation. Dead bodies, missing people, and no clues.

For the longest time, I simply stare out of my window, hoping I'll see something other than that red squirrel robbing the bird feeder. Maybe taking Maggie to work one day might scare the critter away. But then, she'd probably make friends with it and catch the birds.

Before I know it, the afternoon has slipped away. The wailing of sirens rudely brings me back to the present.

Jerome and Newberry have returned.

I'm anxious to go home and get ready for my date with Ruth Ann to hear what she has to say about the un-named councilman.

Instead of ducking out the back door, I wait for my deputy's report.

He better have one.

With nothing better to do, I reach into my pants pocket and feel a crumbled piece of paper. It's the names of Stormie's old *friends*.

I call 4-1-1 and get the numbers of four. The others either moved or died. There's no listing for the remaining five. This Stormie, aka Helen, was one busy gal. No wonder she had so much jewelry.

I call the first name, Alan Rogers. A male answers. Sounds like he's got one foot in the grave and the other on a banana peel. I can barely understand him, his voice is so scratchy. He's very reluctant to talk about her. I assure him I'm only after background information. I've always liked that line, heard it on some cop show.

He tells me he's been wheelchair bound for the past seventeen months. Lost a leg to diabetes.

Another one off the list.

The second fella says he's an engineer for an oil company. "You know. The one outside of Rosemount, Minnesota and north of Hastings. Spent the last twelve months in Saudi Arabia."

Still no word from Jerome. I'm reduced to pacing the floor.

48

Chapter 13

At long last, Jerome swaggers in, looking as smug as that damn red squirrel outside stuffing its cheeks with sunflower seeds.

"Well, deputy, how'd it go?"

Jerome puffs himself up even more. "Man, what a fun trip, chief. Went through Brainerd 'bout 65 m-p-h. Shoulda seen people scatter."

When he realizes what he said, the macho drains out of him like water over Lake Superior's Gooseberry Falls.

I fix him with my *I'm the Chief* stare. "Think that was real smart, Jerome? There'd be hell to pay if you guys had an accident. Run over someone and you'd be in Stillwater." Referring to the State Penitentiary. "I'm going to overlook it for now, but do that again, and your ass is grass."

He gives me a hang-dog look that'd make the SPCA demand *I* be put behind bars for cruelty to animals.

Deputy Jones slouches off to his desk and swivels his chair so his back is to me. I let him stew in guilt for fifteen minutes, then step to his side.

"Jerome, you know what you should do going through a town. Don't do it again. Now, grab a cup of coffee and tell me how things went with the BCA."

He sighs and says, "Sorry, Archie."

After a pause to catch his breath, he continues, his voice bright and as excited as usual.

"After we checked in some gal—boy was she a looker—got in my cruiser. After telling Newberry to follow, she showed us to the back door where cops enter."

I mentally roll my eyes. The "back door" is about thirty yards from the public entrance. They went right by it as they entered the parking lot.

Maybe Jerome is a secret babe magnet.

He scratches his ear. "Newbury fell all over himself, trying to be important. Hell, Archie, she knew he was just a grunt driving an ambulance, but he put on like he was the guvner."

"Not surprising. About the ropes and blocks."

Jerome regains his swagger. "I told Patty, that's her name."

He always had a grasp of the obvious.

"Told her I had some *ev-ah-dense* right there in the back seat. I could tell she was mighty interested. Gave her the complete run down of what happened, how we found the bodies, *our* prelim time of death estimate . . ."

I let Barney, to hell with correcting myself, ramble on. The gist of his tale was the ev-ah-dense was in their forensic lab. I knew it'd go to the top of the work load, being a murder and the vics were prominent people, at least in our town.

"Did you get to the hospital okay?"

"Patty offered to show us. Like you said, it was just a few blocks away."

"When you guys got there, Newberry have *her* unload the bodies?"

"Hell no, why'd he do that? I did."

I didn't tell him about me having to load Rupert and Helen. Guess I forgot to tell Jerome I volunteered him to help ol' Newberry any time.

I shrug. "Then what?"

"At Regions?"

Sometimes talking to Jerome makes even less sense than the Abbott and Costello baseball routine.

"Yeah."

"Man, that's a big place. Good thing Patty's along. I wheel the mayor and Helen in."

"And Newberry sits in the ambulance, right?"

Jerome's eyes narrow and his brows furrow. "Hey, Archie. He's got a wagon full of drugs and stuff in the back. Someone's gotta guard it."

"Sure."

What was it Betty called Newberry?

Oh yeah, lazy.

When he's done explaining, I ask him to write it up, and excuse myself.

"Got an important meeting, have to prepare." He doesn't need to know my *meeting* is a dinner date with Ruth Ann to celebrate the annual opening of the Clover Bottom Inn.

Before I can leave, Dutch and George wander in. Dutch has that silly grin on his face. George tries three times to make it through the door. I'm sure he breathed on the jamb. It looks like a some of the paint blistered.

Humm. Maybe I ought to have him breathe on that red squirrel.

Before they get started with their findings, I cut to the chase.

"No bright red Chevy pickup, right?"

George finds a chair and plops down. I wonder how much coffee's left in his thermos.

Dutch's still wearing that grin. "No, but you should see the outboard motor I pulled up. A twenty-horse Evinrude. I'll have that baby purring like your cat in three days."

"What kept you out so long? You guys have been out over eight hours. I figured you'd be back by noon."

Dutch gestures with a thumb over his shoulder at George; his grin fades. He mumbles, "Had to go back to his office. Five times."

I know the answer but ask anyway, "Why?"

"He ran out of coffee."

Now I'm sure the door jamb will need re-painting.

"George. I'll settle up with you later. My guess is you actually worked four hours. See me when you can walk straight."

That'll probably be a few years in the future. Figure I saved the city forty bucks.

After thanking them, I drive home and start preparing for my date. A shower, another shave. Too bad Ruth Ann isn't here. She'd rush into the bathroom, a come-hither look on her face as she lovingly strokes my smooth, delicate cheeks, like those beautiful, sexy women do on razor blade commercials.

As it is, I settle for Maggie rubbing against my legs. More a demand for something to eat than being impressed with my smooth, delicate cheeks.

I decide to dress semi-formal. Tan, pleated-front Dockers, light blue button-down oxford shirt, recently, within the past month recent, from the dry cleaners. Argyle sox and ox-blood penny loafers. I even give them a fresh coat of polish. I top it off with a brownish herringbone sports coat.

No police cruiser tonight. I'm using my brand new red BMW convertible. It was delivered from the dealer in Bemidji the other day. It's supposed to be a surprise. Ruth Ann loves red BMW convertibles. I spot a splot of bird poop on the windshield and hurry back inside for some cleanser. Failing to notice which direction the spray nozzle is pointing, I adorn my smooth, delicate cheeks with industrial strength ammonia, diluted with blue, god-awful smelling water.

"Oh, just #$!**& peachy!"

Back inside, my hall mirror reflection shows my sartorial splendor is not quite up to 'date quality.' Worse, my face only took part of the fzzzzzzt. My shirt and sports coat, the rest.

So much for the semi-formal look.

Digging through my closet, I find a white shirt that miraculously only has one grease spot on it. Easily covered by my red pull-over sweater.

Even though the drive to Ruth Ann's house will only take ten minutes, I want to see what this baby's got. I roar out of the driveway, slam on the brakes to avoid another red squirrel, and continue.

So far so good.

Screeching to a halt outside her house, and bounding over the door like some Olympic high jumper, I barely feel my knee cracking the rear-view mirror. With a brave face, hobble up the steps. Before I can knock, Ruth Ann opens the door.

My chin scrapes the concrete stoop.

Chapter 14

Ruth Ann looks more gorgeous than ever. She's a corsage away from being the queen of the prom. Her pixie cut, dark auburn hair is streaked with gold and a just a touch of bright red. Not one to wear gobs of jewelry, she's wearing a simple gold necklace with an emerald pendant. Earrings match the necklace, down to the emeralds, albeit they're smaller.

A red spaghetti strap dress accents her hair. The emeralds, her eyes.

Her lips are bright red. Everything is coordinated. Even the black heels seem to highlight her trim ankles and slender, well proportioned legs.

I need a rope and pulley to lift my chin. As the first impression sinks in, I realize my sweater is shoddy and covered with 'pills'. To say nothing about how the color clashes with her dress.

Still, Ruth Ann smiles and stands on her tip-toes to gives me a kiss.

"Care for a drink before we go?"

I feel so embarrassed that some damn bird poop ruined by carefully laid out plans, I quickly agree. If only to get inside before someone walks by and sees me.

"Sit, Archie. I'll fix a couple of martoonis."

The refrigerator opens, closes. Ice cubes rattle and bottles clink. Moments later, she returns with two glasses and sits beside me.

"To the opening of the Clover Bottom Inn."

"To the opening." I sip and look into those green pools of light.

Ruth Ann returns my look and lifts her glass. Half her martini spills on her dress.

"Oh damn. Look what I did. I have to change. It'll just take me a minute." Ruth Ann sets her glass down and rushes off.

All is quiet. No drawers slamming, water running, and no unpleasant words directed at me.

It's like nothing happened when she returns. I can't help but notice she's now in a pair of tan slacks and a yellow blouse. Still, the effect is stunning. There's a smile on her face. "Enough martoonis for me. Ready?"

As we head for the front door, I lay a hand on her shoulder. "Thanks, Ruth Ann. I was all set to leave when I saw some bird poop on my windshield. Ended up spraying myself with glass cleaner. Had to change."

"I guessed."

I take her in my arms and kiss her. What a woman. Betty's question about making her Mrs. Schultz is front and center in my mind.

I've been on pins and needles, anxious to hear her news about the councilman. It's better not to push her. She'd give me a raspberry and wouldn't talk about it until the mood struck her. Probably in a month or two. I hold my tongue and drive to the Inn.

As we enter, I'm greeted with, "Hi ya, cousin."

It's my Mom's sister's teenage daughter, Sally Arlington. Grabbing a pair of menus, she prances through the already crowded dining room and guides us to our lake-view table.

She's going to be a senior in WCB High this fall. Cute as a bug and smart as a whip. Throw in "talented as all get out," and you've described little Sally A.

Aunt Phoebe and Uncle Sam spend most of their conversations talking up their daughter. They also use adjectives like, "popular as honey to a bee." "Comfortable as an old pair of slippers" is another favorite. Guess if Sally had been born Frank, it'd be as comfortable as an old pair of shoes." They also like to add "sharp as a tack" several times in the conversation.

Anyhow, another cousin, I think Janet's actually a second, smiles and takes our drink and meal orders. Ruth Ann opts for a martini and the walleye. I select a Manhattan and a rare rib-eye. When the drinks arrive, we salute each other and I look into her viridescent eyes.

I recall seeing myself in her hall mirror and how shabby I looked next to her. I vow to go to Gill Brothers Clothing tomorrow morning. I'll turn myself over to Bill Jr., grandson of Dave Gill, one of the original owners. Bill's got more fashion sense in his little toe than I have in my entire six foot two frame.

My mind has drifted and I miss Ruth Ann's whisper.

". . . seventy-five grand."

I'm in the middle of a sip and realize she's telling me about a councilman. I cover myself by spewing out my booze. Thankfully, I feel it coming on and aim for my lap.

Add a couple pair of pants, will you, Bill?

"I'm sorry. Went down the wrong throat." As if we have several throats and have to choose every time we swallow.

"I said, Councilman Horace Schmidt deposited one hundred and seventy-five thousand dollars, cash no less, in his bank account twelve days ago. One hundred and seventy-five grand."

Ruth Ann's always been a stickler for repeating herself word-for-word.

I counter with my usual quick grasp of the situation. "Huh? One seventy-five large?"

"That's what I just said. Don't you see the possibilities here?"

Thankfully, Janet arrives with our food and I have a few moments to think before I speak—a rarity.

My steak is the way I like it. Still mooing.

My date rolls her eyes.

She opted for the walleye. I don't question my cousin where it came from as walleye season won't open in our fair state until next weekend.

Ruth Ann asks for two more lemons, and she means two full lemons. I wonder if she wants to preserve the fish for leftovers next month.

I put the donor of my rib-eye out of its misery and cut a chunk of meat.

For the next several minutes there is no conversation. The only noises coming from our table are contented sighs.

I use the time to consider what Ruth Ann said about the councilman's bank account. There could be several reasons. I mentally tick them off:

One. It's a payoff for some reason.

Two. He won at a casino.

Three. It's a payoff.

Four. He inherited it from some relative.

Then of course, it could be a payoff.

Janet strolls by. "You folks finished? Care for dessert?"

There's enough meat left on my steak to keep Maggie happy for three days. I ask for a doggie bag. Funny how restaurants never have kitty bags. I place the bone in the foam container and wonder if she'll take it up one of the trees and store it for later. She likes to watch National Geographic, and I'm sure she's seen her large cat relatives do it.

"The Inn's famous Key lime cheesecake for me. Ruth Ann?"

"Same."

She waits until Janet leaves. "I saw your mouth work over scenarios concerning our Councilman's deposit. What're you thinking? A payoff?"

"Well, that is one possibility. I can think of plenty more."

"Oh yeah? Like what?"

"Off hand, gambling. I heard tell he likes to go to Red Lake and hit the *Seven Clans Casino* or down to *Northern Lights* in Walker. Either of those could've had a big jackpot."

"Snort, snort. Good try, Archie. I'll have you know, crack reporters, namely me, typically check out things like that. I called all twenty Minnesota casinos. Not one in the last month paid out a hundred and seventy-five large."

That catches me off guard. Hate it when she's one step ahead of me. Still, I wonder if any of them were blowing her off.

Chapter 15

When Janet brings our cheesecake we dig in. Well, I do. I wolf down mine, but my slowpoke date is a dainty eater. This gives me time to stare into those liquid emerald pools. I know the answer before I ask, but I have to bring it up.

"You know, this could be a major clue. I need your source."

She responds and I wonder if Ruth Ann is also related to Betty as she launches a chunk of cake at me. I duck and it splatters on the window.

"Nah, nuh, nah, nah. Missed. Had to ask, you know."

Ruth Ann loads her fork catapult but I smash the cheesecake in my hand before she can launch the medieval weapon. I ignore the pain of the tines stabbing my palm and repeat my question.

"Look, love of my life, I'll go see Judge Schultz and get a subpoena for the councilman's bank records. I will get the info. You could save me . . ."

I stop in mid sentence as an ice cube slides down my shirt. I dance and shake it out.

A sly grin spreads across her face. "Need I say more?"

Figuring I won that round, I motion to Janet for the bill. I want to leave before I win again.

On the walk to my BMW, Ruth Ann snuggles up to me . "Sorry, Archie. I was wrong in there. I hope you understand, I can't reveal my sources. You know that."

"Yeah. I just . . .Oh, never mind. I'll see my uncle tomorrow and see if he'll help me get a subpoena."

"Like he's going to turn you down."

"We could save some—"

An elbow to ribs tells me Ruth Ann isn't going to budge an inch.

When I open her car door, she pulls me close and kisses my lips. I feel what Dutch must've felt yesterday on the dock when she just kissed his cheek. My knees go weak and I fear I'm going to turn red and, like him, become a bowl of Jell-O and dissolve.

Ruth Ann breaks away. Her voice all throaty and says, "Better take me home, Archie."

I flow around to the driver's side and start the engine. I detour to the east side of the lake to the city park and pull in. I'm hoping for a little more sugar, but Ruth Ann's out of the car as though she received a jolt of electricity. Together we walk to the shore. Behind us, the moon is rising and casts an orange glow over the water.

We head for the beach. I pull a bench to the water's edge and we sit quietly.

There's a cool breeze coming from the west. It pushes small wavelets before it. Their tips catch the moon beams, looking as though some fairy was turning the water into orange and black Halloween decorations.

In this peaceful setting, I'm thinking of what I have to do tomorrow and guessing my date's anxious about getting the paper out.

She breaks the silence. "Hard to believe little old West Clover Bottom finds itself in this mess."

"Sure is. The town's still reeling from the murders. I don't think the full implication has sunk in."

Ruth Ann reads my mind. "You mean what are we going to do about a new mayor and where are the councilmen? Are they dead, too?"

"Could be."

"I'm thinking I'll have to bring out some special editions. This story's too big for a weekly paper. I'm going to be busy. You too, right?"

"You can say that again."

We fall silent.

The stillness is broken by a night heron's call and the far off squabbling of ducks.

My date snuggles closer. "Sometimes I wish we could turn some magical clock backwards. Then maybe all of this could've been adverted."

As if echoing her sad desire, the warbling call of a loon rents the still night. Its plaintive song cuts to my bones.

Apparently Ruth Ann feels the same. "Hold me, Archie."

I gladly comply.

For the moment, in the warmth of her embrace, I can push yesterday's events to the back of my mind. Little do I know that soon, these will pale.

Chapter 16

It's Saturday morning. Maggie's purring, trying to wake me. That and her rough tongue licking my face does a pretty good job. I didn't use mouth wash before going to bed and she must smell last night's rib steak.

I stumble downstairs to the kitchen and give her the bone. Sometimes I swear she's part dog. She disappears around the corner and into the pantry with her treat. I poke my head in. Only to be greeted by a growl, a razor back, and a tail that'd put a raccoon to shame.

This is going to be a very busy day. I have a lot to do and quickly clean up. Shaving, I prioritize my tasks. Gill Brothers first to tend to my clothing needs, see my uncle about the subpoenas, then call the BCA.

On my way out, I pick up the paper and look at the headlines.

MAYOR AND WIFE MURDERED.
Councilmen Missing.

I pause to skim the stories. Not that I'm not interested, but I am rather familiar with the details. I jump in my cruiser and head into town. Since I have to see about getting legal papers, I dress in my uniform so I look formal before my uncle. Besides, all my other clothes are a mess.

I drop off my laundry at the dry cleaners, hoping I have enough in my checking account to cover the bill, and walk to Betty's *Shoppe*.

She's got a wry grin on her face and greets me with, "Howdy, Chief. Heard you arrested some walleyes the other day. Think they're behind the killings?"

Apparently Dutch's question about me, 'resting a couple walleyes', as I floundered around in the lake, has made the rounds. Instead of some sharp witted comeback that'd set Betty on her heels, I shrug. "My usual."

"Little testy this morning?"

"For some reason, I am. Maybe it has to do with a couple senseless murders. Funny how a little thing like that can get under one's skin."

Betty looks sheepish, her grin washes away, and she hurries to the far end of the counter. I see her talking to the other patrons, apparently warning them not to try joshing me. I'm left alone.

Fifteen minutes later, I put my sartorial needs in the hands of Bill, Jr. Pants, shirts, socks, ties, and two sport coats later, I'm on my way. He promises to have the alterations completed by Thursday.

Before seeing uncle, I stop by the office and draw up a draft subpoena. I audited a legal paper class at Billy Mitchell Law School in St. Paul while attending the U. Before graduating, I acquired a software package that did all the formatting for me. I often wondered why lawyer's papers have to be drawn up that peculiar way. Why not put them in a letter?

Dear Sir (or Madam),

Your presence is required in court on _____.

Sincerely,

Judge _____.

He could add a warning. Something like:

Be there or else.

But, no. They use words like, whereas, heretofore, and whatnot's.

Therefore, being the party of the first part, I figured I might need to draft a few someday. The printer spits it out and after a quick cut and paste change, I re-print my work of legal elegance. Satisfied, I close up the station and head to my aunt and uncle's house.

Aunt Beverly answers my knock and gives me a hug.

"So nice to see you, Archie. Oh, my. All official looking, aren't you? I bet you want to see your uncle."

When I step inside, I'm struck by a most delightful aroma. It's from Bev's freshly baked rolls. "I am, but if you twist my arm, I could be talked into one of your sticky buns."

"You just follow me. He's waiting for one to cool."

My aunt is in her early sixties. She's known all over the county for her pastry. Every year for the past twenty, she walks away with a blue ribbon at the county fair. Not that my plump relation is over-weight, but it's obvious she enjoys her own cooking. I'm sure Doctor Joyce has urged her to lose a few pounds. But then, if she did, would she still be as jolly?

I follow my gray-haired aunt through the front parlor, into their large country kitchen. Uncle Jerry is in a pair of faded blue jeans and a tattered gold and maroon University of Minnesota sweatshirt. He's drumming his fingers on their old pine table, as though his activity will hurry the cooling. He's the Jeff to her Mutt, or is it the other way round? Jerry's as tall as I am, and as thin as a bean pole. I suspect hammering away with a gavel and calling for order in the court uses more calories than people realize.

He's dressed in that sweatshirt, even though it's a fairly warm day, because he suffers from low blood pressure. Perhaps if he worked out, his blood pressure wouldn't be a problem.

He greets me in his deep baritone voice. "Morning, nephew. I heard what your aunt said about wanting to see me. What can I do for you?"

Ruth Ann's paper is on his lap.

"It has to do with the headlines."

Bev jumps in, "And how is Ruth Ann, dear? Any plans for the future?"

I know she and Betty are best of friends and I can imagine them over coffee. "Are Archie and Ruth Ann *ever* going to get married?" It appears that my love life takes precedence over what happened the other day.

"You'll be the second person to know, should anything happen, Auntie."

"And who'll be first?"

"Ruth Ann."

She giggles. I figure she'll be telling Betty that she'll be one of the last people to know, while she, my aunt, will be second.

I just rose to favorite nephew status. Actually, not much of an accomplishment as I'm her *only* nephew.

Uncle Jerry harrumphs.

"Right, Uncle." He likes to get down to business, especially since his wife has a cooling sticky bun waiting. "I've come upon a lead, but need a subpoena for the details."

Keeping Ruth Ann's name out of the conversation, I explain. "I heard from a highly reliable source that Horace Schmidt's bank account jumped a hundred and seventy-five thou a week before Rupert and Helen were murdered."

"And you want to investigate."

"Yeah. It could all be very innocent, but . . ."

Aunt Bev places a plate of frosted buns before us. All thoughts of murder and bank accounts evaporate.

Uncle Jerry and I attack the pastry as though we havn't eaten in a week.

I my case, that's pretty much the situation. Other than Ruth Ann's French toast the other day and the Inn's steak,

I've been visiting Betty's *Shoppe* way too much. That hardly constitutes a *decent* meal.

When we finish devouring Bev's ambrosia, I slide my paperwork to Jerry.

"I took the liberty of making a rough draft for your approval. Actually, there are three forms. One for each councilman."

All is quiet as he reads my offerings. Without breaking his concentration, my aunt hands each of us a cup of coffee. Even though she doesn't understand the incredible skill and talent required to brew a *proper* cup, it's passable.

You don't see this much these days, but uncle, after spooning three tablespoons of sugar in his cup, pours his coffee into a saucer. Then he slurps it from the fine porcelain plate. Perhaps that old-world convention has its last bastion in our fair town.

At any rate, he seems to re-re-read my application and, after burping, says, "You want the records of all three councilmen?"

Less is best when doing business with him, so I nod.

"I can see my way clear to allowing this breach of privacy when it come to Horace, but all three?"

"All three are missing. Is there a connection with the murders and our councilmen?"

Another Uncle Jerry harrumph. Followed by, "Beverly? Bring me my pen."

She sweetly replies, "Get it yourself."

He's the bull in the ring and Bev's the matador. Once again, the bull loses.

Uncle makes a few corrections, pulls out his cell and dials.

"Manny, Jerry Schultz. Our relative needs three subpoenas. I've taken the liberty to correct his drafts. Can you issue them, in proper form, ASAP?"

He pauses. "Yeah. It's about the murders. Thanks."

He's just talked to Clover Bottom's prosecuting attorney, Manny Schultz.

Jerry closes his cell phone and asks for another round of pastry. After Aunt Bev places them on the table he butters his roll and says, "See your cousin in thirty minutes. I'll fax these to him right now and he'll take care of it."

"Thanks, Uncle. I really appreciate your help."

"Harrumph. Glad to help." Moments later, his fax is whirring and spitting out the drafts across the ether.

Thirty minutes later, I'm stuffed and armed with four sticky buns. After I promise to share them with Ruth Ann.

Yeah, that could happen.

With the subpoenas safely in hand, my mind drifts to Rupert. I've known him forever. Every four years all he'd have to do to get re-elected was say, "Think I better run again."

On a couple of occasions, someone would try opposing his candidacy. Guess they got up to five votes. One fellow, got two—he and his wife's.

I feel I owe Rupert as he was the one who argued for the city council to hire me right after I graduated from the U. Two years later, my boss, Chief Latimer, retired and moved to Phoenix. Again, Rupert went to bat for me and persuaded the council to promote me.

I make a mental note to talk to our City Treasurer, Gunner Olson, about the town's finances. I knew Rupert had parlayed the Schultz legacy into a fortune for West Clover Bottom's coffers. Had someone, other than the mayor, been playing around with our several million dollar surplus and he found out?

This thought has taken over my brain cell and before going to the bank with the legal papers, I rush over to Gunner's.

He's busy with a customer and I poke around his store. Never know when I'll need a new shovel. I mean, the design has changed so much in the last two years, almost as much as computers have. I pick out one with a D handle and a red blade. I love the way it'll match my BMW. Guy's gotta beware of stuff like that.

While Gunner rings up my purchase, I pop the question regarding WCB's finances. He gives me the eye. Those steely blue peepers can freeze boiling water.

"Got a reason fer askin' Archie?"

"Actually, Gunner, two. One is Rupert and the other is Helen. I'm doing some investigating. Kinda my job. Need me to subpoena you?"

"No call fer that. I'm pretty touchy when anyone asks questions like that. Since you're who you are, I guess I ken answer your questions."

"Thanks, Gunner. Has there been any unauthorized messing with the town's investments?"

"Well, I don't check on them ever day as they're tied up in bonds and the like."

This deflates my sail faster than a dead wind. I guess it shows on my face. Gunner must see this and says, "Course, there's the mad money fund."

My sail billows out. "What's this? I didn't know we had one."

"Rupert, rest his soul, insisted the town needed one for emergencies. You know, case we were attacked by the Canucks, or some such thing."

"Yeah, there's a huge risk of them descending across the border at International Falls or wherever. How much money are we talking about?"

"A hundred grand."

Chapter 17

I ask Gunner to look into the balance when he gets time and head downtown to Clover Bottom State Bank to serve my papers. There's a parking space two doors down. I get out of my cruiser and step right into a pile of dog stuff. So much for my attempt to look official. Sure can't walk into the bank reeking.

Hobbling back to my car, I sit so my left foot dangles out. Thankfully, my cruiser has an automatic transmission. Three block later, I arrive at *Louie's Repair and Auto Wrecking*.

In an attempt to keep someone's monster dog's excrement from contaminating this half of town, I walk into his shop like I've got a broken leg. My antics of waddling and arm swinging send Louie's entire staff into gales of laughter.

Even Dutch, dismantling a Ford Crown Victoria, drops his hydraulic nippers and joins in.

Great. This will be all over the entire state in ten minutes.

"Watcha got there, Archie?"

"Just get your hose out, Louie." Shaking my leg, I ask, "This from your dog?"

More howls of laughter. "My Chihuahua don't produce that much in a month."

In case any one of his employees missed his comment, he repeats it to each of them.

More teasing as I wash off my shoe. I let them have a short blast of my *sireen* and resume my trip to the bank.

For some reason, Ruth Ann's headlines flash into my mind. It could be the display of the papers in the sidewalk dispenser. I pull out my cell phone and call Jerome.

"Howdy, boss-man. Great article in the paper, right?" His voice's awfully bright. Obviously pleased that Ruth Ann even mentioned his name. I'll have to tell her she made his year.

"Pretty much lays it out."

"I like the part that talks about how me and ol' Newberry raced to the Cities to deliver the deceased to Regions Hospital."

"Me, too. Say, I need you to start digging into the missing councilmen. Get a hold of Jackie. I'm sure she made all the arrangements, and see which motel she booked them into."

"Roger, wilco . . .."

I hang up, make sure my path to the bank's front door is clear, and enter.

"Morning, Archie," Heather Maple, the head cashier says. "Help you?"

"Mornin', Heather. Two things. Could you check my checking account balance?" I had dropped a pile of clothes off at Clover Cleaning and wanted to make sure my check wouldn't bounce.

She smiles and hammers away at a computer keyboard. "Here it is." She flips the monitor around so I can read the screen.

I figure the ten thousand, five hundred will just about cover my dry cleaning bill.

"Second. I need to see Dave."

"Sure thing."

With my astute powers of observation, it dawns on me that her batting lashes, coquettish smile, and ample chest probably mean she might see me as more than a customer. It makes me wonder if all those times in high school when she complained she didn't have a date to the dance wasn't an effort to get me to ask her out.

I take my eyes off her *charms* and spot Dave Feldman, owner, responding to the buzzer.

"Chief. You the one that had Miss Maple buzz me?"

He's always been short of conversational skills. Borrowing a phrase from Uncle George, 'pparently never learnt how to conduct biness in this part of the country.'

One does not jump right into the heart of the conversation, at least not in this area. You have to circle around it like a pair of wrestlers sizing each other up. The circling can last for days. The length of time depends on the topic.

I'll show him how it's done.

"Morning, Dave. How's the missus and kids?"

"Wife divorced me six months ago and the kids are in the Cities, or some such place. Been gone two years."

Congratulating myself for how smoothly the conversation is going, I suggest we head back to his office.

Heather's eyelashes are batting a hundred miles an hour and I'm concerned if her chest expands any more, I'm going to be lacerated by flying buttons.

Since I'm nearly a full foot taller and a hundred pounds heaver than Dave, I take his elbow and maneuver him to be my shield against unguided missiles and steer him to his office.

"What the hell you want, Schultz?"

Looks like my attempt to educate him on Minnesota business etiquette will take more than one lesson. I hand him three subpoenas.

Dave reads through the papers, huffing and puffing. "I gotta do this?"

"Doesn't have to be done by you personally."

"Damn liberals. Always poking into a honest man's work. This country's going to the dogs. Mark my words."

I glance at my left shoe. "Know what you mean, Dave. Fact remains, though, I need those records."

Dave huffs and puffs some more. If the bank were made out of straw, I'd really be worried.

He pushes a button on his desk. Almost before his finger leaves said button, Heather bursts in. She stands behind me. I mean RIGHT behind me. I can feel the heat from her body warming my neck. I dare not turn.

"Miss Maple, read these and give our Chief of Police want he wants. You can use the spare office."

Oh, God. What could be worse than being alone with a romantically starved woman in a closed office?

My fear is answered. My cell phone rings. I have to take it, which means I have to move. Gritting my teeth, I reach into my front pants pocket. This action causes me to rise slightly out of my chair, rubbing her *charms*.

I hear a soft moan of pleasure.

The caller ID says it's my deputy. "Yes, Jerome?"

"Jackie says they were supposed to check into a Motel Ten in Fort Lauderdale."

"You call the motel?"

"Want me to?"

My head is being pummeled by Heather's *charms*, and my deputy's acting dumber than a box of stones. "That's the purpose of checking them out, Barney." I'm so irritated I don't bother correcting myself.

"Gotcha. Roger, Ten . . ."

I snap my phone closed.

She backs slightly away, relieves the pressure on my head, and says, "I can do this for you, Archie. Follow me."

Dave is still huffing and puffing as we leave.

Heather finds it necessary to weld her hip to mine as she leads me to the spare office. Inwardly, I groan. The office has a wall of windows, but they're veiled off. They remind me of pictures I've seen of English homes with their black-out curtains during World War Two. Seeing inside this room would require Superman's X-ray vision.

I try to move away from the hip-weld, but Heather hooks my arm. I discover she's way stronger than she appears. "Won't it be a little dark in there, Heather, what with those World War Two black-out curtains?"

If we stay this close much longer, I'm concerned we'll become co-joined twins and have to be surgically separated.

"No, silly boy. We'll be examining confidential documents. Can't have people peering in now, can we?"

At this point I'm tempted to tear up the papers, but I resign myself and follow her into the dudgeon of iniquity.

Chapter 18

Being in the spare office alone with Heather is worse than I thought.

"Oh, don't sit there, Archie." She pats the chair next to her. "Here, by me. You can see the screen better."

Her eyelashes are about to break the sound barrier and somehow another button on her blouse has come undone.

Reluctant to take the offered seat, I try to break the spell. "You see Ruth Ann's paper this morning?"

Not a smart move, I can almost see claws pop out.

"That girl ought to go to school and learn how to write. I thought it was very childish reporting."

I refrain from mentioning Ruth Ann did go to college to learn how to write. I also fail to mention she maintained a straight A grade average and was editor of the University student paper.

"Now. Come over here." Heather treats the seat like it's a rug and she's beating out a year's worth of dust.

Slowly, I walk around the desk.

When I finally sit down, she says, "Now, isn't that more comfortable?"

I bat away the dust motes and lean on my knees to see the screen. Actually, I figure that's the only way to avoid her *charms*.

Her fingers dance over the keys and the screen comes alive. It says we're entering the Clover State Bank site. Fancy that. What would the user expect? To be plugged into a re-run of a Lawrence Welk concert?

More flashing fingers and a screen asking for name and password. Heather turns to block my view.

"Oh, crap. I don't believe this. Look what it says." She twists out of the way.

ACCESS DENIED.

Her fingers pound the keys, like they're doing some wild tribal dance. For a moment, I think she's going to drive the keyboard through the desk. The same screen comes up. More muttering.

If I look closer, I'm sure the air around her is blue.

A third attempt gets the same results.

"I'm sorry, Archie." Her hand is on my thigh. "I have to work this out. Can I call you when it's fixed?"

"Guess you'll have to. I need those records." I try to ignore her massaging my thigh. As I stand to leave, Heather jumps to her feet. "I've wasted your time. Can I make it up to you?"

She moves too fast. I can't avoid being caught in a bear hug. If her *charms* were balloons, they would've exploded.

I extricate myself and say, "Call me."

In a flash, I'm out of the bank. I head back to the office to cool down. A healthy, thirty year-old man can only take so much.

No one else is here. That's fine with me. I *really* need to cool down. I distract myself by calling the BCA and get patched through to a pathologist. I expect his name will be Doctor Karloff, or something like that. I figure anyone who makes a living working on dead people has to have a little Frankenstein in him.

Actually, the pathologist is not some ogre, but a very pleasant sounding woman named Cecilia Hudson. Her voice is low and raises my temperature even more.

Just what I need, another sexy female. I manage to reach the office thermostat and turn it as low as it goes.

"Yes, Chief. What can I do for you?"

I'm tempted to tell her, but restrain myself and speak in my manly cop voice. "I'm calling about the Mayor of West Clover Bottom and his wife, whose bodies were delivered yesterday?"

I hold the phone away for fear the volume of laughing will puncture my ear drum. When Doc Hudson gains control of herself, she makes a lame excuse.

"One of my technicians just showed me a cartoon."

Sure he did. She's recalling my deputy's antics. I can guess how he behaved. In my mind's eye, I see him putting on his best Fife impersonation.

I put the thought aside. "The reason I'm calling is to see if you routinely send recovered bullets to the FBI so they can run them through NIBIN."

"The National Integrated Ballistics Information Network?"

"Right."

"Our own BCA has done that in the past. I'll talk to them. You suspect the pistol might have been used in other crimes?"

Actually, I'm thinking the gun is rotting away. A 22 is not an expensive weapon. Use it and lose it. "To tell the truth, doctor, I seriously doubt it. But, just in case . . .."

As long as I've got her on the line, I say, "By the way, when do you plan on doing the autopsies?"

"Monday. I'll fax the results to you late in the day. Tuesday at the latest. Your deputy made sure I had your e-mail. Later, Chief."

I hear more laughter as she hangs up.

At least I know the BCA will be involved and scan the deformed bullets. They must have access to the FBI's nifty program. They can examine a bullet or even bullet fragments with a laser. If the gun that killed the Jackmans had been used before, we'll know it.

After talking to Cecilia, I lean back in my chair. Finally, something sounds promising. I can't revel too much as I'm waiting for Heather to call. My stomach growls, reminding me it's close to noon and I'm hungry. Realizing there's no way Ruth Ann will drop everything and fix lunch for me, I opt for Betty's *Shoppe*.

Chapter 19

Even though it's only the first week of May, I've had enough of Betty's Blue Plate specials to last a month. I settle for the soup of the day.

No call from Heather during lunch. My impatience grows. I have to trust she's working on the bug in their computer and not putting me off for some nefarious reason. I decide I'll be less anxious at home.

Once here, I remove my gun belt with all its accruements. It feels as if I've lost twenty-five pounds. The wall rack I use creaks in protest as I hang up the belt. I make a mental note to replace the flimsy drywall screws with six inch lag bolts. My ten millimeter Glock goes into the gun safe.

Out of my uniform into a pair of jeans that've seen much better days, I pull on an old U of M sweatshirt. My dry throat hears a beer silently beckoning.

Maggie hears the refrigerator door open and rushes into the kitchen like she's being chased by a Pit Bull. Her plaintive meows sound like she's been homeless for the past year with nothing to eat.

I wonder if she can read as she hisses when I pick a container of wild salmon. She purrs her approval over my second choice, savory ham. Actually, the ham selection smells pretty good. So savory in fact, my stomach starts growling. For some reason, I can't bring myself to make a sandwich using her food. Betty's chicken noodle soup was okay, if you like the popular canned stuff that I suspect she dilutes. It has all the staying power of plain water. I fix a ham and cheese sandwich and open my beer. My cat's curiosity gets the better of her and she hops up onto the counter. Being a push over, I put a dollop of mayo out. In a flash, it disappears. I get a pleading look and a request for more.

"A little bit, Maggie and that's it. K?"

She polishes it off and looks around for something else. I draw the line when she eyes my beer.

I love mayo on my sandwiches, or should I say I tolerate bread with my mayo? Needing some quiet time, I take my food and brew and head for my inner sanctum. John B. remodeled the original room years ago. It's always been reserved only for John Schultzs. From childhood on, it's drummed into us how private this room is.

I unlock the sliding doors and slip in. The desk was built by Grandfather A. from select trees he cut and milled at the Schultz Lumber Company. The desk top is crafted from some of the finest birds-eye maple I've ever seen. The sides, drawers, and back are crafted from tiger-maple.

It is a pleasure to sit at this desk and connect with my ancestors. The underside of the top drawer has the carved signatures of all five Johns. The privilege of signing is bestowed when we reach eighteen. I guess you have to be a Schultz to appreciate the feeling of rubbing your fingers over those inscriptions.

Years ago, Grandfather John C. installed a stereo system. I ditched the turntable and replaced it with a CD player. I slip in a disk of Beethoven's Fifth.

Leaning back in the chair, my mind drifts to the murders. Two more days before the autopsies come back. The cause of their death is pretty clear, but any trace of DNA on the ropes or under their fingernails will give me something to use, providing there is any.

During the time Heather wrestles with the bank's version of the psycho computer, *Hal*, my mind wrestles with a motive for the killings. Obviously robbery is out. Sex? Some unknown jilted boyfriend of the mayor's exotic dancer wife, Helen, aka Stormie, seeking to right a wrong? Unless it's the old, "If I can't have her, neither can you."

But, two years after the killer, Mr. Violence, lost out to Rupert? Not likely. Then again, who knows what goes through a wronged lover's mind.

These questions are banging around in my head as the list of names I got from her old boss turned out to nothing more than dead ends, save that one guy. And that's tenuous at best.

Money is plainly out. Jealousy is teetering. So, what is it?

Wait a minute.

Maybe money isn't out. Damn. I need those bank records.

Just then, like providence calling, my cell rings. It's Gunner.

"Hey, Gunner. You have some info regarding Rupert's slush fund?"

I've completely forgotten Biness Etiquette. I jumped right into the meat of the discussion. "Ah, what I meant to say was, that sure is a nice shovel I got earlier. Love the red blade."

We continue talking about nothing for the next ten minutes before Gunner gets to the point. "Did some investigatin' about bank accounts."

This sends him into a long dissertation about the banking system. Sometimes I really wish we could cut the crap and go directly to the subject. Then again, might miss something important. What that might be, I have no idea, I'm still waiting for that prescient insight.

He steers back to Rupert. "Strange thing about the mayor's fund. It's down twenty-five thou."

This takes me by surprise. I've known Rupert since I was a little tad. He always stuck me as straight as a Wyoming highway. 'Bout as exciting as well.

"Any idea where it went?"

"Nope. Took it out in one lump sum. Nearly four months ago. Near as I can recall, didn't have any Canucks try to invade us. Got a customer. See ya later, Chief."

First it was Helen being involved with some shady people. Could one of her customers be asking for some hush money? It's not that we all didn't know who and what she was before Rupert came along. Frustrating is what it is. My mind tries to come to grips with Rupert possibly having a tarnish or two on his otherwise sterling reputation.

Before I know it, the day has slipped away and shadows cast by a massive maple tree darken the room. I also realize mayo has the staying power of Betty's noodle enhanced water and my stomach growls. Although, maybe the growls are due to leaving the egg concoction out of the refrigerator for a couple of days last week.

Before I can decide which, my cell phone rings.

"Hey, Heather. Got the computer problem fixed?"

"Hi, Archie." Her tone is low and sexy. It curdles my brain. "You want to come over and get the print-outs? That way I can show you something."

I shake my head to get my mind off the 'something' possibilities. In my desire to get my hands on the statements, I agree. "I'll be right over. If that's okay with you."

"Perfect. See ya."

I lock up the study and rush over to her house. Heather lives two miles out of town in a small cottage. I've been by it several times while patrolling, but never inside.

I pull into the driveway of her brown stained, shingle clad home. With its yellow window frames, it creates a scene right out of Hansel and Gretel. I trust Heather really isn't a witch in disguise.

There is a plume of smoke rising from the chimney, though. As I walk to the front door, I smell hickory. Maybe she's going to bar-b-que something. I hope not me. What-ever, it reawakens my hunger pangs.

She answers my knock. I'm afraid she's going to rip the door off its hinges, it opens so quickly. The door acts as a fan and blows her white peek-a-boo cover-up open.

Heather is about five ten, blond hair that reaches almost to her waist, and thirty-one years old. I know her age be-cause she was one year ahead of me in high school. After graduating, she went to a business college down in the Cit-ies for some kind of certificate. She's been at the bank ever since.

What really attracts my attention, though, isn't her cer-tificate, but that she's wearing a 'something.' A tiny, yel-low bikini. Who cares if it's polka dotted or not. I see she also works out, or she's been blessed with a naturally flat stomach and the female version of six-pack abs. Although I suspect 'six-pack' is the wrong description for a female.

"Come in, Archie. I was in the hot tub."

That explains why her hair is wet up to her deliciously long and shapely neck.

I try to center my thoughts on Ruth Ann. It's very hard to do. Especially since Heather makes no effort to belt her robe. Her very short robe. Incapable of speech, I nod.

"I'm sorry it took so long to get the records, but there they are." She points to her dining room table.

Oh no, it's set for two. A bottle of wine sits in a clay cylinder.

"I thought we could relax with a drink, have supper, and then let the meal digest while we hot-tub."

This is getting out of control. On one hand, I can hardly grab the folder and rush out. On the other, Ruth Ann and I have this . . . what? An agreement? Not really. No one said, let alone demanded, we be exclusive. I'm fairly sure she doesn't date around and I know I don't.

On the third hand, I'm still damn hungry.

Chapter 20

I come up with a solution to hot tubbing with Heather. I tell her, "I don't have any trunks."

She gives me a wicked smile.

"You're wearing underwear, right?"

"Certainly."

"So what's the problem? Or do you prefer commando?"

Her solution unravels me. For a moment, I'm speechless. I manage to stammer something unintelligible, which for me, is no problem. I consider it an accomplishment my brain can generate enough voltage to make noises. As I struggle to speak, my normal manly voice turns prepubescent and reaches high notes I never knew existed.

"Think about it while I fix the drinks. Manhattan, right?"

Her hand is on my chest. I can feel and smell her minty breath. She's so close she seems to suck the air out of my lungs. I can only nod.

With a swish of her peek-a-boo cover-up, Heather goes into the kitchen. I hear ice clinking in the glasses as she prepares the drinks. I turn my back and fish out my billfold to look at a picture of Ruth Ann.

It doesn't do any good when all that exposed flesh is live and right here.

"Follow me, Archie. There's some snacks on the patio we can nibble on."

Like a well trained dog, I obey her instructions.

"Nice house you have," I squeak out. I sound like Beverly Sills reaching a crystal cracking high note.

"That's right. You've never been here before. I'll give you the deluxe tour."

"K."

I sip on the drink. I'm not sure what brand of bourbon she uses, but either it or the view of her bikini clad posterior starts my eyeballs spinning. The image I'm getting definitely sends my mind in another direction.

And it's not on seeing her house.

"You saw the dining room. Here's the living room."

Heather likes pillows. There are pillows on top of pillows. I suspect under the various piles rest a couple of chairs, maybe a sofa. Even the coffee table is covered with small pillows. But, what really surprises me is a wall of bookcases. Three cases worth. Floor to ceiling. Being an avid reader, I gravitate toward them. I guess there's close to twelve feet of old, leather bound tomes.

Among the cases are a few shelves of paperbacks, the rest are devoted to hard covers. I spot a few favorite authors—Kent Krueger, Michael Connelly, Lisa Gardner—I wonder where she gets the money. Her parents never struck me a being rich, but what does a sixteen year-old know?

Scanning down, a few other titles catch my eye. *Investing in Real Estate. Make Your Fortune in Real Estate. Buy Houses Low, Sell 'Em High.*

Her interest in this subject puzzles me. John A and B crafted the town's charter. After all, they owned all the land. They could make any rules they wished. One strictly regulated housing expansion. About the only homes that come up for sale nowadays are where someone moves or the owner dies without heirs. It takes an act of the first John's ghost to get a building permit. At last count, the total permits issued were twenty. That must have been some séance.

Heather stands beside me. "I see you're curious about all my books on real estate. As you know, your ancestors forbad expansion. Although God knows there's a fortune to be made if WCB ever decided to allow it. I do my speculating a little further south. Florida south."

Just when I thought I may have found the motive for Rupert's and Helen's murders, *my* balloon is popped.

"I see. Based on your home and furnishings, looks like you're very successful."

Heather's head is on my shoulder, her arm around my waist. "I try."

Somehow my arm finds its way around her shoulders.

She turns towards me. "Want to see the rest?"

I pretend she means the rest of the house.

"Sure," ekes out.

Heather moves away and I take a gulp of my Manhattan. All the ice has melted and I'm fairly certain the heat of my hand has distilled off most of the alcohol.

"This is the spare bedroom."

I poke my head in. How many bedrooms can a guy look at? "Umm. Nice."

"This is the hall bath."

"Umm."

She makes a grand sweeping gesture that ends up pushing me forward. "And this is my bedroom."

Oh. . .my. . .God. It's the pinkest room I have ever seen. Pink walls, fainter pink ceiling. A foot thick pink carpet. Pink pillows, more pink pillows. Pink bedspread, pink, pink, pink.

"Care to guess my favorite color?"

I make a stab at it. "Brown?"

This sends her into gales of laughter. She falls onto the bed. "Brown. How *did* you know?"

When she recovers, Heather tries to sip her drink and ends up sputtering and coughing. Her face turns red, then takes on a bluish tinge. I rush over and pull her up. The tint disappears, but she's still hacking. I gently pound her back until she spits out an ice cube.

Between coughs, she manages to get out, "Thank you, Archie. I was choking to death. You saved me. Thank you."

She holds her arms out and pulls me down with her. I'm forced to wrap my arms around her. Strictly to support myself, you know.

In my soprano voice I say, "Let's go to your patio until you're fully recovered."

I stand and attempt to pull her up. It seems her pink bedspread is fashioned from Velcro. She pulls me back and kisses me.

Reluctantly, I kiss her back.

We remain lip locked for what seems an hour, my tonsils are being massaged when my stomach lets out a howl. It saves me.

"How rude of me. You must be starving."

I am, but then I've been dating Ruth Ann. I'm starving for a variety of things.

Chapter 21

Heather drags me to the kitchen to refresh our drinks. She hands me a recharged Manhattan, then takes a plastic container from the 'fridge. We continue to her covered patio where she's strung at least two dozen pink Chinese lanterns. They're all aglow and, I must say, cast a pleasant, cozy spell over the scene.

A picnic table that'll seat at least eight has, what else, a pink and white checkered cloth. She fires up the charcoal in a small hibachi and uncovers the container to reveal two steaks swimming in some dark liquid.

I crinkle my nose. "What's that stuff?"

Apparently my grimace irritates her. She gives me a hip bump that sends me to the end on the table.

"Marinade, silly. They've been absorbing the delicate flavors of an old oriental recipe for hours. Wait till you taste 'em. Ever heard of Kobe steak?"

"Is that where Japanese farmers massage their cattle every day to tenderize the meat?"

"Uh huh. Every day."

I point to the container. "That's Kobe? I heard it costs a fortune."

She steps closer. In that same brain curdling tone says, "It's not real Kobe, but some meat I've been working for some time." She pauses and looks at me with hooded eyes. "I find massaging meat to be quite enjoyable."

That makes me wish there was an Argaiv pill. You know, one that acts just the opposite of Viagra.

Her slow licking of her lips turns my gray matter curds into the consistency of cream of mushroom soup. The synapses finally fire and I blather out, "I can't wait to taste it."

I wonder if she's enjoying my extreme discomfort. Why didn't my mother tell me there'd be women like this? And why was I so dense to pass this up when I was in high school? Well, except for that one night in the back of my car. There sure wasn't any action to compare to tonight.

Very slowly, Heather's tongue slips out and back. She says, "They'll only take a few minutes to grill. Excuse me while I finish setting the dinning room table."

Trying to be gallant, I say, "Need any help?"

"You relax. Want another drink?"

"I'm fine, Heather. Just fine."

Yeah, sure I am.

I hear more clanking of dishes, opening and closing of the 'fridge, and the clatter of silverware. The steaks look to be porterhouses. 'Course they're so dark from sitting in that stuff, for all I know they could be painted cardboard.

Moments later, Heather returns, wearing an apron that covers her charms. "Kiss The Cook" in red letters across the front. She faces me and wordlessly suggests I follow directions.

Again, I'm very reluctant, but I am her guest and it would be terribly rude of me to slight her, so I do. I try to contain myself, but her back is extremely soft and warm to my touch. I wonder if she needs massaging. A minute or ten later, I decide, no, she's tender enough.

We break, and after I catch my breath, she places the steaks on the grill. If the aroma that quickly surrounds me is any indication of how they'll taste, I'm in for one hell of a meal.

I know it's not fair, but I think of how hard I have to work to get Ruth Ann to prepare a meal, and how Heather didn't need any coaxing at all. Like I said, it's not fair, but this's damn nice, just the same.

She's all business as she hovers over the food. About a minute into the grilling, her mouth twists as she pokes one of the Porterhouses. She mumbles something about "A tad more."

I see her bare foot tapping as though counting.

"Aha," says she and flips them over.

They hiss and smoke envelopes her face. "Smell this."

I step over and inhale. "I don't know when I've ever smelled anything that good." Then I sniff the steaks.

"Thank you. I try. Not often I get an appreciative audience. I guess guys are scared of me."

"I don't believe that. You're very attractive, obviously a good cook, talented, intelligent." My tongue gets tied up. Besides, I run out of adjectives.

She places the meat on a platter and pulls me close. "Oh, Archie. No one's ever said that to me before."

I hold her tightly and feel her shoulders shaking. Oh man, she's crying. Now what'll I do?

Chapter 22

Heather's crying slows. She puts on a look of bravado and marches off to the dining room, leaving my shoulder sopping wet. Our meal is quiet. Something has happened and I'm not quite sure what. It has no effect on the flavor of the meal, though.

"The steak is divine." This elicits a tiny smile.

"Thanks, Archie." There's no enthusiasm in her response.

"This baked potato's the best I've ever had. For a pure blooded German to say that, well, it speaks volumes."

No response.

Supper is over quickly. I help her clear the dishes. I wonder what has changed. Then it dawns on me. I turn her away from the sink and use my handkerchief to wipe away a tear from her dampened cheek.

"Heather, you're a beautiful woman, obviously well read, a marvelous chef, and a delight to be around. Yet, you try too hard. Would you feel better if we'd made love? You certainly have made your desires known. I can imagine it would've been marvelous, at least for me. Although I get the feeling tomorrow you'd feel used."

She steps closer.

Her voice is soft, yet determined. "Fat chance of that happening. I've had these feelings for you since we were in high school. I knew the way you and Ruth Ann appeared to go after one another, she really loved you and I had no chance whatsoever. But, a girl can dream, can't she?"

I sit at the table not knowing what to say, so I move the salt shaker about.

I open my mouth to speak, but before the words come out, I realize how trite they'd sound. I re-think.

"There must be some men you meet. Don't you go to out-of-town banker meetings? If you deal in the housing market in Florida . . ."

She holds up her hands. Her eyes brimming. "I do, and have. But, they never meant a thing to me. No one has ever interested me like you do."

Heather pauses to brush a strand of hair back in place and takes a deep breath. "I've been carrying around a fantasy about you and me being a couple for so long, I sometimes think we really are."

She needs to say no more. I had no idea Heather carries a torch for me and has for years.

"I'm not sure what to say. I hate to see you hurt, Heather. I really do, but if anything happened, I'd hurt Ruth Ann."

Before she can speak, my work beeper goes off. Something requires my immediate attention. My deputies only use this to reach me as a last resort. I turn on my cell phone, see there are several calls, and dial the office. I know it'll be forwarded to whomever was trying to reach me.

Dreading the unknown, I respond, "Archie here. What's up?"

It's Alexia—Alex, as I call her—my night shift deputy.

"Betty's place is on fire. Maybe injuries. The fire department's turned out in force."

"On my way."

As I rush out of Heather's, I tug her along and explain there's an emergency. I hesitate at the front door and kiss her on the cheek.

I certainly don't worry about being pulled over for speeding and blast my way to town. There's a crowd gathered around the *Clover Bottom Coffee and Tea Shoppe*. At first glance it doesn't look that bad.

Until I get closer.

It is.

The café is a mess, the ceiling has a blackened hole about where I suspect the French fryers used to be. Only part of the Formica counter has survived.

Three hoses are pouring water onto the two story structure. I work my way to the front and see Alex has managed to set up a barrier of yellow tape. She hurries from one end to the other, yelling at people to stay back. I slip under the tape and join in. Between—"Stay back, please." "Give them room to work the fire." "Stay back."—I try to get some details.

Moments later, Jerome joins us and we're too busy working crowd control for me to get any answers. More and more people gather around. Apparently everyone in the area, from Crookston to Duluth, heard the news. I don't see anyone dressed in sealskins, so word hasn't made it that far north, at least not yet. With a crowd this large, I wonder why someone hasn't set up a stand to sell hot dogs and marshmallows.

Not knowing the details is driving me nuts. I finally come up with a well thought out formula to find out.

I grab Alex's arm. "What happened?"

"Pretty sketchy right now, but Betty had maybe ten customers when the grill burst into flame. Someone tried to douse it with water and all hell broke lose. Two people are missing."

"Any idea who?"

She gently takes my arm and says, "Come over here, Archie."

Alex leads me down the street, away from the crush. We reach Gill Brothers and she pushes me down so I'm sitting on a window ledge.

"One of the missing is Ruth Ann."

Chapter 23

Alex has to be mistaken. Or I'm dreaming. I'm going to wake up. Ruth Ann will call me to breakfast. Cream cheese-filled French toast.

Instead, Alex is sitting next to me.

It isn't a dream. It's a nightmare. Not my usual one where I'm stuck in an endless sea of traffic. Now I'm in an even more helpless situation. I want to run into that pile of rubble and rip it apart with my bare hands until I find her.

I feel Alex's arm around my shoulders. Wish it was Ruth Ann's, but . . .

"She could've gotten out the back door. Maybe she's at the paper, working on the story."

I grasp at the straw. "Yeah. Maybe."

She stays with me a moment longer. "I gotta get back, boss."

I nod.

Several minutes later, not knowing what to do, I put on my cop face and join my deputies.

The fire's well under control and one firefighter, decked out in a scuba tank and mask, wearing an aluminum colored suit to protect against heat, wades into the char.

Apparently, the chief had the foresight to have our ambulance standing by. The guy, or gal, in the shiny suit waves to him. Another fireman quickly dresses like his colleague, grabs a stretcher, and runs in Betty's, or what's left of it. Together they haul out a blanket covered body.

I can't make my way over to them before Newberry drives off, scattering the crowd, racing to the hospital. Thank goodness it's only three blocks away.

The siren barely gets to full volume before it fades away. I take off at a dead run. I have to see if . . .

I burst into the ER, my badge out. I'm not about to be slowed down by someone telling me I can't go in.

I shove my credentials in the face of the first person I see. "Who just came in?"

The appearance of a yelling, half crazed man tends to make people unresponsive.

My face is an inch away from his. I grab him by the collar. "Who?" I scream.

"I, ah, I don't know. I'm just a janitor."

Great. I just abused a janitor.

"Sorry." I look for a white coat and spot Doctor James Joyce.

"Doc."

Ignoring me, he looks one way, then another, and he hurries towards a nurse.

I run to his side. "Who?"

For the moment he ignores me and speaks medical talk to the nurse. The conversation ends with "Stat."

On his way back to whomever, he says, "We're busy."

That's a help. I want him to explain what the hell's going on. Was the person they brought in Ruth Ann? I take a breath and realize if it was her, *my* wants are immaterial.

Another nurse comes up and tells me I need to leave the area. My badge has little effect. I stumble to the small waiting room and sit.

The minutes go by as if they're in a race against a snail. The shelled animal is leaving them behind in the dust. Another guy joins me in the ten by twelve room, carrying a cup of coffee.

"Where'd ya get that?"

He must have his own problems and gestures at the double doors.

Since he doesn't seem to be in the mood to talk, I nod my thanks and follow Map Quest Guy's directions.

The janitor I abused earlier is pushing a dust mop down the hallway. "Sorry to interrupt you, ah Mr. . . ."

He gives me a sour look and backs away.

"Look, I was—hell still am—concerned about my lady friend, she was in the big fire. I'm trying to find out if she was the person brought in. I'm really sorry I went at you like that."

"I didn't know about the fire until a little while ago. They wheeled someone in. I overheard one of the orderlies say it was a Ms Boyer."

"Ruth Ann Boyer?" As if there are any other Boyers in town.

His face falls. "No. Not little Ruth Ann. Man, I'm so sorry. Any word?"

"Nah. She's still in the ER. I'm going crazy waiting. You know where the coffee machine is?"

"That crap? Hell, Betty's asphalt is way better than that . . . well you know what I mean. Follow me, I got a thermos of *decent* coffee. Might be a tad strong fer ya."

A man after my own heart.

He leads me through a maze. "Come into my office," he says with a grin.

His office is the boiler room. I hear strains of what has to be, *The Hundred Best Loved Classical Tunes.*

For a moment, the strains of the *Blue Danube* help me forget upstairs and what's happening to Ruth Ann. I calm down, knowing my worrying won't make her any better and it'll tear up my stomach. The scene around me is so different from what I expect what most of us would classify as a simple hourly worker. The beautiful music, a poster of Mount St. Helens erupting, an old wooden desk with pictures of, I guess, his family. I'm reminded of a guy who worked at the University of Minnesota animal hospital. I wandered into his office one day. It was a room full of monkeys, dogs, rabbits. All right, I admit it, I was lost out of my skull. He was an wizened old fellow and we got to talking. Said, "I got the most important job in town."

"Why's that?"

"I take care of these animals and if I don't do it right, all them scientists upstairs?" He waves in a direction that could be downstairs for all I know. "Well, they depend on me. Wouldn't be able to do their research if my animals get sick. Yes, sir, best and most important job of all."

A book and its cover. Be careful what you think.

My new-found janitor friend pours a cup of coffee that puts mine to shame. I ask how he makes his and he gives me his secret. I have to swear I won't tell a soul.

I start to talk and he holds up his hands and cocks an ear.

"They're paging you, Archie."

Quickly, I thank him, then tear off to the waiting room. Half way there, I realize somehow he knows me and I didn't take the time to get his name.

Doc Joyce is waiting, unsmiling. He looks drawn through the proverbial knot hole. I do not like this and, by projection, him either. I want to be back in the basement talking to my friend.

In three words, he sends me to hell. "Sit down, Archie."

Shit, shit shit. Tears flood my cheeks. I know what's coming. I can't face it, but I sit like a trained dog.

"We have to fly her to the Duluth Burn Center. There's a lot of damage to her head. Luther Bronson has his chopper set to go. Ruth Ann's being prepped for the trip as we speak. She'll be in their capable hands in about thirty minutes."

I'm speechless.

He senses my distress and puts a hand on my shoulder. "They are a certified burn center, Archie. One of the best in the state."

I manage to croak out, "How bad is it? Will she make it?"

He answers with those most encouraging words, "It's too early to say one way or another."

If I thought I was suffering through a nightmare earlier, it's was nothing compared to his, "It's too early to tell."

Joyce continues, "She's heavily sedated and will be for the next couple days. Go home, Archie. Go to Duluth late tomorrow."

I'm in a stupor and barely manage to leave. I have so damn much to do. Everything goes out the widow until I know what's going to happen to Ruth Ann.

Besides, I don't want my flow of dimes to come to a crashing halt.

Chapter 24

In the hospital parking lot, I watch Ruth Ann being loaded into the helicopter for her trip to the burn center. As the chopper becomes a speck in the eastern sky, I can't see myself going home to do nothing but worry, so I wander down the street towards my office. On my way I glance back at Betty's place. The crowd has dispersed. All that remains are shards of yellow tape flapping in the breeze and the firefighters cleaning up. In the station, Alex is waiting for me. Guess she knows me pretty good. She hugs me for the longest time. It helps. All my concerns seem to flow to her. She doesn't have to ask how I'm feeling. Her eyes do.

"It's not good. They're flying her to Duluth. Doc James says there's a lot of damage to her head. I couldn't see her and then she was in Luther's 'copter. James said I'd be wasting my time if I tried to visit her right now. I should wait for a couple days. Whatever *couple* means."

She holds my hands. I feel her expression of "I'm sorry."

I try to change the subject. "Any idea what happened?"

She shrugs. "The Fire Chief says it looks like it started in the deep fryers. Like I said before, someone threw water."

I could see it. The water instantly turning to steam. The grease explodes, catching fire at the same time. Some lands on Ruth Ann's head. I cringe at the thought. The pain. I wonder if a skull can insulate the brain. Guess it depends how on long her hair was on fire.

The door opens and in walks Betty. She's covered in soot and ashes. Her dress is mostly charred holes. There's a bandage on her right cheek.

"Archie, I'm so sorry about Ruth Ann."

I tell what I know about her condition. "She's in Duluth as we speak."

"We, Ruth Ann and I, tried to get a hold of you earlier."

Her eyes are boring a hole in me and I immediately feel guilty.

"She had something to tell you. All she said to me was she was looking all over for ya. Something important."

Damn. And I was at Heather's enjoying her advances.

"Any idea what she wanted, Betty?"

"Nope. I can speculate, but that's all."

"Speculate, then."

"Well, I got this ability to read stuff even if it's upside down. Little Ruth Ann was making notes. She kinda shielded them from me, but she gots arms like a bird gots legs."

Yes, Ruth Ann's slender. Almost to the point of Twiggy-dom. "Go on."

Betty shakes her head. "Sorry, Archie. All I read was, 'real estate.' She spelled it in capital letters and underlined it three times. Mean anything to you?"

Oh, did it ever.

Instead, I answer, "No." Shaking my head back and forth so rapidly, I'm concerned it'll fall off. Or I might get struck by lightening for telling a lie. Now that'd really be a sign, as there isn't a cloud in the sky. Although, since it's dark as all get out, for all I know there could be a storm about to hit.

Betty heaves a sigh. "Well, I gotta go and get cleaned up. Lots ta do if I'm gonna be open by next weekend."

I can imagine her in coveralls, wielding a hammer and Skill Saw, directing a crew. Betty's place is a West Clover Bottom establishment and I'll bet she'll have fifty people reconstructing the *Shoppe*.

My day's been one of constant tension and the last drop of adrenalin finally melts away. I realize I can barely stand as I wave good night to Alex and head home.

I'm expecting to collapse into bed and sleep until noon tomorrow, but by the time I park, I see in the rear view mirror that my eyes are fixed and dilated. Not from some drug, but by Ruth Ann's note. REAL ESTATE.

My competent-editor-crack-reporter/girl-friend has stumbled onto another clue. My mind swirls. If I expect to get any sleep, I better calm down. My recliner looks inviting, yet all that does is give Maggie another place to curl up for her fifteenth nap of the day. I counted them once, so I know.

Her incessant purring and demands for attention are hardly conducive to my calming down. I unhook her claws from my arms and retreat to the study.

There isn't any storm brewing, in fact the sky is clear. A half moon beams forth and lights the clearing down to the lake. I flip the dock light switch on, and a hundred watt bulb sputters on. A slight breeze is rippling the water.

Something on the far shore catches my eye. Before it registers, it's gone. My mind begins to play games. *It was something you imagined. You like to brag about your imagination, don't you?*

Oh yeah, that's really instrumental in bringing on sleep. I make a Manhattan instead and contemplate what I saw, or imagined I saw, or hypothesized I saw.

Could it be related to 'the note'?

I check my watch. Eight PM. What the hell? I'm so wired I fumble around and locate the list of names.

There's a recorded message stating the number has been disconnected. A quick call to the phone company and I'm told Mr. Lee left the area in December. Another scratch off.

A woman picks up. "Is Richard Stewart there?"

"Who is calling?"

"Chief Archie Schultz of the West Clover Bottom police."

"May I ask what this's about?"

"I'm investigating a double murder and he may have information about one of the victims that'll help with the case."

"Please hold." I hear Mrs. Stewart bellow out, "Dick. For you."

He comes on the line. "Yes?"

I explain who I am and the reason for the call. I can almost see him turn all shades of red, then white as he hems and haws when I mention Stormie.

He tells his wife, "This is a business call. I need to take it in the den."

A minute later, he's back on the line. "Look, Chief. I fooled around with Stormie three years ago. I haven't seen nor heard of her since. Do you have to tell my wife?"

"How long were you involved with her?"

"Less than a month. She was nothing more than a wild fling. When she suggested I should give her a diamond ring she spotted in Macy's, I broke it off."

I noticed something in the way his voice cracked when he talked about the bauble Stormie requested. "So, was she really pushy about getting this gift?"

"For awhile, yeah."

"Ever price the ring out?"

I imagined him hanging his head. "Twenty-five."

"Let me get this straight. She wants a ring, you balk, and then break it off."

"Pretty much so."

"Any contact since then?"

He answers too quickly and too forcefully. "Not on your life. Why all the questions, by the way?"

"Stormie was found shot to death recently. I'm doing a background investigation. Strictly routine."

I get to use another line from the cop shows. Do people really believe cop questions are strictly routine? And what does that mean anyway?

Another half dozen questions and I reluctantly hang up, after I reserve the right to call him again. With only one questionable tie-in with Stormie's past, that leaves me with Rupert and the missing money. Although, I find it strange that the ring and the deficit in Rupert's mad money just happen to coincide.

I know the mayor of Bagley, a town near-by West Clover Bottom. He's another Jackman. Since it's not that late, I get his number from information and dial.

He must be an early to bed type, as he sounds sleepy when he answers. I explain who I am and the reason for my call. After I repeat this two more times, he agrees to see me tomorrow. I wonder if he's related to Rupert. After all, Jackman isn't that common of a name. Besides, I have a few other things on my mind.

A severely injured girlfriend, to name one.

Chapter 25

The events of the day have sapped me mentally as though some alien stuck a straw in my brain and sucked it dry. Hope they have a small appetite, since there's not that much to draw on.

I'm exhausted. My first drink goes down too smoothly and my mind begs for another. Two Manhattans do the trick and I fall asleep. Not in my comfortable, adjustable firmness bed, but in my way less conforming executive chair.

I wake to the sounds of rattling dishes. For an instant, I think it's Ruth Ann. Somehow she's recovered and back in town. I jump up. My skull feels as though I head-butted a steel I beam.

I try to wipe away the stars and crazy $#%%, symbols. Two drinks did this to me?

Again, the rattling sounds make their way through the den's inch and a half thick mahogany pocket doors.

This time they're accompanied by a "MEOW."

I open a fresh bag of Friskies. At least Maggie gets breakfast prepared for her.

Purrs and leg rubs tell me she's forgiven me for being tardy. Moments later, she's off to her after-breakfast-and-before-a-snack-nap.

I can't go to Betty's since it's in shambles, so I make two watery scrambled eggs and char some toast. While eating, I decide to hell with waiting, change out of my uniform into civvies, and strike out for Duluth. Along the way I call the station to tell Jerome I'll be in after I check on Ruth Ann. I trust he'll not be faced with some sort on an emergency that might require him to be armed.

Heading east on Highway 2, lost in my thoughts about Ruth Ann's condition and Betty's remark about real estate, I'm aware I've passed Cass Lake. I'm also aware of a set of flashing blue and red lights behind me. Figuring it's just the Minnesota Highway Patrol going to some accident, I continue on my way. I probably should pull over, but I need to see Ruth Ann. Besides, he can pull around me. There's hardly any traffic.

Perhaps it's his seven thousand decibel *sireen* blaring alongside of me, or the sight of his shaking fist that gets my attention.

I respond by smiling and waving. Then it dawns on me. He does want me to pull over. I slow from eighty and stop.

As I start to get out of my car, his voice over the loudspeaker—its volume obviously set to 'wake the dead'—bellows out, "Stay in your car. Hold your hands out of your window. Get your license and registration ready where I can see them. You armed? Anything illegal in that car?"

Jerome obviously has a relative in the Patrol. He must be a recent graduate still following every procedure as if it's gospel. I'm not sure how I can do all these things at once.

I see him in my mirror. He's thin as a rail looking like the wash from a passing car'll blow him into the ditch. The creases in his uniform shirt look sharp enough to slice bread.

He's in a half crouch. Stalking up like I'm a wounded grizzly, his BB gun-sized pistol out, and he looks to be speaking into his shoulder mounted mike.

By the time he gets to my rear bumper, his pistol looks like a twenty-two. Then I read the small note on the bottom of my mirror, "Objects may be closer than they appear."

I twist my head to speak and see the 22 now looks like it's a 50 caliber firearm.

That barrel is huge!

"Officer, I'm the West Clover Bottom Chief of Police. What's wrong?"

"Sure you are. Now, open the door."

My hand drops from sight as I comply.

"NO! From the outside."

Now I know this guy's right out of class. He could let me open from inside. I find this somewhat complicated and fight to push the button under the handle. I twist and turn, trying to get some footing. I part the air with a few well chosen words and stop to catch my breath.

"Mind if I try to open this damn door from the inside?"

"Hell, yes, I mind. Keep working on it."

After what seems ten minutes later, I see the frustration on his face as if I'm trying *his* patience. A heavy sigh and he pulls my door open.

"On the ground."

"Just bear with me here. I'm going to pull out my billfold and show my badge."

I ignore his screams to get on my face and slowly pull out my credentials. Shit. In my hurry to see Ruth Ann, I've left my wallet on my dresser.

"Well, buster?"

"You might as well lock me up and throw away the key. Or—"

"Or what, smart ass?"

"Or run my plates."

"Yeah, sure. I'm gonna cuff ya. You look like a major risk to me. Now, put your hands behind your back."

All of this hassle because I was going a *few* miles an hour over 60. Had I not been so honest and used my cruiser for personal business, I coulda been halfway to Duluth by now. I contemplate arguing with Fife Jr., but I know it'll delay me even more, so I stuff my frustration and play along.

I put my hands behind my back. The kid cuffs me. I say kid because he looks like he doesn't even shave yet.

"Did you call this stop in?"

He doesn't answer.

"You know, according to Code 17, Section 2a, as amended, you're required to call this in before you approach. What if I'm really on the FeeBee's Ten Most wanted, rather than West Clover Bottom's Chief?"

I can tell he's confused, so I press some more and say in my most humble voice, "Tell ya what, officer. Let's pretend you just stopped me. Call my plates in. K?"

I read his eyes and he knows he's screwed up.

A car pulls up. The driver asks if everything's okay.

The kid nods and waves the car to continue. He acts as though it's common for a scrawny kid to be holding a hundred caliber pistol on someone.

As the car leaves, the kid backs away and he mumbles into his mike.

This is too much. I wait until he's done. "Officer. Don't *ever* do that again."

"Huh?"

"You turned your back on me while you were talking to headquarters. I could have jumped you."

His mike barks, "That's the Chief of the West Clover Bottom Police. What the hell you doin'?"

I admit, he's pretty quick on his feet. "Just checkin'. Over and out. Roger. All clear. Wilco. Ten-four."

Jerome's relative, all right.

I hear a click as the conversation ends.

His shoulders droop, his face drains. After he frees me, he holds his hand out in a peace offering. I apologize for speeding and explain I'm in a rush to get to Duluth and see how my girlfriend's doing after the fire yesterday.

"I ought to be the one apologizing, Chief. My cousin, Jerome? Said there was a big fire. The gal they airlifted is your girl-friend? Man, I'm really sorry 'bout all this. Tell ya what, Chief, I'll escort ya to Duluth. Let's go."

The countryside speeds by and soon we're in downtown Duluth. I wave my thanks and pull into the Burn Center parking lot. I pause for a moment, almost afraid to enter and find out how she's doing. I have this strange reaction when confronted with an emotional crisis. I get sarcastic and make light of things. Like yesterday with the janitor. I don't know why, but it helps me get through.

The receptionist tells me Ruth Ann's in Room 412. I forgo the elevator and bound up the stairs. I'm guessing the sound of pounding feet, along with my huffing and puffing, disturbs the quiet. The gal at the nurses station scowls at me and holds her finger to her lips. She's got this pinched face that looks more like the stereo-typical vision of a spinster librarian than a highly trained nurse. Even her hair is in a bun under her blue striped cap.

I start to speak—my voice raised in response to my frustrating morning.

"Shush, now. We must be quiet on this floor."

I don't give voice to my response, but I want to tell her, "I wasn't aware this hospital also served as an auxiliary station for the public library."

There I go again.

"Now, sir, may I help you?"

I explain who I am, a task made more difficult by my lack of identification. She calls my office and, somewhat mollified, tells me I can only spend five minutes with Ms Boyer.

"Is *Ruth Ann* awake?"

"*Ms Boyer* is very ill and under heavy sedation. Certainly the doctor told you that yesterday."

My frustration seeps to the surface. "I'm not exactly sure why I only have five minutes to see my girlfriend, if she's not awake."

My defense mechanism takes over my thoughts. I'm getting the impression Nurse Ratchet in her highly starched uniform would shatter if she attempted to bend. Wish I'd brought Dutch with me. She'd make a nice lawn ornament, after he throws her out of the window. Head first.

Cautiously, not knowing what I'll see, I enter 412. I suspect, somewhere in the jungle of wires leading out and tubes leading in, lies Ruth Ann. Perhaps where the blanket ends is her head. It's hard to tell because she's got enough wrappings round her to make an Egyptian pharaoh's mummy jealous. She looks absolutely terrible. I wonder what she looks like under all the dressings. Good thing she's out and can't see my expression. Her condition tears me apart.

As I stand there, trying to figure out if I can touch her, or where I can whisper sweet nothings, I feel my eyes leaking. I quickly wipe the tears away. Just then another nurse enters.

She looks as though I'm not there and starts writing on some form. For all I know she's doing a crossword puzzle. She stares at the thingy that's beeping. Drawing on my vast medical knowledge, I'm pretty sure those red, squiggly lines are Ruth Ann's heart beat. That other thing, the one that is silently dripping, is putting something in Ruth Ann, about where I'd expect her arm to be. There's another drippy thing going into her other arm.

The nurse lifts the bed sheet and looks at a drippy thing where something yellowish is coming out. Then she stares at the beepy gizmo once again. I'm guessing this time the numbers are Ruth Ann's pulse. I hope 60 is good.

The nurse finally notices I'm in the room. "Who are you?"

"Her boyfriend. How's my Ruth Ann doing?"

Apparently the staff here tends to be on the formal side. "You'll have to speak to Doctor Thompson about Ms Boyer's condition."

She swishes out.

There's nothing for me to do except wait. I pull a chair close and rest my hand on what could be her stomach.

I bend down and whisper into the ball of gauze, "I love you and I know you'll be up and around in no time." Then I relate the tale of getting here. Probably my imagination, but I swear I hear her chuckle when I mention the cop and his relationship to Jerome.

There's some disturbance by the door and I look up to see Nurse Ratchet's arms waving as if she's a windmill. She's whispering something to, I assume, Ruth Ann's doctor.

I figure him to be a doctor because he's got a stethoscope artfully draped around his neck. Not only that, he really looks like a TV doc hawking some pill. Whatever Ratchet said to him puts a pained expression on his face. He catches my eye, and motions me over.

I quickly change my opinion of him when he says, "Thank you, Nurse Ra, ah, Jamison. I'll take it from here."

He and I step into the hall and he explains Ruth Ann's condition. After he tells me not to bother Ms Boyer.

Chapter 26

Alone in the antiseptic smelling hall, Doc Thompson informs me in a quiet, confident voice, "She'll be sedated for two more days. If her vitals continue in a positive direction, we'll slowly start removing the dressings."

My sarcastic side rears its head. I make a statement tantamount to The Grand Canyon's really just a ditch, isn't it, when I say, "Then she can come home."

His patience is tried, but he's much better at hiding it than I am.

He responds, "No way."

I move aside as a patient goes by in a wheelchair. The orderly pushing is saying something as he whips by, " . . . they'll give you something for the pain."

The doctor doesn't offer any explanations and with a sigh continues with Ruth Ann's condition. "She has both first and second degree burns. We're keeping them under a thick layer of Silvadene cream. It's cooling and mitigates skin trauma."

"Then she can come home."

"Chief Schultz, I know you're anxious, but that is not going to happen for at least two weeks."

I'm not being told something.

"Just how extensive are they?"

He illustrates by placing his hand in the middle of his head. "It goes from about here," then his hand sweeps down the back of his neck, "and extends to about here. In addition, there's less severe damage to her right hand. Fortunately, her face escaped the flaming grease."

My next words are difficult to get out. "Ah, is, could there be, you know?"

That earlier patient is wheeled by again. He's wearing a huge grin. Apparently he likes the pain shot.

The corridor clears and doc puts his hand on my shoulder. This is not going to be good.

"It's too soon to tell. Like I indicated, the burn area is extensive, but the treatment she received before coming here was excellent. The reason we're keeping her for longer than if she was burned, say, on an arm, is to check for any brain damage. MRI, etcetera."

He pauses, apparently to pick his words. "I have every hope she'll be fine."

"Every *hope*" lodges in my brain. Not, *she will be*. I go back to her room. Her meds have her in, what appears to me, a coma. I hope she can sense my presence so she knows how much I care.

A half hour later, a nurse enters and tells me my five minutes are up. I lean over and whisper a sincere "I love you" and leave for home.

My heart is heavy with worry. I want the doc's words about his *hope* to be a prophecy. He wasn't very convincing.

I pull into Grand Rapids' huge Musky-shaped restaurant for a burger and fries. This plaster replica of a fish makes all the pictures of road-side novel structures. But, my mind's on Ruth Ann's condition. A thought seeps in. Could her accident have been planned? Did the note Betty saw really spell 'DOOM'?

I shake my head to clear the thought. How improbable is it? Still, I gobble down my food and stroll to the end of the counter. The fryers are about three feet away from the edge. If Ruth Ann were sitting here, she'd be less than six feet away. I picture Doc Thompson's illustration of her burns.

I try to vision the *Shoppe*'s layout. Was it like this one? The fryers opposite the end of the counter and close to a wall separating it from the back room?

Did a hand with a tumbler of water come around that wall? If so, she must have known what was about to happen, and ducked. That would explain the burns starting in the middle of her head and going down her neck.

I look for a minute longer. I'm not sure, but they sure resemble what I recall of Betty's place. So, I ask myself, how did the fire actually start?

Having prepared so well for this trip, not only did I forget my billfold—good thing I have a ten in my back pocket—but my cell phone, as well. No way of taking a picture. I do it the old fashioned way. I make a sketch.

To hell with that kid cop. I race back to West Clover Bottom and then on to my meeting with Alan Jackman, Mayor of Bagley, Minnesota.

When I pull up to their municipal building, it looks shabby compared to ours. Then again, Bagley didn't have a couple of Schultzs years ago to leave a bundle of money behind.

Before going in, I take in the buildings on the street and note they're respectable. A good starting point to my conversation with Alan.

He greats me warmly and I offer my condolences for his loss.

"We weren't that close, Archie. Being second cousins and all. But thank you anyway."

I spend about fifteen minutes dancing the dance of Biness Etiquette before getting down to my real business.

"So," I say. "Like I mentioned, I'm investigating Rupert and Helen's death. One thing has come up that bothers me. Rupert had a slush fund for his use in case on an emergency. Some of it's missing. Were you unaware of his fund and have any ideas why some is missing? Any family difficulties he may used it for?"

"He had a fund he could tap into? I know you folks have a pretty healthy reserve, but like I said, we weren't that close. Never said anything to me about any money."

Another dead end. I head back home to lick my wounds.

Chapter 27

A swarm of people are working feverishly on Betty's place. They're mostly guys, but several women saw and hammer with the best of them. In the middle of the gang stands the owner, looking like a combination of Rosie the Riveter and Ma Kettle. She's wearing bibbed coveralls, a pair of rag-tag combat boots, and her hair's up in a bun. Fists on her hip, giving some poor fellow a chewing out.

When she's done, he meekly shuffles off to some task. Maybe Dutch, if he wasn't such a pussycat to start with, might have objected to her language; other than cuz, I doubt anyone would even try standing up to her.

I catch her eye and nod to my left.

Betty hollers at someone and stomps to my side. "How's Ruth Ann? Heard you were in Duluth. She holdin' up?"

I explain what her doctor said. In response, she fixes her eyes on me, lays a leather gloved hand on my shoulder and gives it a little squeeze. I make a note to visit Doc James right after this and have my shoulder X-rayed to see just how badly it's damaged.

"Also heard you spent the better part of the evening over ta Heather Maple's place. Something going on there, Archie? Better not be, buster."

I shudda known in this town if you sneeze, a dozen people call to say "Bless you."

"Look, Betty, I love ya to death, but that was over the line."

I get a smile and another bone bruising squeeze.

"Better been biness, boy. And I don't mean monkey biness."

I'm not about to tell her what really went on. Instead, I say, "Two questions about the fire. Were the French fryers next to the back room wall?"

I get a nod.

"Second. Who was in your place that night? All regulars?"

I watch her scrunch up her face. She does that when she's trying to recall an event. Her mouth moves back and forth. She runs her hand through her hair, apparently forgetting it's up in a bun.

Her language turns the air blue as she extracts her fingers from the knot. "Less see, the Farmer family was there. So was what's his name, he works at the sewage plant? Ruth Ann, of course." Betty rubs her face and turns ninety degrees. "Helps me remember iffen I stand like I'm at the counter."

We're interrupted by one of the workers asking if she wants the same sized front window as before. She answers him with a cuff on his head. "I said I want everything the way it was, buster."

Betty turns back to me. "Ruth Ann was on my left, two stools down. Wait. There was a couple guys next to her. Never seen them before. Said they're working on that new oil pipeline coming down from Canada? Other than them two, I knew everone else."

I hadn't paid much attention to the pipeline. Supposed to be a thirty-six incher. I heard the route was going to be close to the north end of the lake.

"Mayor Jackman was opposed to it, wasn't he."

"Was he ever. Said it would be put in. . . ." Betty pauses. Her face looks stricken. "Over his dead body."

I never would have believed it if I hadn't seen it with my own eyes. A tear spills down her cheek. A honking sound partially covered up by a red checked handkerchief. She gives me a wide-eyed look. "You think that's why he was—?"

"Hard to say right now. I don't suppose those strangers gave you their names."

"Nope."

"Would you reorganize them?"

"Sure would."

"Can you describe them?"

Betty waits until I have my notebook out. "Big. Both had full beards. Long straggly hair. One was fat, the other fatter. Fat wore glasses. Fatter has a scar on his right cheek."

Wasn't much, but I thank her and head to the office. I need to call my cop friends over in Bemidji where all the pipes are being staged.

My route to the station takes me past the mayor's home. Talk about being embarrassed, I haven't taken the time to search his place. Torn between calling Bemidji and searching, I flip a coin.

Damn!

I miss and it rolls down a street drain.

Deciding it was heads, I walk up the sidewalk to Rupert's. I squint through the first floor windows. Everything looks neat and orderly. His VW Bug sits in the garage. The right rear tire's flat. I mosey back to the house. The front door is unlocked. I mean this is a small town and people would look down their noses if someone actually locked their doors.

What am I looking for? Signs of disturbance? Blood? A smoking pistol? I don't touch anything and go from room-to-room. I detect a stench that seems to be coming from the kitchen.

Not sure what it might be, I attempt to unholster my service revolver. Fortunately, I don't keep a round in the chamber. The strap across the grip proves to be difficult to undo. Grunting, uttering words that would stop deer and antelope from playing, had they heard my exclamations. Finally, I drop my gun belt, which also holds up my pants.

My frustration builds to new heights. I try to kick off my trousers and fall flat on my face. To say the air turned blue is an understatement. It was purple.

My damn shoe-boots prevent getting my pants off. I fling them across the room. Too bad about that mirror. I'm sure the Jackmans won't be filing a complaint, though.

Peter Sellers in that *Pink Panther* movie had an easier job getting out of the bucket.

Standing in the middle of their living room, in my boxer shorts, wrestling to free my Glock, I see the trouble. After exploring the lake bottom the other day, I forgot to wipe down my belt. The snap is rusted shut. Cheap thing.

I also carry a Swiss Army knife in my pocket and use it to slice the leather strip. Finally, I can investigate the smell.

"Freeze! Police! Hands up."

Oh, God, it's Jerome. "What the hell you doing here?"

"That you, Chief? Boy, your legs are really skinny."

He bends over laughing.

"Say a word about this and you'll be on permanent duty cleaning toilets in City Hall."

"It'd be worth it."

By now, I'm hopping on one foot getting my pants on. Finally presentable, that's a laugh in itself, I ask Jerome, "What brings you here?"

He can't stand anymore and plops down into a chair. "Boy, this is really comfortable, Boss. Ought to try one."

"Never mind that. What brings you here?"

"The Jackmans got a silent alarm system, remember? You must've set it off when you broke that window."

Apparently my other shoe went through a living room window. "Oh, yeah. I forgot about that. Never understood why they had one. Never locked their doors."

To add insult to insult, Jerome's nose is twitching worse than Ruth Ann's after I bagged the Jackmans.

"Phew. That sure smells like spoiled cat food. Right?"

"That's what I thought. Although it could be another body. I didn't want to take any chances during my thorough examination of their house."

"Should have told you sooner, Archie. That's what took me so long to respond last week. Ruth Ann called to see if you were in the station. Said the mayor was dead. I stopped by to search before going to the pier."

Reclaiming my dignity, I dismiss Jerome and made a quick pass upstairs before going back to the station to call about the two strangers.

I pat all my pockets and realize my phone's back home. I mumble a reminder to retrieve it as soon as I'm done here. Before I leave though, a thought strikes me and I head down the hallway to see if, by chance, Rupert has a home computer. Sure enough, in what appears to be a converted bedroom, I find a well, equipped office. A fax machine, color ink-jet printer and a Dell computer. There's a small bookcase with a handful of computer related titles. I page through them looking for a tip or two.

In the book called *Computers for Dummies*, I come across a three by five recipe-like card. Good old Rupert. He has copied down his password. Moments later, I have his *Inspiron* booted.

I open his e-mail and page through. Most are notes to friends and don't concern me. There's one sent to the councilmen confirming the date for their retreat, But, the one that really interests me are four back-and-forth's to R. Stewart. The earliest one, a mere five months ago, Stewart claims Stormie—Helen—has been contacting him off and on since Richard broke it off with her. He goes on to say she's now demanding the ring, or 'else.'

The next couple are Rupert's denial his wife would resort to any such thing.

Rupert makes a mistake and calls Stewart's bluff. The last e-mail from Richard is his answer. An ultimatum. Either Rupert gives her the ring or he's going to the press.

Apparently that worked as when I found her body, she was wearing one honking ring.

I find all this hard to believe, or should I say, accept. On the other hand, Rupert married an exotic dancer, much younger than he. I suppose in order to keep her satisfied, and by extension, himself satisfied, he did stuff out of character.

Now the question remains, did it stop or does Stewart still have a sword hanging over his head?

Chapter 28

I feel a little tarnished myself as I leave. My mentor has some dark secrets I really don't care to know. No sooner do I pick up my cell phone, it rings. It's Jackie reminding me I'm expected to speak at Rupert's funeral.

Great, just what I need knowing what I now know. Did I make another dumb promise I can't remember? It's not like I don't have a few other things on my mind. Like how to live down the episode in the Jackmans' house. Jerome probably has it posted on YouTube by now. Then there's Ruth Ann's condition, of course. To say nothing about who killed the mayor and his wife. Minor details.

I grunt my acknowledgement, drive to the office and, along the way, stop for a minute to marvel again on how much progress has been made on the *Shoppe*.

Betty's ability to organize is truly amazing. All the chaos of the other night has resulted in order. Still work to be done, of course, but Betty will be slinging hash by the Opener. God, the opening of fishing season starts midnight Friday.

I dash into the station and close the door. Finally, I can call Bemidji uninterrupted.

Before I can pick up the receiver, Jerome busts in wearing a sly look. I know he thinks he's got me over a barrel. I'll show him.

"Need you to patrol East Clover Bottom. Then you'll have to set up a radar trap out on Highway 2. After that—"

"No need to worry, Chief. My lips are sealed."

Sure they are. "In that case, go to the pier and make sure everything's ready for Friday. We're going to be inundated by fishermen Thursday, if not sooner. I'm thinking this year we ought to set up one-way traffic into the lake parking lot as well as going out. Get some city maintenance people to put up the signs. Main Street will be one-way west and First one-way east."

"Gotcha."

I'm put through to my counterpart in Bemidji. I relay what info I have and ask him about the strangers seen just before the fire.

"Not too many folks working on the pipeline just yet. I'm guessing a dozen or so. Want to poke around and see if anyone matches the descriptions?"

"Yeah. I'll stop by tomorrow on my way to Duluth "

"Look forward to seeing you again. We'll take a swing through the equipment staging yard."

I hang around the office to talk to Alex. Want to see if she can adjust her hours starting Thursday. Our town will more than double its population on opening day. The folks who take money at the pier will need a cop watching out for their safety.

Long ago, when my great-grandparents came up with the idea of damming Clover Creek to build Lake Clover Bottom, their son, John B, foresaw all the money the town could generate. As the lake took shape, they stocked it and established strict fishing rules. Membership costs $2,500 with another two fifty a year dues. Most people pay by check some time in January, but several wait until opening day.

At any rate, there's a lot of money floating around. Little wonder Betty has people working three shifts to get her place ready.

Alex breezes in, asks about Ruth Ann, and how I'm doing.

"As well as can be expected, in both cases. Say. I wonder if you'll be able to arrange your classes so you can start your shift at 3 p.m. starting Thursday. Probably stay that way until the rush settles down."

Alex is working on her bachelor's in Criminal Science at Bemidji State. Although with my luck, she'll follow in Michele Leonhart's lead and end up as head of the DEA.

"Can do. Kinda planned on it. I see they're making one-way streets this year. Should really help traffic. Your idea?"

"Yeah."

"Good thought."

"Thanks. It's late and I've had a long day. I'm heading out. Appreciate you adjusting your hours, Alex."

"Glad to help. Oh, got something for ya. I hear old WD-40 really works on rusted bolts and stuff. Here."

Chapter 29

It's nearly eight when I get home. Maggie lets me know I'm late with her food. She seems to quickly forgive my trespasses when she receives a handfull of kitty treats. Must be like feline ice cream.

A burger along with some fried potato wedges and a couple of pickles constitute supper. After my meal, I take a busman's holiday and watch *Mystery Theater*.

It's a British story about a crotchety old Lord of the Manor meeting his end at the hand of an unknown person. Inspector Morse and his side-kick solve the problem and eventually arrest the scullery maid. She explains the Lord did her wrong.

In my world, it seems Mayor Jackman did Helen, the equivalent of the maid, right when he married her.

Too worked up to sleep, I wander down to the lake to think about Rupert's eulogy. I apply a half can of OFF and sit relatively undisturbed by mosquitos, the Minnesota state insect.

This afternoon's clear heavens are quickly becoming this evening's cloudy skies. Perhaps the weatherman had it correct when he called for showers by morning. The wind picks up and blows our hated insects into the Dakotas.

Floating across the lake, borne on the wind, I become aware of faint conversations. They stop and are replaced by engine noises. Not heavy diesel equipment, but much softer sounds. Like small gas-powered equipment. I'm tempted to rush over, but that'd require turning on some lights, alerting whomever. Like last time I saw activity in the same general area. Instead, I call Alex to very discretely check it out. Whispering, I say, "Keep in contact. Don't hang up. It could be nothing, but this is the second time I've seen or heard activity over there. I'm guessing it's by the park. Be careful. Approach with your gun drawn. K?"

The sound of the office front door closing tells me she's leaving. Her cruiser starts and she gives me a street by street report of her progress.

"I'm going dark now." She says this as she announces making a left on County 38, the road that goes by East Clover Bottom Park.

Her cell phone picks up her tires crunching gravel. Her trip seems to take forever. Either she's outside pushing the car or my internal time clock has gone into overdrive.

"Alex? Getting close?"

"Yeah. I'm probably a couple of blocks away from the entrance. I'm stopping. Gonna make sure my interior lights don't come on when I open the door and go the rest of the way on foot."

"Way ta go, gal. Remember, be careful."

"Will do."

There's a soft click as she opens her door. A few footsteps clinking on the gravely path, then all's quiet. I guess she's walking on the grassy shoulder.

I know she has to be silent from now on. I wish to hell I was doing this, or at least with her. To make sure no light, no matter how weak, can be seen, my baseball cap is hooked over my cell phone's screen. I sneak a glance at the time-display. Only three minutes have crept by.

I try to think of a way I can join my deputy. My boat is too noisy, even if I use the trolling motor. Besides, it'd take a half hour to get there. Rowing would take even longer. I haven't quite mastered teleportation techniques, so it looks like I've got to wait. For a nano-second I consider calling Jerome. That'd be like holding "Running of the Bulls" in a china shop.

I can't sit here and let Alex face this all by herself. I crawl on my hands and knees to the shore-end of the dock. I refuse to cry out as my left knee attempts to bend that nail. The same one I've promised myself to pound down. I think I've had a tetanus shot in the last ten years.

I help ease the pain by grinding some dirt and gravel into the wound as I crawl. It feels a *lot* better.

When I'm sure I'm on solid ground I hobble towards my detached garage. Good thing I leave the side door un-locked. Inside I smack the other knee into the front bumper.

Ah, that's better. The pain is equalized now.

Flailing my arms around, I grope the red tag on the open-er. I jerk it and it's disengaged. Now I can manually open the door. Providing I don't step on a red-bladed shovel I bought at Gunners.

Too late.

Good thing I twisted my left ankle. Be hard to drive if it's my right one.

"Where the hell did this box come from?" I ask as I try to sit up. Oil spots tend to make the floor slippery. If I roll over on my back and scoot, maybe I can sop it up with my shirt.

At least something goes according to plan.

A little moonlight spills in and I get my bearings. On the other side of the garage I have a work bench. I grab a ham-mer and pound out the tail and back-up lights.

Moments later, they're two piles of red and clear plastic. I get in, start the engine, kill the interior lights and back out of the garage.

I drive backwards—in the dark—for a hundred yards.

Hopefully the rose bushes will recover.

On the main road. I drive in the dark until I intersect with the west end of Main Street. Now I gun the engine and race to County 38. All the time, hoping the activity in the park turns out to be nothing serious.

As I make the left on 38, Alex's voice roars out, "Freeze!"

Chapter 30

It's obvious, even to me, Alex has the drop on whomever's messing around in the park. Hit my lights and siren and attempt to jam the gas pedle through the firewall. The next three miles flash by. With little light to see, the entrance catches me by surprise and I have to slam on the brakes using both feet. My twisted ankle doesn't complain, much. I crank the wheel hard left.

The cruiser skids around the corner. It hardly shudders as the right rear quarter panel bounces off an old oak. I figure Alex is by the lake. I keep pressure on the accelerator and sash-shay through the park like a highly talented square dancer. 'Cept they seldom Allemande left off saplings.

The picnic area looms out of the darkness. A pair of light standards each supporting a weak bulb cast a feeble glow. Throttling down, the lights show Alex has the drop on two guys imitating night crawlers.

Grimacing, I hobble out of my car and assist in 'cuffing them. "Good job, Deputy. Any idea of what's going on?"

"Haven't had a chance to pull any fingernails yet."

"We'll get to that in a few moments. Something to look forward to, fellas. Got your pliers handy, Deputy?"

"In my jacket."

Before we turn them over, Betty's description flashes through my mind. These guys are big.

And fat.

Alex covers me as I wrestle them onto their backs.

Full beards, one is fat, the other fatter. Mr. Chunky Guy has a face scar.

"Well, well. What have we here? I was going over to Bemidji tomorrow to look for you guys. Thanks for stopping by. Saves me a trip."

"You know these two, Chief?"

"I know *of* them. They were at Betty's just before the fire started."

Fat speaks, "So?"

"So. My girlfriend is in bad shape in the Duluth Burn Center. You fine specimens know anything about how the fire started?"

Both shake their heads.

"Care to tell me and my deputy what you're doing here, besides breaking and entering, trespassing, and a few other things?"

Alex joins in. "You guys walk from Bemidji?"

Fatter tries to sit up, fails, and says, "Nope."

Fat turns his head and tells his accomplice, "Shut up."

Taking no chances, I bind *Fat's* legs with plastic ties and pat him down. In his right front pants pocket is a set of keys. I fish them out and hand them to Alex. Struggling to roll him back over onto his stomach is akin to getting a beached whale back in the ocean. I remove his billfold.

Fatter also has a set of keys and billfold.

Opening their wallets I see there are no driver's licenses. A few bucks, but no credit cards or any other identification.

"Alex, these nice people are going to be our guests for a bit. Take my cruiser and see if you can spot their cars. Just in case their off the road, use the spotlights. If you find them, run their plates. K?"

She holsters her weapon and takes my keys and drives slowly away. The spotlights sweeping either side of the park road.

Meanwhile, I pull a park bench over and sit down.

Both of my prisoners are squirming. Figure they're being investigated by ants and providing a feast for the recent hatch of mosquitoes. We're surrounded by a thick stand of pines. No breeze makes it through the boughs to blow them away.

"Little uncomfortable on the ground, fellas? We may be a small community, but have we got a real nice jail house. Cool, comfortable, and pretty much free of bugs. 'Course, I'd need your names to register ya. Care to share that tidbit of information?"

Fat's response isn't one I'd like to repeat with a woman near by, even if Alex isn't *that* near by.

All attempts to engage these two in conversation meet with the same results. I finally ignore them, waiting for my deputy.

Maybe another fifteen minutes passes before I spot three lights approaching. I guess one headlight Allemande left off something larger than a sapling. Oh, well, bulbs are fairly inexpensive, I think.

Alex stops, but keeps both spots on Fat and Fatter. She strolls over and points to Fatter. "Name's Bruce Trolly. The skinny guy's Len Davis. Last reported address is in the Cities suburb, Eagan."

"Okay, guys. I've got enough here to arrest you for all the items already mentioned. Time to rest a bit in our posh resort. Read 'em their rights, Deputy."

Chapter 31

I have to cut the intruders' leg ties to walk them to my cruiser. Fat starts kicking as soon as I slice the strap. Fortunately, I'm moving away when one of his feet connects with my chest. Even so, it's like being hit with a side of beef.

It takes me a minute to regain my breath. "Add resisting arrest to the list, Deputy."

A slight tap on his head with a nearby stick quiets him down. And helps make up for the kick.

I call my cuz. "I need your assistance loading a couple of unruly prisoners."

"They need dunkin', Archie?"

For several seconds I contemplate this, but decline, saying, "Next time, Dutch. Right now, I just have to get them into my cruiser."

"On my way."

"One moment, cuz. I'm at the park. The gate's open, take your time."

This is tantamount to telling an eight year-old boy to go easy on his Halloween candy.

During Fat's quiet time, I re-refasten his legs so he's ready for Dutch. He's coming to and moaning about a headache when cuz arrives. I tell Dutch, "One of these guy's been un-cooperative."

"Which one?"

I tap Fat a couple of times with my stick. Just to make sure there's no misunderstanding which one I'm referring to.

Maybe Dutch is a *touch* too eager to deposit him into my back seat. Fatter doesn't argue one bit when it's his turn.

He's actually as meek as a church mouse. Dutch is quite gentle as he deposits him on top of his colleague. Before I get behind the wheel I examine the rear door, to make sure it's closed, mind you.

"Those dents have been there for a long time, Alex."

"Don't you mean bumps, Chief?"

I pretend I didn't hear and say, "We'll seal off the area before we haul our friends to jail. Too dark to see much to-night, anyway. Besides, I think I just felt a drop of rain."

"Need any more help, Archie?"

"Yeah, Dutch. Get your car out on 38. Park and wait for us. Alex, padlock the gate. Our friends' cars will be safe here."

While the autos are being moved, I rummage around in my trunk for a roll of yellow tape. With the scene secured, I tell Dutch to follow us back to town. "Might need your help getting the boys into the hoosegow."

His quizzical look tells me he's unfamiliar with the term.

"Jail."

His face brightens.

We take off. Alex in the lead, me and the prisoners sec-ond, Dutch trailing. To assist their unloading, I make a Uee in front of the station so Fat and Fatter's heads are curb side.

Without even breathing heavy, my cousin posit's the boys in Cells 1 and 2. He did this on my specific instruc-tions. They're the first on the heating/AC line. After a *slight* adjustment to the air flow damper, and another to the thermostat, the term, 'in the cooler' will make sense to our guests.

After everything settles down, I turn to Alex. "Would you book 'em? I need some shut-eye. Tomorrow, after I get back from seeing Ruth Ann, it'll be time to do a little questioning. Night."

"Night, Chief."

Before leaving, I add, "Thanks for a great job, Alexia. You handled what could've been a dangerous task like a true pro."

She blushes and steps closer. "I owe it to my training. Want me to look in on them from time to time?"

"Use your judgment. If they feel like talking, all the better."

Alex wears a wry grin as I leave.

Chapter 32

The next morning, since the *Shoppe* is still under repair, I have to fix my own breakfast. Bisquick pancakes, Egg Beaters, and sausage compliment my coffee. Compared to Betty's offerings, mine is at least savory and delectable. It fills the kitchen with a divine redolence.

As I eat, Maggie eyes me. She showers me with affection. At least I choose to interpret her claws digging into my shins as affection.

The day will be busy and I head to the jail to spend some quality time with the latest residents and to instruct Jerome to do a grid search of the park. "We have to find out what those bozos have been doing."

"I'll get right on it, Archie."

He heads for the door.

"Ah, Jerome? No sirens. K?"

His shoulders slump and he's out of the door. Next, I call the Clover Bottom Inn and order two light breakfasts.

As an afterthought, I buzz Jackie and inform her that we have two guests in jail and she'll see some meal charges from the Clover Bottom Inn.

"Will you pass the bills along to the treasurer, Jackie?"

"Be glad to, Archie. Caught someone speeding?"

"Nope. Alex and I arrested two guys we spotted in the park last night."

I hang up and slip into my winter jacket to visit the prisoners. Both men wore light weight clothes when we brought them in. Our thin cotton sheets hardly offer any insulation. Their chattering teeth reminds me of the noise my red squirrel friend makes when it's upset.

"Howdy, boys. Sleep well?"

Fat stammers out, "DDDDamn near froze to ddddeath. Can you wwwwarm this place up?"

"You're chilly? I feel fine. I ordered some grub for ya guys. Should be here in a few minutes."

Fatter jumps in. "To hell with fffood. Want some heat."

"Make a deal with ya guys."

"Yeah?"

"Tell me what you've been doing in the park and we'll get your cells nice and toasty. K?"

"Heat first."

Figuring they've experienced the 'cooler' long enough, I crank the thermostat to 80.

In moments, pipes start banging and there's a warm, musty odor seeping into their cells. As they move under the outlets, the delivery boy from the Inn arrives with two Styrofoam carry-out style boxes.

"Breakfast is here, guys. Sure smells good. Steak and eggs. Want a sniff?"

They move to the barred front of their cells as I hold the food out for inspection. Fatter starts to drool. He reaches out to take his share, but I keep it away.

"Oh, come on. I'm starving."

There's a small table between the two rows of cells where I place the boxes. With a plastic knife, I slice off a tiny chunk of steak, spear it with the spork, and dangle it in front of his nose.

For a fat man, he can move quickly, and snatches the morsel.

"Good, huh?"

I can hear his stomach growling. "Got's ta have a little info first, boys. Names, and what you were doing in our park."

'Course, I already knew their names. Bruce Trolly and Lenny Davis

Fatter retreats to the back of his cell, although he keeps an eye on the food.

"Call when you're ready, K.?"

I leave and go to my office, not before I return the 'stat back to 60. And turn on the intercom.

The aroma of the Inn's food is making me hungry all over again, so I call and order another breakfast. "A little heavy on the steak and lighter on the eggs. K? This one's for me."

For several minutes quiet reigns in Cells 1 and 2. About the time my food arrives, Fat, aka Len, speaks in a stage whisper. "Bruce, why don't we just tell him? I could eat that damn box, I'm so hungry."

"Don't know 'bout that, Lenny. Remember what that guy said."

The conversation stops.

My food comes covered by one of those stainless-steel thingies. The steak is an inch thick T-bone. Done medium-rare. They even included a side of potatoes and a dollop of horseradish.

Halfway through my meal, Bruce bellows out, "Come back here."

Savoring another bite of T-bone, I saunter into the cell room, nibbling on a steak fry.

"Yes?"

"Okay, you win. Lenny and I were doing some soil sampling. Someone wants to build a development of eighty-five houses in the park."

The news stuns me. First off, the city charter strictly forbids housing projects within city limits. The city boundaries completely surround the lake. Further, any new construction has to go through rigorous reviews. If someone wants to subdivide their lot, they need a permit and, if it's to build a house, it has to be approved by the architectural committee, down to the type of nails used to attach clapboards.

John A. and son John B. designed the charter generations ago. Since they owned the land and the lake, they could do whatever they wished.

Now, someone appears to be challenging this rule.

"So, why were you two picked?"

"We work for the pipeline and have a lot, I mean a lot, of experience in these matters."

I couldn't resist. "Including causing Highway 2 in Bemidji to collapse?"

"Not our fault. Said that soil was unstable. The water table is high there. Wouldn't listen to us and went ahead, tunneled under the roadway anyhow."

I got friends who live in that area, by the airport. Every so often, for some reason, the water table rises. Hell, one year, back in the mid-nineties, there was a shallow lake off the west end of one of the runways. He could be right.

"Okay, boys. Tell ya what. You're in the system so we have to follow through. You'll—"

Lenny pipes up. "Wadda ya mean, *system*?"

"Means you were booked and charged with several infractions of the law, that's what it means."

Bruce steps up to the bars. "Your deputy didn't book us last night. I hinted that maybe we could reach an *agreement* with you."

Well, well. That does change the picture.

Chapter 33

Now I'm in a quandary. I want to get to Duluth to see Ruth Ann and these guys weren't booked. This could be to my advantage, so I press them.

"No big deal, Bruce. I can book you right now. Probably take a couple of weeks to get a hearing, then prep time for your trial. You'd need to get a lawyer, probably two as the chances of trying you together are none and even less. Or—"

"Or what?"

"You could give me all the details of who, what, why, and where."

Did I leave out any of Ruth Ann's journalistic 'W's'?

"*If* we don't cooperate?"

"You won't get bail. The pipeline is moving every day. Too much of a risk of flight to grant bail. Nope. You're here for the duration."

"Not much of a choice, eh?"

"Think it over. I have to be away on another matter. See ya 'bout noon."

"How about turning up the heat again?"

"Sure."

Back in the office, I call Jerome to see how he's doing.

"Found a small electric auger, some cigarette butts and a couple candy wrappers. 'Bout all."

"Search their cars?"

"Suppose to?"

"Yes, Jerome."

"What if they're locked?"

"These guys committed a crime, several in fact. Think about this for a minute."

A looong pause broken with nose sniffles, throat clearing, and a couple coughs.

"Oh. I know. I get a warrant, right?"

Oh, man.

"No, Jerome. Break one of windows and search their cars. We're looking for ev-ah-dense about who hired them to do what they did. Look, I'm on my way to see Ruth Ann. Take your time searching the cars. We need to find out who they're working for. I'll be back no later than one. Call me if you have any questions."

"Roger. Wilco. Over . . ."

I snap the phone closed and make a bee-line for my cruiser.

There's the tiniest sliver of hope creeping into my brain cell. With Ruth Ann's note spelling out REAL ESTATE, and now these bozos admitting they were doing pre-construction prep work, maybe, just maybe, I have a solid clue.

Before starting out I call the Bemidji PD and tell the chief what happened.

"Thanks for your offer to assist finding the pipeline workers. I'll fill you in on the details as soon as I can, Dave. Might not be for a couple days, though."

"Call me anytime, Archie. Good luck."

Next, a call to the Highway Patrol to inform them, I'm heading to Duluth with my lights on. Business taken care of, I head east.

No sign of Jerome's cousin this time as I race to Duluth. At the beginning of the city I slow and turn off my lights. It takes two passes through the Burn Center lot before I can park.

Nurse Ratchet's attitude, apparently brought on by seeing me in uniform, is quite pleasant. I still expect to see her crack into a thousand pieces, should any part of her bend. I actually get a smile, if you consider the corners of her mouth moving upwards one millimeter a smile. "She's resting, Chief Schultz. We removed some of the bandages last night. Her doctor is slowly reducing her sedatives."

With that, she floats off. Causing nary a crease in her uniform.

Ruth Ann's room is four doors down from the nurse's station and I, too, float down there, actually bending my knees and ankles.

What a change. I can see those green eyes, even though they're best described as droopy, that perky nose, and her lips, albeit, they're far from 'rosy.' All-in-all, she's beautiful.

As I get closer, she raises a finger. I hope it's a wave.

"Hi, beautiful. Care to dance?"

Ruth Ann's obviously struggling to speak. I'm thinking she's still loopy.

"Never," pause, "see you," pause, "'gain."

"That's my gal. Did I tell you, you look ravishing?"

Her finger waves at me again, this time I can tell she wants me to come closer.

"Kiss."

I give her a soft kiss on her chapped, cracked lips. Her eyes close and I hear a subdued snore.

Just in case, I brought the bank record print outs. I lean back in the designer plastic chair. Sure wish I had one as unpleasant as this one in our interrogation room. Have people spilling their guts in a flash.

Nevertheless, I start to peruse the data. I didn't know bank records were in ancient Aramaic. At least to my accountant-challenged mind, they look that way.

Fifteen minutes later, I give up and make a mental note to contact Heather Maple for help in deciphering her bank's equivalent of the Dead Sea Scrolls.

I'm both excited and reluctant to see her again. The anticipation causes certain reactions.

Ruth Ann moves and draws my attention away from Heather and her *charms*.

My testosterone level falls sharply.

Chapter 34

Ruth Ann's eyes show the effects of her drug-induced sleep. I think she's trying to focus on me, but I'm looking into the face of a seriously cross-eyed person. For an instant, I follow her right eye gaze to the wall.

"Over here." Her voice is weak but she says this with a crooked smile.

I look back at her. Both eyes are now in sync.

"How ya feelin'?"

"My head hurts. They tell you anything 'bout me?"

"Other than you're gong to be here for a while and you're doing real good."

"I'm scared."

"Of what?"

"What you're going to do when I get outta here."

"Mean I might drive a little fast taking you home?"

Cough, cough. "No. You might find me ugly and—"

I lean down and kiss her lips. A long passionate French kiss. "Answer your stupid question?"

Ruth Ann purrs her response.

"Here's what's gonna happen, babe. You're coming home with me and taking over the guest room. The one that looks over the lake?"

"Tomorrow?"

"Not till next week. You'll have to go through a few tests first." I don't mention the Burn Center will have to debride her scalp to remove dead tissue.

A college friend of mine spilled boiling water on his stockinged foot. He said the debridement was ten times as painful as the initial burn. Ruth Ann doesn't need to worry about the treatment.

She smiles and drifts off.

Hopefully tomorrow I'll be able to bring up the REAL ES-TATE note. I kiss her again and drive back to WCB to have another discussion with Fat and Fatter.

Along the way, I call Heather and ask her if she'd be available to help me go over the records.

"I can see you after work. We're finishing an audit. So as long as my brain is concentrating on numbers, tonight would be fine. Care for supper?"

My mind brings back the yellow bikini. "Ah, I guess so. What time?"

"About seven."

"Can I bring anything? Steaks? Burgers?"

"No, silly. Just bring your appetite."

"K. Seven it is."

Looking at my speedometer, I realize I've once again exceeded the speed limit by twenty miles an hour. The cruiser quickly slows without my foot trying to shove the accelerator through the firewall.

Cass Lake zips by and I wrestle my mind away from Heather and out of the gutter. I concentrate on questioning Bruce and Lenny.

Just outside town, I realize we have little information about these two. I know the pipeline work is only a few miles ahead. Why not poke around, interview some of their co-workers?

The line moved rapidly as long as they were punching through fields, but now they're in an area of low lying, swampy marshes.

The path is easy to spot and I see draglines and earth movers. A gravel road, actually a driveway, gives me a place to pull over. I carry a pair of Wellingtons—rubber boots—in the trunk and I slip them on and head over to the work area.

Funny. You'd think there'd be more noise. People yelling, diesel engines growling, pipes clanking. Yet, all is quiet. There is one guy sitting on the tracks of a 'dozer, smoking a cigarette.

"Afternoon. Work-day over already?"

"Kinda. Ran out of pipe. Last shipment was short. Everone else back in town. Waitin' for the next load. I'm jus watchin' stuff here. Had some theft early on."

"Yeah, I can imagine there's a big demand for thirty-six inch pipe. Wish I had a length or two."

Apparently, he finds this hilarious as he collapses off the bulldozer and lies on the ground laughing.

I decide to head to the office. Maybe the autopsy reports are in. I'll stop at the yard, although, and make arrangements to see folks later.

Chapter 35

Entering West Clover Bottom, I again hope the Jackman autopsies have been completed. I asked the pathologist to e-mail me the results.

My parking spot is clear. Guess Jerome decided to leave it available after the chewing out I gave him over transporting the Jackman bodies to St. Paul.

The gas gauge is flirting with empty, but I'm anxious to see if Doc Hudson transmitted the data to me.

"Jerome, will you take my cruiser over to Louie's and fill it up? Put it on the City's tab and sign for it. K?"

He's out of the door faster than I've ever seen him leave. I wonder why.

Moments later I know the answer. There's an e-mail from Doc Hudson. I bet he saw the results and can't wait to tell people. Hell, he's faster than Betty when it comes to spreading rumors and gossip.

Before I can tell him to keep a lid on it, my car disappears around the corner. Even though I'm certain the radio is off, I try reaching him. Then I try his cell. One last chance. I call Louie.

"Jerome there yet?"

"Yup."

"Put him on."

Moments later, I hear Jerome's scratchy voice, "Yeah, Chief."

"Not one word to anyone. Got that?"

The sound of air leaving his body can be heard over here.

I return to my computer and bring up Hudson's e-mail.

Cause of death was in fact a 22. Nice to have it confirmed. The lead's at BCA for ID. She added a note:

The state of Minnesota no longer uses NIBIN. It takes a lot of time and the results are very problematical. Call El Sullivan. He's their firearm expert. He can tell you more.

Damn! I was hoping it'd been used in other crimes. Another lead down the drain.

I read on and find there was no sign of a struggle. That answers the question of why no tissue under the victims' fingernails. If there had been any, I guess being in the lake washed it away. She also confirmed the time of death was sometime between Friday and Saturday. I was indeed off by a day. The time was established based on the state of decomposition and finding fly eggs. Especially deep inside Rupert's head wound. This throws me, as it means the bodies were in the open for a spell. Blow flies are quick to colonize.

I skim the rest of her report and spot a statement at the end:

Tissue and blood samples were sent to the BCA for toxicology testing.

The printer spits out the report and I file it in the Jackman file. It's late in the day and I'm sure the BCA is closed, so make plans to go to the Clover Inn for a walleye supper.

Before I can leave, Jerome enters.

"All right, Deputy. How may people did you tell?"

"How'd ya know?"

Hudson's e-mail was right there.

"Oh. Ahh. Not many."

"Like everyone in *Louie's*, right?"

"Well, maybe a couple more."

"Including Betty?"

Jerome nods.

So much for keeping it quiet. I marvel how few of the town's residents knew about the mayor's murder until I told Betty. Now my crack deputy has notified the entire upper Midwest, if not North America. Good thing he can't speak Spanish.

Alex comes in and I give her the report.

She speed reads and asks, "Tox testing?"

"I think it's fairly routine. Unfortunately we have to wait another week or two before that data is in. I'm going to the Inn for dinner. Need anything, Alex, buzz me."

Shit. Before I go I realize I haven't talked to Fat and Fatter.

"Alex, do me a favor? Talk to the boys in the back and see if you can worm out any info about who hired them. Anything'll help. I'm going to the pipeline staging area and talk to a few people."

Even though the day is waning, I have at least an hour before dark. The site is a beehive of activity. Apparently the load of pipe arrived. I hop out of my cruiser and stop the first person I see. "Can you point out the foreman?"

"He's the one in khaki pants and yellow shirt."

"Thanks." I head straight for the yellow shirt. "Hi. I'm Archie Schultz from West Clover Bottom. Got a few minutes?"

"You being a cop, yeah. But, damn few. What can I do fer ya."

"Bruce and Lenny are sitting in my jail. Broke a few laws."

"Oh, shit. You're joshin' me, right?"

"Not at all."

He excuses himself and says he'll be right back. Two minutes later, he and three other workers show.

"What's this about Bruce and Lenny?" one fellow asks.

I explain to my interested audience their colleagues were arrested for breaking several of our laws. "I need some background."

"What they supposed to done?" This from a real tough looking guy. Skinny, but looks like he eats nails during break-time.

I check off our list, being sure to upgrade 'resisting arrest' to 'assaulting a police officer.'

"Anyone kilt?"

"Nope. Not yet, anyhow."

"So what's the big deal. These guys are my buddies. Think you can drop the charges?" He says this as he starts moving towards me. The implication is plain to see.

"Hasn't been charged yet. That happens after the City attorney reviews the case. But, they will be brought up."

As we talk, it probably looks like we're a gaggle of wrestlers sizing each other up before we attack. I'm easy to spot as I'm the one who's back pedling. I figure there's close to a thousand pounds of Unfriendly bearing down on me.

The sun sets and I manage to get a tad of info from them. Mainly, my prisoners are well liked and I'm not.

I thank them for their help, and start back to my car. I have to pick my way, as equipment is on the move, the lot is muddy, and I forgot to put on my Wellingtons. As I dodge around an eighteen wheeler, my cell phone buzzes. While I'm struggling to get it out of my pants pocket and see who's calling, I suddenly come face to face with a mud puddle.

Several minutes later, I rise from the mud into a sitting position. My head hurts like hell. Then it dawns on me, someone clobbered me with something hard and heavy.

I look around and there's no one to be seen. All the smaller trucks are gone.

Rubbing my neck helps relieve the pain, at least a little bit, when my phone rings again. Given it's in the mud, maybe I ought to change the ring-tone to, *Singin' In the Rain*.

Even though the screen is dirty, I can make out the caller's ID. It gives me another jolt.

It's Heather. I forgot our meeting.

Chapter 36

"Hello, Archie. Did you forget we're going over those bank statements? Or are you giving little ol' me the brush off?"

"Heather. I got tied up, but I'll be over in a few minutes, K?"

"I can wait, Archie. Barely."

Is that a double whatever you call it? I'll pass my house on the way. I'll be able to clean up. On the way to my place, visions of tiny, yellow bikinis keep filtering into my mind. The visions have a marvelous effect on my head and for some reason, the pain subsides. A very fast shower and a change of clothes takes me seven minutes and twenty-two seconds and I'm back on the road to see Heather.

When I arrive and she opens the door, the vision of yellow leaves. Heather is dressed in jean shorts, a modest, but shear, white blouse.

A few seconds later, I close my mouth and my senses slowly return. Her blouse is very, very shear. "Damn. The file is my car. I'll be right back."

I hope a sudden cold snap'll descend on her property. Hopefully one that brings minus forty degrees. I need something to cool me down.

After gathering up the spilled papers, I head back. To my disappointment, the temperature's still in the low seventies.

Heather's waiting by the door and ushers me into her living room. A tray with an ice bucket, two highball glasses, and a decanter of what appears to be bourbon sits on her coffee table. Another tray has cream cheese logs rolled up in slices of proscuitto ham. Another has an assortment of crackers.

"My. This is some spread."

"Please. Sit. Make yourself comfortable. I thought we could have a drink and some appetizers before getting down to work. It shouldn't take too long, then supper. Okay with you?"

"As long as you make sense of these statements, sounds fine."

She stands to make the drinks and offers me the cheese and ham rolls. As Heather leans over at the waist, I'm not sure what's being offered. I fight down my male impulse and take a cracker and cheese-ham appetizer.

She tucks her long, shapely legs under her as she sits and looks at me over the rim of her glass.

"What part didn't you get?"

She long since left the double thingy in the dust. She's now up to quadruple.

Ignoring the implication, I respond, "Look. I can barely balance my checking account. Trying to decipher what appears to be highly complicated transactions involving large sums of money is beyond me. Let me tell you what I'm trying to find."

Her hand moves to my knee. "That would be sooo helpful, Archie. I'm sure I can help you find whatever you need."

Maybe I should leave and find a CPA someplace. But, that would definitely be an invasion of the councilmen's privacy. Probably breaking some law as well. I have to stick this out.

Wrong choice of words.

I develop a coughing fit and move away from Heather. That lessens the sexual tension, by point oh oh one. I stand up and explain.

"I have reason to believe there are dastardly deeds afoot in West Clover Bottom."

Gad. There I go slipping into Arthur Conan Doyle speak again.

Heather looks at me. "How so?"

Then I recall her interest in real estate. "I really can't go into it right now. But I'm thinking the events of the past week are all wrapped into one tight ball. I need to understand these statements."

"To see if they're related to the, what did you call it? Skullduggery?"

"Correct. For instance, Councilman Schmidt deposited one hundred seventy-five thou. Every month, for the past several, he deposits between one and two hundred. Why? Where does that money come from? In Klinestadt's and Van Pelter's accounts, similar amounts are deposited. How did they accumulate it to begin with and where does it go?"

Heather studies the items I've highlighted. "To the computer, Sherlock."

"You a fan of Doyle, too?"

"*The Hound of the Baskervilles*, is one of my faves."

"Mine, too. I must have three different copies of his entire works." My impression of Heather goes up three notches.

We retreat to her back bedroom slash office and she boots up her Dell. Her hands fly over the keyboard. If I was interested in memorizing the key strokes, she left me behind after the first five seconds. The bank site comes up and she enters a couple of passwords and Schmidt's account appears.

The screen scrolls every way including sideways. I give up trying to follow what she's doing. My eyes drift away from the screen and before I realize it, I'm enjoying the view of her *charms*.

To get my thoughts off them, I ask, "Care for a refill?"

She dismisses my suggestion with a curt wave of her hand. "Help yourself. Bring me a cheese roll. Please?"

In the living room, two rolls find their way into my mouth along with a couple of crackers. I add a half shot of bourbon to my glass and six half-moon ice cubes.

"Archie! Look at this."

Chapter 37

Balancing a cheese roll and my drink, I hurry back to Heather's office. "What?"

She slowly stuffs the log into her mouth. Strangely, a gesture I find erotic, and points to a line on the screen.

"Right here." She moves several lines lower. "And here."

In a similar manner, Heather indicates four other entries. "See those?"

"I see them, but they mean nothing to me."

She moves over and pats the cushion next to her. "Sit, silly."

Half of my butt is off the chair. I stick my right leg out to keep from falling. Heather puts her arm around my waist and pulls me closer. To make matters worse, she turns slightly to give me more room. My left arm is being impaled. By a *charm*. A sensation not entirely unpleasant.

Seemingly unaware of my situation, she points to one of the strings of numbers. "This is a wire transfer to another bank."

"Can you tell which one?"

Her fingers are a blur as this page fades to a dot and another takes its place.

"It's in the Second Bank of Brooklyn."

"Brooklyn? Why there?"

"I don't know." There's a pause. "Humm. Maybe it's a drop on it's way to another bank."

"That kinda sounds like he's trying to hide the money."

Heather turns even more towards me. Good thing she's not wearing sandpaper on her chest or my left arm would be severely abraded.

This is too much and I extract myself and stand away to sip my drink. "Punch up Klinestadt and Van Pelter."

Her hands are a blur and Van Pelter's account appears. Rather than sit, I stand behind her and lean down.

Bad move. Now I know for certain she's wearing neither sandpaper nor a bra.

I try to keep my eyes on the screen.

Sure as shootin' Van Pelter's transferred money to Brooklyn. A minute later, we confirm Klienschmidt's done the same.

Pacing the twelve by twelve room, I stop and ask, "How do we find out what happened to the money? Is it still in New York?"

"You need a subpoena. One to see those records. Can you do that?"

"I have relations in high places."

"I should've known. Judge Schultz. Right?"

"We have a very avuncular relationship. Sometimes I even call him Uncle Jerry."

"Excuse me, Archie. Ma Nature's calling."

She dashes off to the bathroom. A minute later I hear the toilet flushing and she returns.

She takes my hands and says, "If you need any further help with this mystery, you know how to reach me."

While she's talking she's moved into my personal space and I'm aware of her perfume.

The fragrance is like inhaling rich vanilla. It brings back memories of high school and the one date we had. Specifically, in the back seat of my chopped Chevy. She wore a very similar scent then. It drove me crazy. We fogged my car windows that night.

I have to leave before her house widows suffer the same fate. Besides, I need to talk to the boys in jail. Can they shed some light on this money thing?

"Excuse me, Heather, I have to go to my office."

"We didn't have supper."

For a moment, I debate supper or Bruce and Lenny. My stomach wins. Beside, my trip to the pipeline yard has given me an appetite. Fat and Fatter can wait.

A decision I'll regret.

Chapter 38

Heather smiles. A moment later, her printer starts up. "You'll need these reports. I'm going to put the finishing touches on our meal."

She runs off to do whatever she needs to do.

"How long before we eat?"

"A few minutes," comes her reply.

"I'm going to put the papers in my cruiser. Back in a flash."

The fresh air allows me to put lurid thoughts aside. Visions of Ruth Ann encased in layer upon layer of gauze helps put tonight in perspective.

Reentering Heather's house is pleasantly akin to entering a food fair. The aroma of roast beef surrounds me. Funny I didn't notice it before. Maybe because my mind was on other things.

She's setting the table with a rib roast, mashed potatoes, baked broccoli, and glasses of red wine.

"Hope you like beef, Archie."

"One of my faves." I mimic her earlier choice of words.

The need to get back to the jail causes me to eat quickly.

"This is fantastic, Heather. I've stuffed myself."

"Care for dessert?"

"I couldn't eat another thing." I'm hoping she hasn't fixed something like baked Alaska and cherry cheesecake. I've got to get back to the station.

Heather pouts, then sighs. "Food's not exactly what I had in mind."

Things are really getting out of hand. I excuse myself with, "Thanks to your efforts, the Jackman case has taken a leap forward. But, there's something I have to take care of at the station."

She takes my arm as I head to the front door. Before I know it, she's got me in a lip-lock. I can't help but respond. Eventually I break the vacuum, pull away and head to my cruiser.

I roll down all the windows, turn the A/C to high and drive into town.

By the time I reach downtown, I've cooled down and anxious to see if Alex's learned anything from our guests.

I push open the office door and freeze.

Chapter 39

Alex is in a wooden guest chair with eyes as large as the proverbial saucer. Her left cheek is abraded and starting to turn black and blue. Her ankles are tied together. The rope winds around the legs of the chair. In addition, even though I can't see them, it looks as though her hands are tired in back of the chair.

Duct tape stretches across her mouth. She's trying to speak, but only makes a moaning sound. I rush to her side and carefully remove the tape. Before I can ask what happened, she yells, "Go to the back. Hurry!"

I stop freeing her, unholster my Glock and carefully go through the door separating the jail cells from our office. As I push the door open, I drop into a crouch. My pistol in a two-handed grip.

The jail room is deathly quiet.

Literally.

A set of keys hangs from Bruce's cell door. Both he and Lenny are in the same cell. Both are staring, sightlessly, at the ceiling. A pool of blood puddling around their heads.

It comes from their foreheads, both of which have sprouted a third eye. Just like the Jackmans.

Holstering my pistol, I go back to Alex and while releasing her, she tells the story.

"I just finished my meal, after delivering one to the boys. I figured if they were fed, I might get something from them."

Her face is drawn and she appears to relive the event.

"Two guys burst into the office. They're wearing ski masks so I know this is not going to be a social call. One has a sawed off, double-barrel shotgun pointing right at my head. I make a slight move to my gun and he says. 'Keep that up and your brains will be all over the wall'."

Even though I'm anxious to hear the rest, I interrupt. "What did his voice sound like?"

"Low and gravelly."

"Can you describe them?" I want to get this information out as quickly as possible while everything's fresh in her mind.

"The guy with the shotgun was about six, six. Thin, but well built. He was dressed in jeans, a long sleeve shirt, and a ski mask, so there wasn't much to go on. Still, I could tell he's pretty well built. You know, like he worked out a lot. His muscles filled out the shirt. I can't even guess his age."

I get two cups of coffee and add cream to Alex's.

"Here. Take your time."

She takes a couple of sips, heaves a long sigh, and continues. "The other guy, he was way smaller, never uttered a word, but the one with the shotgun said, 'Keys.' He pointed to the jail room.

"When I didn't jump to his demand, he stepped closer and cocked one of the hammers."

"You gave him the keys, I see. Good. In a situation like that, don't try to be a hero. You did the right thing."

"Thanks, Archie. I was so scared and worried what you'd say. I—"

I didn't let her finish and hug her. My normally cool, collected deputy let the terror of the event overtake her, as she begins to sob.

I hold her tightly and the tears flow. What goes went through my mind is we're becoming the Cabot Cove of Minnesota. Four murders in a week.

Alex gets her emotions under control.

"Thanks, boss."

"They took the keys and...?"

"The quiet one did, actually. As soon as he left, the one holding a drop on me stepped up and popped me a good one. I must have gone down like a load of bricks. Before I was aware, he had me tied and taped.

"I didn't see much after that. He turned the chair so my back was to the cells. But I heard what happened."

Alex looked to be hyperventilating so I told her to slow down and gave her some water.

"I was surprised they left the door to the cells open."

"They wanted you to hear."

"Ohhh. Anyway, they spoke in low tones. Bruce and Lenny started pleading with them, at least it sounded like that to me. I heard a cell door open. One said, "Move.""

"I can guess the rest as Lenny is in the same cell as Bruce. Did they question our prisoners?"

"Nope. At least not that I heard. Two shots and they came out. Neither one looked at me as they left."

"When did this all go down?"

"I think it was close to seven. It was about fifteen minutes after the Inn delivered their meals. Maybe it was twenty minutes."

Christ. That was just about the time I was debating whether to come and see Alex or have supper with Heather.

I try to put it out of my mind, but it won't leave. How come Heather came on to me like gang busters after I told her to back off the other night? Did these thugs bust in knowing Alex was alone?

Then, what about Heather having to go to the bathroom and coming out wearing that perfume? She had to remember our high school night. Did she really have to pee, or did she call someone? With some code the coast was clear?

I keep my suspicions to myself.

Alex and I begin the gruesome task of dealing with the corpses in the back room.

As we work, my headache returns with a vengeance. I have to ask myself, did my talking to the pipeline workers have anything to do with this? Or does my earlier suspicions about Heather going into the bathroom tie into these murders? I can't deal with it right now continue with what needs to be done.

Chapter 40

I call our intrepid coroner. Thank goodness Uncle George and his coffee isn't around. To say nothing about a nearby body of water. Doctor Peter Hansson sounds groggy when he answers.

"Yeah. What's up, Archie?"

"I see you've got caller ID, doc. Need you to come down to the jail."

"What fer?"

"Not over the phone. Just hustle on down, see ya in five."

Alex has been quiet, no doubt thinking of earlier. I try to come up with something to get her mind off events. I suggest the only thing I can think of. "Feel up to making a fresh pot?"

She jumps up and throws herself into the task. A year's supply of rancid oils in the glass coffee pot slowly disappears under her frantic scrubbing.

By the time she's cleaned the pot, all our cups, the small sink and counter, and is looking at the floor, Pete barrels in.

"That fresh coffee I smell?"

"Evening to you, too, doc. How ya been?"

"Fine. Got anything to spice up my cup? Work better with a little old ethyl mixed in with my caffeine."

"Sorry." I'm guessing Uncle George is passed out in his bed and not answering his door.

"Okay. Pour me a straight cup, boy."

Like his servant, I obey.

He takes a sip and says, "Now what?"

"In the back room."

Pete's quiet as he looks at the bodies. He steps into the cell and stares at Bruce and Lenny. He finally speaks. "You do this?"

I don't bother responding.

"They're dead. So, why get me out of my nice soft bed and bring me here?"

He's probably still mad at me for dumping him on his lawn. "You're the coroner, right?"

Now he ignores the question and says, "So what happened?"

I'm not sure I'm pissed at myself for not being here when those guys busted in, or I'm pissed at Pete's attitude. "They both had heart attacks?"

"No call to be flippant, Schultz."

"Sorry, doc. No reason for me to act that way," I lie and proceed to explain what happened.

He turns to Alex. "You handled everything just the way you should've, deputy. If you hadn't, I'd probably be looking at three bodies. Too early to tell, but this looks just like our mayor and his flu, ah, wife's murder."

Hansson squats down to examine them closer. A few minutes later, he straightens up and tells me they can be hauled away.

He leaves without another word. Alex and I just look at each other.

I hate to do this, but I call Newbury. "Need you to come to the jail. Two more for you. Pull up in the back. No sirens and bring someone with you. No way I'm doing your job this time. Oh, keep this quiet. K?"

He grumbles something, but agrees.

Next, I call Jerome. He'll have to make another run to St. Paul tomorrow. Surprisingly, within fifteen minutes, he shows up. We fill him in on what happened.

"They talk anymore about what was going on in the park, Alex?"

"Not a word, boss. I thought Bruce might, but then, well, you know."

By midnight the deceased pair are in the hospital morgue waiting delivery to Regions Hospital. The BCA won't have to get involved until the lead is retrieved. I'm guessing it'll match those from the Jackmans.

As I finally head home, I can kiss my well thought-out plans for tomorrow goodbye.

Chapter 41

In the morning, before driving to Duluth, I have a short meeting with Jerome and Newbury.

"If you guys want to be employed tomorrow, you will *not* use your sirens, you *will* obey the speed limit, and you will *not* race through towns. Got that?"

They hang their heads and mumble. "Got it, Chief."

With that I dismiss them. Then I instruct the city maintenance crew to clean up the cell. "Be sure to scrub it down with soap and hot water, then rinse it with bleach, two times. K?"

I made arrangements before leaving last night for Alex to be on call should some emergency arise. Not that West Clover Bottom *ever* has an emergency.

Since the Minnesota fishing opener is two days away, I'll probably not be able to see Ruth Ann after today until sometime next week. I'm anxious to see her and fill her in on the latest, providing she isn't all doped up.

Unlike Jerome and Newbury, I have an excuse to blast my way east. And blast away I do. Two times, traffic on

Highway 2 is backed up. A short blat of my *sireen* clears the route.

I pull into the Burn Center lot and hurry inside. As I make my way toward Ruth Ann's room. Nurse Ratchet is nowhere to be seen. Maybe it's her day off. In her place is a middle-aged woman. She stops me before I can get to Room 412 and asks if she can help.

"Thanks, nurse. I've been here before. I'm here to see Ruth Ann Boyer in Room 412."

"Right down the hall. Fourth door on the left. "

"How's she doing today?"

"Fine, but you'll need to see her doctor for specifics."

This stops me in my tracks. "Has her condition changed?"

"You'll need to talk to her physician. Do you want me to page him?"

"By all means."

I hear the announcement over the PA system. Now I'm really concerned. I know nurses aren't supposed to give out any information, but Ratchet would at least give me some clues, even if they were non-verbal. A pleasant smile can convey a lot of information. This nurse is somber and won't make eye contact.

Instead of hanging around with Nurse Droopy, I head to Room 412. To my surprise, there's a Duluth cop guarding her door. He looks me up and down as he rises from his chair.

"You here to see Ms Boyer?"

This guy is a formidable looking fellow. He's maybe, if he stood on a soap box, five ten. It'd have to be a sturdy container, though, as I estimate he weighs close to three hundred. He'd make an excellent defense lineman for the Vikings.

"Yes, officer, I am."

"ID."

My uniform probably isn't ID enough, so I whip out my badge. He examines it and then asks for my drive's license. I dig out my billfold and show him my picture ID.

"Sorry, Chief. Have to make sure after last night."

My heart is someplace other than in my chest. I can't tell if it's rattling around in my shoes or in my throat. Wherever it is, it's pounding. Feels like some jungle drum sending out a message to Tarzan. "Bring on the elephants."

"Can you tell me what happened?"

"You being a cop, I guess I can. We got a call right after midnight. A night duty nurse said someone had been caught messing with one of their patients. Trying to inject some drug into her IV bag. An orderly saw it and tackled the guy. We responded and have the bum in jail."

"I want to see my girlfriend."

Before I can open the door Ruth Ann's doc arrives. He goes over the story and explains the 'drug' was actually strychnine.

"Since this was an obvious case of attempted murder, I requested a round-the-clock watch on Ms Boyer."

"Thanks for that, doc. It's not that I don't think the Duluth PD isn't doing a fine job, but I want someone in her room as well."

Officer Whatshisname speaks up, "You'll have to take that up with my boss' boss."

"Not to worry, Officer. West Clover Bottom will supply just the person. My cousin, Dutch Schultz. Anyone gets by you guys, well, look for them out there in the lake. They'll have broken arms and legs. Probably a few other things as well. Dutch thinks the sun rises and sets on Ruth Ann. Any chance he can have a talk with the bastard who tried this?"

"If it was up to me—"

I turn my attention to her physician. "I want to thank the orderly who stopped this, doc. But, first I want to see Ruth Ann. She okay?"

"Physically, yes. Emotionally, not so well. She's been calling for you, so go right in."

Which I did.

"Boy. Am I ever glad to see you."

Either she's totally off her sedatives, or the trauma of last night burned them off.

"Hey, babes. How you feeling?"

"Fine, now. You heard, right?"

"I did. Dutch is going to be with you 24/7 from now on."

"They posted a guard."

"Great. But he isn't Dutch. You know how he feels about you. No one will get within a hundred feet of you while he's around. I'll tell the nurse's he'll be watching you, and inform Dutch some people will have to be around. We'll work it out."

I can tell she's pleased cuz'll be watching out for her. She smiles and motions me down.

"Did I ever tell you I love you, Archie Schultz?"

Chapter 42

Talk about mixed emotions. Part of me doesn't touch the floor. Another part is seeing red, I'm so angry at the attack. But I have to put the feelings aside, at least for now. The first thing I do is call my cousin and tell him to get his butt over here. Then I have to see the Duluth PD and talk to whoever the hell tried to murder my girlfriend.

Knowing it'll be close to two hours before he shows, I poke my head back into Room 412, kiss my sleeping girlfriend, and ask the cop outside to call his office and inform them I'll be there in thirty.

I leave the Center and drive to a lakeside park. I walk down to the water's edge. The recent warm spell we experienced in WCB hasn't had any effect on the frigid waters of Lake Superior. I think maybe I should just keep walking. Instead I stare at the breaking waves. Must have been a storm somewhere over the lake last night ,as the waves are about four feet high. The wind is diminishing, yet it passes right through my lightweight clothes and raises goose bumps as though I was naked. The crashing waves sound as angry as I feel. Why the hell didn't I immediately send for Dutch? Her attempted murder would never have happened. The bastard who did this would still be stuck head first in the bottom of Superior. Even though she survived, I feel as if I've lost her. It's like someone has cut out my heart.

What makes it worse is I have this nagging feeling Ruth Ann's accident wasn't some random event, but planned malice.

I realize I can't go on about whatta, shoulda, but I have to live with my mistakes and slowly walk back to my cruiser. All the way, trying to convince myself, that it'll all work out in the end.

By the time I get into my car, I'm trying to think up a convincing argument why I should be left alone with her assailant for about thirty minutes. Although if they give me a lead-filled pipe, five'll be enough.

I zip out of the park and head for the DPD. I find a parking place and hurry to the front desk, tell the woman who I am, and need to see the detective handling Ruth Ann Boyer's case.

"May I ask who's calling?"

"My name is Archie Schultz. I'm the Chief of the West Clover Bottom PD. Ruth Ann is a special friend of mine and the editor of our local paper. Her welfare is of utmost importance to me and WCB."

"WCB?"

"West Clover Bottom."

"Oh. The best fishing spot in Minnesota. Know it well. One moment, please."

I'm still hopping mad at John E. Schultz and his lack of foresight when a grey haired woman appears.

"Chief?"

"Yes."

"Hi. I'm Detective Bonnie Noble. I believe you want to see me?"

Bonnie is a fifty-ish woman who appears to have some Indian—American Indian—blood. Her hair is as black as a moonless night and her eyes are like lumps of coal. If I were twenty years older, and not committed to Ruth Ann, I'd be knocking on her door.

"Pleased to meet you, Detective. I go by Archie back home. Ruth Ann and I are nearly engaged, well, going steady. Is that a term still in use these days? At any rate, I've been working on a line so sooth and convincing, you'll give me a lead pipe and let me interview the, ah—I better cool this down a couple of notches. You'll let me talk to the rotten son-of-a-bitch who tried to murder my far better half."

"I just wish I could have done that when we brought him in. Seriously, want to talk to him?"

"You betcha."

"You packin'?"

"Yeah."

"Follow me."

Gad. At times I can be so smooth and convincing. The Lady Detective is actually going to let me at this pond scum while I'm armed. I start to swagger, like Jerome does when he's feeling cocky.

She leads me into a unisex locker room and dials a combination lock. "This'll be yours while you're here. Put all weapons—pistol, mace, and anything else—in here."

Rats. I comply and she takes me to the cell room. Duluth has a few more cells than we do. It's two tiers high. She motions to a guard and when he comes over, she says, "Get that guy we brought in last night. The one that tried to murder the Burn Center patient?"

"Yes, Ma'am. The interview room?"

"Right. Cuff and shackle him."

The guard hurries off and we pass through two sets of double doors and into the interview room. It's maybe ten by twelve. Gray painted concrete block construction with a stainless steel table, two chairs. One I can see is bolted to the floor. Hope it's for asshole. There's a one way mirror on the wall. I suspect Detective Noble eventually will be watching and recording my interview. Probably trying to learn a few techniques.

The door rattles as it opens. The suspect is between the detective and guard.

No wonder the orderly subdued him so easily. He's got to be all of five four and on a good day, a hundred and twenty. He has a plethora of tattoos. There's a blackish ship's anchor on his right hand, a naked woman decorating his right forearm. Probably something on his biceps as well, although it's covered by rolled up sleeves. The right hand knuckles spell out HATE. A boa constrictor-looking snake, with a red darting tongue, starts on his hand and disappears under rolled up cuffs of his shirt.

His hair needs washing with an industrial strength detergent. I'd recommend one that contains at least ninety percent lye.

A crown of thorns apparently slipped and winds around his neck. Brown teardrops leak from his left eye

All in all this is one bad looking dude. Maybe he wouldn't be a pushover at all. I've got to send the Burn Center orderly a twenty pound box of chocolates.

The guard pushes him down into the chair and straps his legs and chest to the chair with wide, leather belts.

Pond Scum fixes me with a sneer while my inspection and his trussing continues. The guard leaves and Detective Bonnie stays.

"Chief, this Randy Booker. Lately from East LA." She doesn't bother to introduce me. I approve, as this tells Scum Bag he doesn't deserve the courtesy of knowing my name.

I stare straight into his eyes. I hold this for at least five minutes. He breaks eye contact and tries to squirm. Finally, I lean close so I'm inches away and whisper. A very soft whisper.

"Tried to convince the detective, here, to let me talk to you down by the lake. See, I got a cousin who'd love to get his hands on anyone who messes with my woman.

Dutch is three times your size and his way of dealing with shit-heads like you is to ram them head first in our lake. Hell, Superior'll work for him just as well. My detective colleague here knows Dutch and seen what he's done to people. In your case, he'd probably break your arms and legs before giving you a bath. Oh, one other thing. He hates tattoos. He'd have to remove them first."

Booker probably thinks he's a tough guy. Maybe he is. Maybe he's used to getting his way. The threat of having him worked over by Dutch seems to be getting to him. Beads of sweat litter his brow and wet patches are showing under his arms.

I turn away and let him stew.

He finally speaks, maybe trying to sound arrogant, but a high-pitched cracking soprano doesn't work. What comes out is, "Can't do that stuff anymore."

Slowly, I turn around and grin. "You're not in LA, Booker. This is Minnesota. We handle things a little differently in the North Woods. Detective? Can I take him to the lake? My cousin will arrive in," I look at my watch. "About ten, twelve minutes."

She goes along. "Don't see why not. We're pretty partial to Ruth Ann, too." She approaches him from the back and starts to undo his leg straps.

"You gotta be kidding me," says Booker.

"Sorry. Dutch'd do *me* over if I didn't give him a chance to talk to you."

"What you want?"

Chapter 43

"Oh, not much," I tell him. "Detective Noble says you're from LA. No way you would know about my woman. Some-one hired you to kill her."

Most of the time, my voice has been a whisper. I change tactics.

At the top of my voice, "Who?"

Booker rears back. Probably my scream. Or, it could be my garlicky breath.

"Don't know."

"You telling me you get a FedEx from someone with in-structions that a newspaper woman in West Clover Bottom, Minnesota is troubling them? And this unknown person di-rects you to bump off the patient in Duluth's Burn Center, Room 412? That what you're telling me? I think you need to talk to my cousin. Let's go."

Bonnie has already removed the straps and I grab Pond Scum by his shirt collar and yank him out of the chair.

For someone who tries to portray himself as one bad ass tough guy, he's really a wimp.

"No, man. Not what I'm saying at all. Take it easy, man. I tell ya."

"You got thirty seconds, buster."

"Look. East LA is one tough place. Man's gotta look out fer hisself. Gotta be tough. Look at me, man. Think I can stand up to them real tough dudes? No way. I gotta make them think I'm better than they are. This is some *init-e-ation* thing for me."

"Cut to the chase, K?"

"Huh?"

Pond scum is fidgeting and sweat pours off his nose. I'm wondering it he's also a druggie. Maybe starting withdrawal. I'll leave that tidbit for later.

My voice becomes calmer, like I'm taking him into my confidence.

"Look, Randy. I just want to be your friend here. The gang in LA is probably going to slice and dice you, now that you've failed. I'm betting someone approached them and offered your leader a pile of money to get rid of my Ruth Ann, right?"

If Pond Scum nods any harder, his head'll fall off. "Right, man."

Now I'm worried. These hoods aren't about to send a low life alone to do this job. That means Ruth Ann's not out of the woods yet.

"Excuse me. There's something I have to do. You okay with him, Detective?"

"No problem, Chief."

I step out and phone Dutch. "You at the hospital yet, cousin?"

"Bears eat ants out of a tree?"

Apparently that fractured metaphor is stuck in his brain. "Great. I know I don't have to tell you this, but talk to the guard outside Ruth Ann's door. I—"

"What guard, Archie? There's sposed to be someone else?"

"I can't spend much time right now, Dutch. I think there'll be another attempt on Ruth Ann. I'm guessing it might be with a gun. Lock and barricade her door. I'll call the hospital and let them know what's going on. If anyone knocks, DO NOT ANSWER. I'll be there as soon as I can. Got all that?"

"Bears eat ants?"

I call hospital security. My frustration is building and I get some lame-brain who tries to argue with me. I demand to speak to his supervisor. Reluctantly, he passes me off. This guy sounds reasonable and after I tell him what I said to Dutch, he agrees to post two security types outside Room 412.

After several deep breaths, I return to the interrogation room and Pond Scum. "Okay, Randy. I need your top man's name."

"No, man. Doan ask me that."

"You got three choices. Tell me his name, get on a flight back to LA, or talk to Dutch."

"Look. I tell you his name, I'll be a dead man iffen I go back."

"Who says you have to return to LA, Randy? I think you're actually a decent kid. Tell me what I want to know and you can live in West Clover Bottom. We'll clean you up and get you a job."

"True, man?

"True."

Chapter 44

Detective Bonnie's has been quiet most of the time. I ask, "You okay with this?"

"It is a little unorthodox."

"You guys book him yet?"

"No. That was scheduled for this morning, but then you arrived."

"Great, then the Duluth PD can release him into my custody."

"Look, Chief. Booker, here, tried to poison your girlfriend and you want us to release him into your care?"

"Let's step outside for a moment. Excuse us, Randy."

"Like I'm going somewhere," he says with a smile.

As we exit the interrogation room, Bonnie motions me to follow her. "I gotta have a cup of coffee and a donut. How about you?"

"Sounds good."

She takes me to a lunch room. It's about the size of a closet. There's a strong order of burned coffee. She tosses a buck into a Nash Coffee can and hands me a finely crafted 'Made in China' foam cup.

This is the worst coffee I've ever tasted. Still, I choke it down. Although it does do a fair job of softening my stale, hockey puck-like donut. Probably soften cured concrete as well.

She gets to the point. "Chief. I'm not sure we can simply let you take Mr. Booker."

"Look at this from my point, Detective. Randy'll be dead within a week after you lock him up. If it takes that long."

"How do you figure?"

"My deputy and I arrested two guys the other night. They were doing some ground work for an illegal housing development in WCB. In a—"

"WCB?"

"West Clover Bottom. Anyway, little over twenty four hours later, they're dead. Shot in the head. Just like our mayor and his wife. Heard about them?"

Bonnie's heard and she signifies her understanding by dropping her coffee. Thank goodness, besides being the worst tasting stuff in North America, it's cold. My feet are only wet, not scalded. I quickly wipe it off my shoes. Just in case.

"You've had four murders in, what did you call it? WCB?"

"Nearly five if you count, whatshername? Oh yeah, Ruth Ann."

Bonnie flushes red.

"If you want to find Randy's brains splattered all over his cell, be my guest. But, I guarantee you, he'll be dead. Let me take him and I'll put him to work with my cousin. You have to see Dutch to realize I'm not kidding when I say he loves dunking people in our lake. Ask the Liner twins, or any of our former troublesome teenagers."

Noble seems to ponder my impassioned statement and paces the break room. *Pacing* in this place means taking two steps forward, then two back.

"I'll have to run this by my boss. Can you come back in an hour?"

"Be here on the dot. I have to do some WCB cop stuff anyhow."

Once outside, I call Jerome.

"Hey, Archie. Newbury and I are being good boys. We'll have those guys at Regions in thirty minutes."

"Good. Keep your phone on. There's been some developments here. I'll fill you in later. Do me a fave, Jerome. Go to the BCA after you're done at the hospital and ask to see El Sullivan. He's their gun expert. See if he's had a chance to examine the lead taken from Rupert and Helen. Tell him to expect some more when the autopsies are done on Bruce and Lenny. K?"

"Got it, Chief. Over and out. Roger—"

My next task is to get in touch with Doc Joyce. Unfortunately, he's with a patient. I tell his nurse to have him call me. "It's urgent I speak to him. K?"

Next, I have to get something to eat. It's noon and I'm starving. I spot a street vendor hawking hot dogs and I order two with all the fixings and wash it down with a diet Pepsi.

As I toss the paper wrappers into the trash, my cell phone warbles. It's Joyce.

"Afternoon, doctor. Thanks for getting back to me."

"My nurse said it was urgent. What can I do for you?"

I explain why and what I need. After some hemming and hawing he agrees.

"Thanks, doc. I really appreciate this."

My phone beats out its tune again. It's Jerome.

"Hey, Chief. Just talked to Sullivan. Get this. The gun used on the mayor and wife was a .22."

He says this as if it'll make CNN interrupt their programming for Breaking News.

Jerome continues. " He's thinks it could be a Colt Woodsman, First Series. The rifling is 6 right. You know what that means?"

"He said a Woodsman, right?"

"Absolutely."

That tells me a lot. The pistol used on our city official and Mrs. City Official is expensive. I mean really expensive. In the thousands of dollars expensive. I can see someone tossing a cheapie, but not a gun that goes upwards of three grand.

That means if the slugs from Bruce and Lenny match those from the Jackmans, the same person killed all four. How does Ruth Ann's attack tie into this, if at all? Could it be instead of the picture becoming clearer, it's getting muddied? Now I know how the character in Edvard Munch's *The Scream* felt.

I've got fifteen minutes before I hear from Bonnie if they're going to release Randy.

Certainly not normal for me, but I begin to doubt if this is the smartest move I've ever made. That question takes a lot less than a nano-second to answer. The hell it is, Schultz.

Something about that kid, though. Even though he's mixed up with a bad crowd, he actually seems to be decent. Just searching for acceptance. Decent deep down. I sure hope I'm right. Our small town will work its magic and turn him around.

Either that, or I can probably start looking for a new job. Maybe Bemidji has an opening for a dog catcher or a garbage truck driver.

Chapter 45

I use the final minutes before seeing about Randy's release to call Ruth Ann's physician at the Burn Center. I reintroduce myself, in case he's forgotten me. There's a very good chance he has. I say, "I have a favor to ask."

"Now what, Chief?"

His admiration for me has obviously grown by leaps and bounds. "I want to take Ruth Ann back to West Clover Bottom this afternoon."

He laughs. "You are kidding, right?"

"Not at all. I have reason to believe she's not off the hook yet. Another attempt will be made on her life."

That takes him back. I'm sure there's never been a patient attacked while under his care. Probably not any other Burn Center physician has either.

"Look, doc. I'll go into detail later. I have my deputy and an ambulance arriving in about two hours. We *are* going to take her with us. I've already talked to Doctor Joyce back home and he says he can watch over her. I'll be in your facility shortly. We can finish then. I have to run."

Then I call Jerome.

"Hey—"

"Jerome. Pull over. Tell Newbury there's been a change of plans. I want both of you here as fast as you can make it. Use your lights and siren. Just watch it going through towns. Proceed without lights and sirens when you get to Duluth. You are to go directly to the Duluth Burn Center. Got that?"

I can visualize the gleam in his eyes. Official permission to go like a bat out of hell.

"Yes, sir."

I stare at the phone. He disconnected without going through a litany of sign offs. Will wonders ever cease?

My hour is up and I waste no time going back to the station. The receptionist remembers me and tries to engage me about the prospects for the fishing opener this weekend.

I tell her it'll probably be good, as usual, but I need to talk to Detective Noble.

Bonnie comes down the steps, catches my eye before she reaches the last one, and waves for me to follow.

She's mum as she takes me into the inner sanctum of the Duluth PD. She knocks on a panel door. I can't help but see a small, engraved plastic sign telling me we're about to enter Luther Holmgren's office. He's my counterpart. Duluth's Chief of Police.

Yeah, we're equals all right. I've got two deputies. If, with a straight face, you count Jerome. And he's probably got fifty on his force. Hell, their station alone can probably hold half of the town of WCB. Buildings and all.

I'm thinking I'll walk right in, sit in one of his padded chairs, put my feet on his desk, and light up a big seegar.

Sure I will.

He bids us enter.

"Archie. Good to see you again. How's tricks in WCB these days? Fishing going to be super this weekend?"

To the best of my recollection, I've never been introduced to the him before. Being the shrewd politician I am, I flash what I hope passes for a huge smile and take his offered hand. "Chief. Good to see you as well. We expect the walleyes will jump into your boat, they'll be so anxious to see humans again. Going to come on over?"

"Wish I could. But, you know, duty calls."

"Boy. Do I ever know what that means, hah, hah."

Sure I do.

He sits and gets to the point. "My Detective, here, tells me you want to take responsibility for our attempted murderer. That *really* right?"

The question smacks as though he's talking to some small town hick. Come to think about it, I am. Well, not necessarily the hick part, anyway.

This whole thing with Luther is so condescending I make an equally smart come back.

"Cross my heart."

Boy, did that get him. His mouth drops and he stares at Bonnie.

"Mind telling me why you want this scum bag?"

Gad, do I have to?

Sure I do.

I go into detail about the situation. The murders of the mayor. The murders of Bruce and Lenny. The attempt on Ruth Ann and my suspicions about further attacks, not only on her, but Randy as well, if he's locked up. That gets to him and he spins around in his executive chair that probably costs more than I make in three months.

His only comments throughout my explanation are a few "Hmms." When I finish, he makes two more circles in his chair and takes out a few papers. Looks like a full ream to me, and asks me to sign them, releasing the DPD from all liability.

By the time I'm done, I've got a severe case of writer's cramp. Doubt a full bottle of Aleve can solve it.

Soon, after I remove my gear from the locker, Randy is cuffless and shackleless and in my cruiser heading for the Burn Center.

Randy's head's on a swivel as he looks at all the stuff in my car. "First time I've ever been in a cop's front seat."

"One thing, Randy, my boy, don't ever give me reason to put you into the back. K?"

"I'll try, Chief."

As we park in the Center's lot, it dawns on me that Ruth Ann has no inkling what's been happening. She doesn't know about Bruce and Lenny, the autopsy reports, and certainly doesn't know that last night's assailant is about to walk into her room, free as a bird. Nor does she know we're whisking her home.

As we head for the front door, my phone beats out a line from Simon and Garfunkel's *Scarborough Fair*. It's Jerome. Probably with an update.

"We're on I35 approaching Moose Lake."

"I gather you're not wasting any time, right?"

"You said ASAP."

"I did. Be careful. See ya in about thirty minutes?"

"Probably a lot sooner."

"K."

Since we're only a minute or so away from Room 412, I call Dutch and tell him to expect us. I knock three times on the door.

My raps are answered with, "Who's there?"

"It's Archie, Dutch. You can open the door."

"Is that really my uncle there?"

I'm surprised he's quick enough to try that.

"I'm your cousin. Open the door."

"What's your real name?"

"Dutch. Open the door."

"Not until you give your real name."

I've said this before. Dutch follows instructions to a T. Although, sometimes he stretches it all the way to Z. I give up and call Ruth Ann.

"Hey, babes, tell Dutch to open the damn door."

I hear her speak and, I swear, two minutes of rattling chains and furniture scraping later, the door opens a crack. Apparently he's satisfied it's really me and lets us in.

Ruth Ann screams.

Chapter 46

Oh, great. Another stupid mistake. I never told her about Randy. I rush to her side and hold her hands and tell her, "It's okay. It's okay. He's with me. It's okay."

My usual melodic, sweet, soothing words have their effect and Ruth Ann drenches me with water from her full, ice filled glass.

After I tell her she's going home to my place, she calms down, a bit. Although I notice her eyes never leave Randy.

There's another knock on the door and her caregiver enters. Apparently he's never seen Dutch and backs away for a moment. When I tell my cousin who he is, the tension leaves the room. He suggests Randy and Dutch wait outside and proceeds to tell Ruth Ann and me he's against having his patient leave before she's officially released.

Ruth Ann isn't aware of why I've insisted she leave. I give doc a stern look. "We've been over this, doctor, and as I said earlier, she's going home. The discussion is over. K?"

"It's against my better judgment, but I'll sign her release as soon as *you* sign a release absolving the Burn Center from any future liability. Okay?"

He spits the last word out like it's drenched with Tabasco sauce.

As I follow him to his office, I call Jerome.

"Hey, Archie. What's up?"

He says this as though we just met after not seeing each other for a month.

"Where are you?"

"I'm gussin' we're four, five block away. Goin' nice and peaceful like."

"Good. Go to the front entrance and wait there. K?"

"Ten-four, rog—"

I end the call.

My new, best-friend doctor goes into his office and *forgets* I'm following. Luckily, I put my hand out to stop the door from slamming into my face. I don't think my wrist is shattered. Probably just severely sprained.

I sign another ream of forms and vow to learn to write left-handed, should I ever have to sign more releases.

I hurry back to Room 412 and go through a repeat with Dutch of my earlier entrance. I suggest Randy and Dutch wait outside while Ruth Ann changes out of hospital garb. She fixes me with a stare. Here I thought ice was cold. I offer to show the boys where the door is and join them in the hallway.

Moments later Ruth Ann pokes her head out and says we can re-enter. A nurse indicates an orderly will have to wheel her outside and supervise getting her into the ambulance.

When said orderly arrives, I demand he submit to my frisking him. Ruth Ann's brows furrow. She still isn't aware of my concerns about Randy's failure and a possible second attempt.

He's clean. But just in case, I tell Dutch to stick like glue until Ruth Ann's safely in the ambulance.

Apparently, being followed this closely unnerves the orderly. Once in the elevator, he reaches for a handkerchief, apparently to wipe his sweaty brow. Dutch's vice-grip-plier-like-paw clamps around the guy's right arm. Dutch looks down at him and shakes his head.

The door opens when we reach the first floor and I hold everyone back and scrutinize the foyer before we get out. I tell everyone to speed it up. We must look like we're being attacked by a swarm of killer bees.

With Ruth Ann secure in the ambulance, we form a four car caravan and head back to WCB.

To safety.

I hope.

Chapter 47

I decide Randy's probably a nick name for Randolph, or something like that. Oh, he's randy all right. I turn the AC on high and electronically lower a rear window.

I try to engage him in conversation. What was it like being a gang member? Was he from LA? Did he complete high school?

Most of his responses are typical teen-ager. Shrugs and one or two word answers.

We're midway between Duluth and WCB when he begins fidgeting, starts, then stops talking.

"Want to tell me something, Randy?"

A long sigh. Then it's like a dam bursts.

"I ran away from home when I was seventeen. I'm originally from Vegas. Mom and dad were into drugs and booze, when they weren't fighting. They work at some small, out of the way casino. Not one of the big ones like the Mirage.

"I got tired of being beat up by my dad and left."

"I'm sorry, Randy. You'll find West Clover Bottom a whole lot different than LA or Vegas. Do you want me to contact your parents and tell 'em you're okay?"

"Not especially."

We drive several more miles before he speaks again. "It'll probably take me some time to adjust to a small town."

"Mind if I say something 'bout that?"

"Like what?" His tone is a little defiant.

"Your tattoos. WCB is a great place, but maybe a little conservative when it comes to kids and their dress."

"A lot of places are like that. Hell, even in LA some stores'll kick people like me out on our butts. Nothin' new there."

I look at him. He seems to be pretty sharp and savvy about people in general. I'm betting he'll work out.

"Something you should know. My tattoos are henna. Won't last much longer. Another thing."

"Yes?"

"Name's not really Randy. I took that when I left home. Thought it sounded better than my own."

"Which is?"

"Al. Short for Aloysius. Aloysius Throckton, Junior."

I really can't associate the formality of his name with his outward appearance. It's probably a teenage rebellion against his home life. Hopefully he'll come around. But, it might take a Dutch-dunking or two.

A little fiddling with my two-way radio channels and I'm connected to Newbury.

"Yeah?" is his response to my call.

"How's Ruth Ann doing? She still sedated?"

"A little. I hear some sounds coming from back there."

"Keep you eye on her, K?"

"You tellin' me how to do my job, Schultz?"

Not only is Newbury lazy, he's a smart ass and insolent. I bite my tongue. "Just checking on my girlfriend. You know you're taking her to my house, right?"

Apparently he does as my radio goes silent.

Al looks at me. "What happened to your woman?"

"Besides—?"

"Look, Chief. I'm really sorry about that."

I believe him, or he's a great actor. Tears are flowing down his cheeks. I put my right hand on his shoulder and give it a little squeeze.

"There was a fire the other day. Ruth Ann sustained burns to her head."

Al digs out a well used handkerchief and blows his nose. Sounds like an irate gander fighting off a fox that's after his goslings.

"Was it real bad? Her burn?"

"Yeah. She was all doped up for a few days. You ever been burned? Badly?"

He shakes his head. "Got burned on my arm once, but it was nothin' compared to what she looks like. All them bandages."

"She's gonna need a lot of care."

"Anything I can do to help? You know, to help make up for—"

"The best thing you can do is be a great kid. I see it in you, so do me proud. K?"

"I'm gonna try, Chief. I'm gonna do my best. You'll see."

I smile, but inside I'm cautious. Is this a well crafted ruse to get to Ruth Ann?

Chapter 48

We pull into town and Al is all swivel-necked and gawking at our town.

He points. "That where Ruth got hurt?"

I correct him. "It's Ruth Ann and yes, that's where the fire was."

I'm so amazed at the progress, his question slips right by. Betty's place looks exactly like it always did. Although she's added a large banner proclaiming Grand Opening Tomorrow, May 13.

I turn left at the corner onto Second Avenue and *Louie's Repair and Auto Wrecking*.

"This's where you're gonna work, Al. Louie'll show you the ropes. Dutch is going to be busy during the days watching Ruth Ann. You'll bunk with him at night. Today, however, you can come home with me to get cleaned up. I'm gonna insist you cut your hair and start working on those tattoos. I'm guessing some hydrogen peroxide will do it. Any questions?"

Knowing anyone who's hired Dutch has a pretty low bar, Louie shouldn't have any problems with what looks like a gang-banger. We pull in.

"Gonna need some ear protection," I holler to Al as we go inside.

I motion him back outside and drag Louie along to introduce him to his new helper. "Louie, Al. He'll start in the morning, K?"

Louie looks my ward up and down. "Know anything 'bout car repair?"

"Nope."

At lest Al is honest.

"Care to learn?"

"Sure."

"Good enough for me, Archie. How's Ruth Ann?"

I admire how Louie has the ability to get to know all about a person so quickly. Maybe I ought to use his techniques the next time I need to interview a candidate.

"She's on her way home. She'll be staying with me for the duration. Dutch tell ya he's watching her?"

"Yeah. Heard she was attacked in the hospital. Gather whoever tried, failed. That right?"

I'm pleased to hear Dutch apparently can keep some things private. I'll have to buy him a sixty-four ounce steak at the Clover Bottom Inn. On second thought, better not. They have this deal that if anyone can eat one, they get another, free. He'd probably ruin their month's profit. Instead, I'll buy him a hind quarter from the Clover Butcher Shop.

"Right, Louie. I insisted she come home. Doc Joyce and Nurse Nightingale are more than capable of handing her medical needs."

Louie gives me a strange look. "Nurse who?"

"You know. The gal who works for Joyce."

He finds this funny and slaps me on the back several times. I stumble back a few paces and slam into his building.

"You mean Mary Jane Hooper?"

"Yeah, that's her name. Between them and Dutch, Ruth Ann'll be in good hands."

Introductions completed, Al and I drive to my house. He heads for the guest bath for a much needed shower and I toss his clothes into the washer.

By the time he's sort of presentable, Newbury pulls in.

"I was getting concerned, Newbury. Ruth Ann okay? What delayed you?"

"She had to make a potty stop. Pretty embarrassing helping her to the little girls' room."

I'm tempted to smack him over the head. I tower over him and say, "You tried any funny stuff, Newbury, I'll dump you in the lake, got it?"

He slinks back to the ambulance, muttering.

Ruth Ann needs assistance out of the ambulance. I manage getting her out on my own and vow to have a talk to the fire chief and get Newbury's ass fired.

I only trip once and slam into a doorway two times, but I get my love into her bedroom.

She sits on the edge of the bed and I probe to see if I need to toss Newbury into the lake. I'll be sure to use a pallet load of concrete blocks. "You okay? Have any problems on the way?"

"I'm K. Still groggy. Wanna sleep. Take my sweat pants off."

This is way more than I bargained for. "Ahh. You sure?"

She drapes herself an my shoulders and nibbles on my ear. I attribute her action to a reaction to her travel meds. Hmm. Could I find out what she took? Unfortunately, for me, this is quickly followed by snores.

I know I'm blushing. Probably my toes are red as well. I undo the knot on her pants tie and pull her sweats off. If I was expecting some French cut panties, well, the surprise is on me. She's wearing a pair of old fashioned knickers.

I lower her into bed and pull the covers up. Her snores increase in volume. I kiss her, make sure the light-blocking window shades are pulled and the drapes closed. I turn on a cat-shaped night light and slip out.

In the kitchen, Dutch and Al seem to be getting acquainted. I notice a lot of Al's tough-boy gangland speech has suddenly disappeared. He and my cousin are telling jokes, although Dutch's center around knock-knocks.

I interrupt their conversation. "Dutch, Ruth Ann's sleeping and I need to take Al into town for some clothes and a haircut. Check all the doors and windows to make sure they're locked. We'll be gone for a couple of hours. Want me to have the Inn deliver something for you?"

This is a foolish question, but just in case he's not hungry, I had to ask.

"Burgers and fries. One of their malts, too."

"I'll phone it in. You know little Sammy, right?"

"Yup."

"I'll make sure he delivers your food."

Al and I leave and on the way I call the Clover Bottom Inn with Dutch's order. Six double cheese burgers, three orders of fries and three strawberry malts.

"Sammy on duty today?"

I get an affirmative and insist he deliver to my place. "This is for Dutch."

The guy chuckles and I hang up.

Al draws a lot of attention when we enter *Louise's Barber Shop.* She is Louie's Auto Repair's wife. As good at fixing hair as her husband is repairing cars.

Al sits in her chair and as soon as Louise's done gowning and fitting the paper collar around his neck, says, "Heard you're gonna be working for husband. Got a tip for you, young man, do what he tells ya and don't grumble 'bout it."

Al is quick on the pick up as he responds, "K. Will do."

I see Louise smile. She leaves his hair fashionably long, but neat.

Our next stop is Gill Brothers. Bill Jr. fits him out with four pair of stone-washed Levis, four long-sleeved shirts, socks, and a pair of tennis shoes. Bill puts it on my account, and a handsome teenager exits the store.

I detour to Betty's *Shoppe* to see the progress and to let her meet my ward. There are several volunteers putting the finishing touches on her place and they get a chance to size Al up. Another reason we stopped.

He's polite and differential to all. Again, I'm amazed how well he's fitting in. Bill Jr.'s suggestion of long sleeved shirt goes a long way hiding most of Al's tattoos. I figure a couple more shots of peroxide should make them nearly invisible.

I'm feeling good for the first time in days and we stop by the police station.

Jerome seems all excited about something and gives me a head wave. I excuse myself from Al and my deputy and I go into my office.

He's bouncing from foot to foot with excitement. "Just heard from the BCA. El, the gun expert? He got the slugs from Bruce and Lenny already. Guess the path-olo-gist did the autopsies real quick. He says they're same as Rupert and Helen's."

"I'm not surprised. That pretty well ties all four murders together."

Jerome's eyes become slits and he rocks back and fourth on his feet. Talk about smug. "That's what I figured all along."

"Then give this some thought, deputy. Why?"

Chapter 49

With all my running around, I've missed lunch, again. Al and I head over to the Inn and get their half sandwich and cup of soup. I order iced tea and he a Coke. When we finish the food, I decide to ask him who he took orders from out in LA.

The gang must have done a number on him for he starts to sweat and looks about as though some tough was at the next table.

His reply is inaudible.

"If speaking his name is hard, Al, write it out. K?"

He leans over. "You don't know how hard this is. I've seen guys get cut real bad for even being in the presence of a cop."

He breathes deeply for several counts, closes his eyes, and whispers, "Blue Dog."

"Blue Dog? What kinda name is that?"

Al puts his fingers to his lips. "Not so loud, Chief. Blue Dog means he thinks he's top dog of the Crips. Blue's their color, you know."

Maybe I know that. If I do, it's tucked away right close to a recipe for Beef Wellington. On second thought, it's several slots lower than the recipe.

I've got Chief of Duluth's PD office number in my cell phone's contact list. He answers on the second ring.

"Afternoon, Chief. How's Ruth Ann doing?"

I'm a little jealous he's not interested in how *I'm* doing. I ignore his lack of courtesy and ask him if he happens to have our counterpart in LA's phone number.

"Not at my finger tip, Schultz. Call 411. Everything under control?"

"We got confirmation the same gun was used to kill the two guys I told you about and our mayor and his wife."

"From what you told me, that's hardly a revelation, is it?"

"Not really, but now we have proof."

"Good. Say, Schultz, I've got to run to a meeting. Thanks for the update."

So much for him. I swallow my pride and tell Al I have to get back home. After I pay the bill, we head out. In my den I get a brilliant idea and call information for the LAPD.

It's obvious they don't know who they're dealing with here and I'm shuffled off to a detective.

I can tell she's very impressed that a Chief of Police would lower himself to talk to her.

Her, "You're the Chief of Police of Clever Button? That next door to Podunk, Minnesota?"

We're off to a great start. I explain about Ruth Ann and the attempt on her life. Not once, but more than likely, twice. If I could come up with a third, I'd really have her attention.

"What do you want me to do about it? LA is just a little ways away from Minnesota, let alone Copper Bitter."

She's got a great sense of humor. I nearly laugh. I reply, "Look, Detective, I thought you people in San Dago might be interested in the fact that some dude named Blue Dog is behind the last attempt."

"You know 'bout Blue Dog, Chief?"

"I sure do. I know he considers himself the head of the Crips. Out here, next to Podunk, we think Crips is a derogatory term for handicapped folks. But, in Cal-i-forny, you associate that name with rampant crime, right?"

"No need to get nasty, Chief."

"That's what I thought. Now, want to talk about this?"

Chapter 50

Jerome apparently broke from the caravan and went to the station. He calls me to find out where everyone is. I remind him the plan was to deliver Ruth Ann to my place.

He covers by saying, "I know that. I just needed to make a stop at the office. How's Ruth Ann doin'?"

And, in case I didn't notice, he tells me all the one way street signs are in place. He informs me he also checked with George about the upcoming onslaught of frenetic fisher-people.

"Guess what, Archie."

"What?"

"He's sober."

That is a surprise. Don't know if I've ever seen him in such a state. Jerome continues to fill me in on the preparations Alex made for the opener, now just three days away.

I thank him and pass along that Ruth Ann's sleeping off the travel sedation, but she seems fine. "I'll probably be late tomorrow. Doc wants to see Ruth Ann at nine."

"Coming in today?"

"For a little while. Got some things to work out with Al. Oh. I forgot to mention that's Randy's real name. Al Throckton, Jr. Thanks again, Jerome. Call me if something comes up."

After I hang up, I wander into my living room and find Al watching cartoons. "We need to go into town and get you started with Louie. Why don't you change back into your old clothes? They're in the dryer."

He hops up, kills the Cartoon Channel, and quickly changes. A few minutes later, after I check to see how Ruth Ann's doing, I let Dutch know we're leaving.

"I'll lock the door behind me, cousin. But, check all the doors and windows to make sure I didn't miss anything. K?"

I walk away to bears eating ants.

We drive to Louie's, and the owner takes Al under his wing, introduces him to the rest of the crew, then takes him back into the depths of his shop for some hands-on training. I hear Louie say, "Gonna show you how to change oil, check the tires and fluids under the hood and . . ."

The rest is lost as they move out of ear-shot. What with the noise going on, that takes a trip of about twelve feet.

Before going to the station, I travel around town to see for myself how the preparations for opening weekend are going. So far, so good. I want to see a sober George and go to the landing. Much to my surprise, he's got the parking lot cleaned, legible signs with instructions for boat launching, and reminders about parking restrictions.

I suspect being off his 'coffee' has given him a burst of energy. I see a small wisp of smoke coming from his office and head in that direction. He answers my knock and invites me in.

"How's my niece doin'?"

"She's recovering nicely. I'll bring her by tomorrow after she sees Doc Joyce."

"'Preciate that. Any leads on them murders?"

"A couple, George. A couple." I don't want to go into details so I change the subject. "Everything looks set for the weekend. You've done a great job."

"Thanks, Archie."

He looks worried. He's fidgeting and starts pacing. He's acting like he has something to say. I remain silent.

"Something I should tell ya, Chief."

He goes from my first name to my title. "Yeah?"

George is getting more nervous. He looks out onto the dock, closes the door, and shuts the windows . "Don't want anyone to hear." He pulls his chair closer and wets his lips. "I need a little coffee first."

This time, he doesn't bother to use actual coffee, but takes a pull straight from his bottle of Jack Daniels.

"That's better," he says, wiping his mouth. "Okay. Last evening, I was just about to turn on the lights." He pointed towards his left. Probably indicating the light standard at the edge of the dock.

"Go on, George. It was getting dark."

"Yeah. Before I flipped that switch, I heard some voices. I froze and listened. They was real low. Menacing, I thought."

I wait while he takes a second sip from his bottle. I think about taking it away, but it apparently gives him a sense of security.

"How many people were outside?"

"I don't know for sure, but I think three. One guy did most of the talking. He seemed pissed at the others. He said, 'You fuck-ups missed two times. I'm not paying youse to miss, right?'"

"I heard some mumbling. Two different voices. That's why I think there were at least three guys."

"Okay. Good reasoning, George. Then what?"

"This main guy says, 'She's paying big bucks. Can't miss again or we'll get it. Now, what happened at that Burn Center?'"

"He said Burn Center? You're sure of that?"

"Pos-i-tive, Archie. Said it clear as can be. Another guy speaks up. Says that kid was looking to be accepted. Promised he'd do it, no sweat."

That has to be Al. Now my hackles really rise. What George was saying, sounds like the attempt on Ruth Ann. Was Al still after her?

Chapter 51

Like someone once said, "The plot thickens." It was about to harden into cement. I press George and he tells me something that knocks me off my chair.

"'Look, Blue,' this guy says and then I hear a real loud slap. The guy called Blue says, 'Shut up. No names. Case the cop's joint. Goona be lots of confusion in a cuple days.'"

This not only knocks me off my chair, it takes away my breath. Why would they need to case my station? Are they hatching a plan to attack us as well? Or are they going to use the opener to finish off Ruth Ann? I've put off interviewing her because of the meds she's been on. I can't wait. What does she know about the case that has unleashed these attacks? Who's behind them?

I've got to get home. "Thanks, George. Keep your eyes and ears open, K?"

The trip is made quicker with lights and siren. I skid to a stop by the back door, and fly to the door. Damn. I told

Dutch to lock up. He's got to have heard the siren, so I call hoping I'm right.

He answers on the first ring. "That you, Archie?"

I have to take into account Dutch's intellectual capacity. My name shows clearly on his screen. "Yes, Dutch. It's me. I need you to unlock the door right now!"

"Don't have ta yell. I'm on my way."

The dead bold scrapes back, the door chain rattles, and he cracks open the door. "That's you, all right." He steps aside to let me enter.

"You okay, Archie? Heard the *sireen*. Sumthin' up?"

"Yeah. Ruth Ann awake?"

Ruth Ann shuffles into the kitchen. "I am now. The siren woke me."

I heave a sigh of relief. "How're you feeling, honey?"

"Okay. A little drowsy. Fix me a cup of your coffee?"

The grinder reduces the beans into a microscopic powder and they're carefully transferred to the pot. Three minutes later there's a thunck as the spent grounds fall into the trash can.

Cautioning Ruth Ann about the temperature of the coffee, I drop an ice cube into her cup. I'm not sure, but it sounds like the cube sizzles as it hits the liquid.

Two sips later, her eyes are wide open.

Using the Minnesota approach to conducting 'biness' I start the dance with Ruth Ann and carefully circle. "So, what did you find out about the murders that has made you the target of a bunch of hoods?"

My subtle approach pays off.

"I'm not sure I follow."

"Betty said, before the accident, you had written something on a napkin. She said you spelled out 'real estate.' Said it was in capital letters and underlined. Had to have been important."

"I did that?"

"Betty said so. The note was lost in the fire."

"Fire?"

Oh, man. She doesn't even remember there was a fire. "You recall anything about Saturday night?"

"No."

"You know why you were in the hospital."

"My head hurt like crazy. Still bothers me. That why?"

"You do know who I am, right?"

Chapter 52

"Sure I do. You're Archie Schultz. Why?"

"It sounds like you've got a case of temporary amnesia. At least I hope it's temporary."

Her eyes widen and her face drains color like bleach being poured over a pair of jeans. Her voice rises. "What do you mean, amnesia? Was I in an accident or something?"

I put a hand on her shoulder. "Bear with me here. You don't remember the fire at Betty's or the note you made about real estate?"

She touches her bandaged head, grimaces, and gives me a slight head shake.

Everything seems to cave in on her and tears flow down her cheek. "Am I going to be okay?"

Not wanting to give her a cheery smile and say she'll be just fine in a few days, like nothing happened, I take her hands. "Maybe it'd help if I tell you about what I've found since we had supper at the Inn. You recall that, correct?"

She nods as she wipes away a fresh flow.

I continue. "You said someone told you about Horace Schmidt and the large deposit he made. I got a subpoena for his records. The money left here, went to Brooklyn, then to the Bahamas. The other two councilmen's money followed the same route. Each one of them has at least a million bucks stashed in the Sixth Bank of the Bahamas. If you recall, those guys are missing, but I'm betting they're lounging on some sunny beach."

I see Ruth Ann's eyes gleam. "It's coming back. I kinda remember something about a real estate deal. The details are still fuzzy, but I think it was pretty shady. I wish I could recall more."

"It's a start. Don't worry about it. Concentrate on getting well. K?"

"I want to hear more about that fire. Tell me what happened."

"Let me fix you a martoonie. Then we'll talk."

That brings a smile to her face. She's apparently recalling the incident at her place before we had supper at the Inn. I hurry to my home office with its well stocked liquor cabinet and fix our drinks.

This gives me time to think out my approach to her accident at the Shoppe and the attack by Al at the hospital. I know I have to be careful not to upset her. I'll ease into the situation. Maybe hold her close. Hold her hands. Rub her back. She always likes that.

I fix our drinks and carry the glasses to the living room.

Ruth Ann is standing by the fireplace. Her foot is tapping the floor. She speaks before I can hand her the martoonie.

"Why the hell did you bring that guy here? The one who tried to mess with my IV."

So much for plans A, B, and C. I read somewhere that temporary amnesia can clear in a blink of an eye. Someone must've blinked.

"Sounds like your memory's returning."

Her face is clouded. I've noticed on more than one occasion when she's upset her brows become straight lines, as does her mouth. I expect to hear her tell me she never wants to see me again. Her teeth appear to be so clenched, I'm sure she can't open her mouth to get the words out.

I hold out her glass hoping the gin will loosen her up. She refuses.

"K. In case you aren't fully clear on the events, let me explain."

I launch into the story of the fire, my concerns she was the target due to what she knows, the death of Bruce and Lenny, the thwarted attack by Al Throckton, Jr., aka, Randy. I finish with her Uncle George's tale of Al's gang leader, Blue Dog, and him being here in good old West Clover Bottom.

By the time I finish, her demeanor changes and she downs her drink in two long pulls.

She slumps down into a chair. "So, I'm not out of the woods yet?"

I don't answer, but think, babes, you're so deep, I don't want to even think about it

Chapter 53

I guess the booze reacted with her meds. In moments her head falls to one side and she starts snoring. At least she looks peaceful. Soon, a smile tries to beak loose. I watch her for nearly an hour before checking and double checking the doors and windows. It's times like this I wish I had a dog the size of the one that left its calling card addressed to my lett shoe.

I pick her up and take a hundred and ten frightened pounds to her bedroom. Apparently she's not fully asleep. As I try to lay her down, she's got a death grip on my neck.

She whispers, "Stay with me for a while. I need you close to me."

I slip off our shoes and socks. I'm not sure it's Ruth Ann or it's Maggie that joined us, that's purring. At any rate, even though her gin soaked breath is gently blowing across my neck and Maggie's cat food breath is caressing my face, I'm contented.

I stay next to Ruth Ann until the hallway clock strikes eleven and extract myself and head up to my bedroom.

I'm tired, but sleep avoids me. I remember hearing a single gong and must have drifted off wondering if it was one or just the strike on the half hour.

My alarm rouses me at six-thirty the following morning and I drag myself into the bathroom to get ready for the day. A long hot shower washes away my tiredness. I need to get some food, and hurry downstairs. I make a quick check on Ruth Ann. She's still asleep under the watchful eye of Maggie.

My coffee making process must have worked on both of them, as Maggie is suddenly on the counter. No doubt learning the secrets of brewing a real cup when Ruth Ann slips behind me and blows on my neck.

"Got plenty of cream, mister?"

"Farmer Jones' truck should be delivering a semi-trailer load any minute. Sleep well?"

She nibbles my ear lobe and I feel her nodding her answer. Scenes of Heather flash in my mind. I debate if I should add that bit of information to the saga of last Saturday night. Maybe later, when Ruth Ann's further down the road to recovery.

"Today's the day Betty reopens. Care for breakfast there?"

"Might be fun. As long as you're there to act as body guard."

I point to my kitchen clock. "Seven-thirty. Your appointment with James is nine. Why don't you take a bath and we'll leave in fifteen?"

"Fifteen, as in minutes?"

"Yeah. That's how long it takes me to get ready."

"You have sooo much to learn. Fifteen minutes. Geeze."

While Ruth Ann is doing her toilette, I call the *Shoppe* and after a dozen rings, Betty answers.

"Wadda ya want, Schultz?"

"Good morning, Betty. Congratulations on your grand re-opening. Brisk biness today? Happy to be behind the counter again?"

"Cut the crap, Archie. I'm busy. So, wadda ya want?"

"Just making small talk, Betty. Nice to see you're in such a fine mood. Ruth Ann just went into the bathroom to start getting ready for her doctor appointment. We should be leaving here in about fifteen minutes to get breakfast."

I thought Doc Hudson's reaction to my call about Jerome and his antics was ear-drum bursting. It's nothing compared to Betty's.

Midst the uncontrolled bouts of laughter, she barks out, "Buster, you are so dumb at times. I'll see ya in an hour. Want to order now so I can have it ready? If I'm not forgetting, that lovely young—still single, I understand—lady loves my pancakes. I'll plant some wheat right away. It'll be ready to harvest by the time you get here."

The rest of her laughter is cut off as she hangs up.

Chapter 54

I certainly understand Ruth Ann much more than Betty ever will. I swear I never exceeded ninety on the trip to the *Shoppe*. We arrive fifty-three minutes flat after my call.

True to her promise, Betty has two stacks of 'cakes under the warming lights. Ruth Ann smiles and digs in. I notice several people staring at my lady-friend. They act as if they've never seen a woman with her head wrapped in gauze and wearing a stocking cap. Ruth Ann's oblivious to the attention and inhales her food. Doc Joyce never said anything about her fasting so I assume there will be no work done on her head other than to change the dressing. I've avoided mentioning debriding her scalp. I don't tell her it can be as painful as the original burn.

Some stranger comes over as though to either speak to Ruth Ann or get a closer look at her. My mind wanders back to the conversation I had with her Uncle George and his recounting the discussion regarding Blue. My hand drifts down to my holster and I slip open the strap holding my Glock in place.

Ruth Ann's busy finishing off her blueberry 'cakes and doesn't pay any attention to the stranger in our midst. He reaches between us and grabs a menu from its holder. I heave a sigh as he leaves.

"Not hungry?" Ruth Ann says to me.

My head's been swiveling around like it's on ball bearings as I check out Betty's opening day crowd.

"Been busy checking things out. Good sized crowd, huh?"

"Yeah. 'Bout time to go?"

"One minute." I stuff a pancake into my mouth and wash it down with some OJ. After catching Betty's attention, I mouth, "Put it on my bill."

I throw down a ten to cover the tip and we make our way to Ruth Ann's appointment.

As we leave, I return to scanning the crowd. I have no idea of what Blue Dog looks like, but based on his name, I suspect someone with a pointed nose, a set of fangs, and uncontrolled drooling. Probably has long hair with tufts sticking out of a T-shirt, as well.

No one matches that description.

We make it through the crowd and into my cruiser with no problems.

"Town's getting crowded already," I observe to Ruth Ann.

Her mind is on her immediate future. "I'm a little scared, Archie. Think everything's going to be okay?"

To myself, I say I sure as hell hope so. To her, I reply with what has to be the world's most comforting words ever spoken, "Ummm."

The Clover Bottom Clinic is on Third Street in the mostly residential area of town. Main Street contains most of the businesses, all six of them, as well as the lake front. Second

Street has Clover Bottom State Bank, the dwelling place of Heather, a shoe repair slash dry cleaning establishment, Ruth Ann's paper, and Louie's Auto Repair shop.

There are no other streets beyond Third.

I pull around to the back of the Clinic and escort Ruth Ann in. Joyce may be a recent graduate of med school, but the waiting room is stocked with ten year-old *Readers Digests* and a few ancient issues of *National Geographic*.

After she signs in and hands over her medical card to be copied, we sit and wait for her nine o-clock. Fifteen minutes later, Joyce's nurse, Mary Jane Hooper, calls for Ruth Ann.

"You want me to come along?"

I figure she wants me too, as even Hulk Hogan couldn't hold onto my arm with that kind of a grip. Nurse Hooper gathers Ruth Ann's weight, (after Ruth Ann shoves me away from the scale), her height, and blood pressure, then ushers us into an exam room.

Very gingerly, Ruth Ann removes her hat and holds it in her lap. The muscles in her face are so tight, I wonder if she's suffering from lock-jaw. I stand behind her and massage her neck. I can feel her tenseness start to ebb.

Joyce bounds in. "How's my favorite patient?"

Ruth Ann forces a smile.

Without any further ado, he starts to remove a mile of gauze. When he gets to the last yard, he says, "This may sting a little, Ruth Ann."

Her "Owwwww" confirms he was spot on.

I never would have guessed tearing off a hunk of one's skin would be painful.

"Your head is looking good. First time I saw this burn, it looked pretty bad. A lot of times the initial impression is worse than it really is. You're proof of that. I think we'll give you a few more days before proceeding."

"Will my hair grow back, doctor?"

"It'll be even more beautiful than it was. I want to check your vision. Any problems?"

"Nope. Other than when I woke up this morning."

"Oh? What happened?"

"I saw Archie."

As he leaves he says, "I'll send in Mary to redo the dressing. See you in four days?"

After Hooper redresses her burn, Ruth Ann and I leave the clinic. We drive by Louie's and I make arrangements for Dutch to accompany us. He's only too happy to act as guard.

Once everything is settled, I head to the office and get a surprise.

My old grade school buddy, Roy Fritz, is waiting for me. I look closely to see if that black eye has healed. He tried to stand up for me against all the hazing Ruth Ann gave me for spending so much time at the St. Louis arch. On the way to the famous court house across the street, he bumped Ruth Ann. She wheeled around and landed one mighty punch on his left eye.

We embrace. "Roy. How the hell are you? Long time no see."

"Hey, Archie. You're looking great."

I haven't seen my friend for a few years. He went to St. Johns, down in St. Cloud, to major in business. Then his folks left WCB for Crookston, so he seldom makes it here anymore.

"Say, bud, I stopped at the newspaper office to see Ruth Ann. Her assistant said she was sick. What's up?"

A pang of jealousy creeps in. He and *my* Ruth Ann were an item during our sophomore year. During those years she and I were at each other's throats.

"Yeah, I gather you haven't heard about all the commotion."

"News of good old West Clover Bottom seldom makes the front page of the *Times*. Tell me about this, *commotion*."

I fill him in on the murders of Rupert and his second wife and the two construction workers.

"If that weren't bad enough, Betty's *Shoppe* burned. Ruth Ann got caught up in the fire. Suffered a bad injury to her head."

Roy fires back ""God! Is she okay?"

I nod.

"That's good. Must say, I've kinda missed my old girl-friend since I've been out east."

I've heard people's eyes turn green with envy. I'm sure mine are florescent emerald. "*I've* been spending a lot of time at the hospital and now *I'm* taking care of her during her recovery. She's very appreciative *I'm* around to watch over her."

I fail to mention cousin Dutch is acting as her bodyguard or her life is in danger. Even though Ruth Ann's never spoken of Roy, I remember the way those two carried on after classes. Talk about puppy-love. Talk about star-struck teen-agers.

I'm not about to give him any reason to try to re-kindle that romance. Besides, I wonder why he picks this time to show up. Is he part of this scheme involving the attack on *my* gal? Or maybe even the disappearance of the slush fund?

Chapter 55

Roy doesn't seem to pick up on my jealous ramblings and asks more about Rupert. "So, what's going to happen to WCB without a mayor and council? Will there be a special election?"

"Probably. The town's still reeling from the murders and the fire. With the fishing opener at midnight tomorrow, no one's thinking about replacements. At least not yet."

"One person seems to be."

This bit of information throws me. How could some outsider know this? But, being a person who's up on everything going on in town, I can't let on I haven't the faintest idea of who he's talking about. I yawn, "That so?"

"Don't be so coy, Archie. You know Jackie's getting together a group to run for mayor and council. With her as mayor, of course."

Another yawn. "Oh, that. I guess it slipped my mind, what with taking care of Ruth Ann, and all."

Jerome walks in and for a moment he and my buddy Roy are engrossed in catching up. I hear Jerome giving Roy all the details of finding Rupert and Helen, and my falling into the lake. Jerome switches to a whisper and before I know it, Roy is roaring with laughter.

"Dutch really said, 'You 'restin' some walleyes,' Archie?"

I answer. "Hah, hah."

Jerome says something about having to check on traffic and leaves.

Roy ambles over. "Seriously, Archie, any clues about the murders?"

I answer by asking what he's doing these days.

"I'm working for a large investment company on Wall Street."

This gives me an idea and I use my practiced 'Minnesota Biness' technique. The one that worked so well with Heather's boss, Dave Feldman. You know, a little chit-chat and gradually work the conversation into the real subject.

"Great." That takes care of the chit-chat. "So, you could use your computer skills and get some info for me, right?"

Roy was hacking computers even when we were in fifth grade.

My subtle approach works like a charm.

"Huh?"

"Let me explain. Come into my office."

I lay out my idea.

"Jeez, Archie. That's a little unorthodox."

I don't voice my thought. You're working for an investment company on Wall Street and concerned about being orthodox? I figure their motto is: We have no idea of what orthodox even means.

Roy wipes his face. Apparently thinking of a response.

"You know, buddy. That might just work."

"You remember Heather Maple from school?"

"Kinda. Why?"

"Oh, I was just thinking she needs to know the plan. You could work with her."

Roy's eyebrows furrow and his mouth twists. "She's back in town? Wasn't she ahead of us? Kinda gangly, as I recall."

I smile to myself. Gangly, Heather is not. Horny, she is. In spades. I can take Roy's mind off Ruth Ann and Heather's off me. I hate to admit it, but if anything, Roy's better looking now than he was in high school.

"People change, guy. People change."

He gets a look at her in that yellow bikini, he'll call work and demand a month's vacation.

"Let me get back to you. You going to be around tomorrow?"

"It's the opener, Roy."

"Right. I forgot. I'll call ya."

As soon as he's out of the station, I call Jerome. "I've got a break in the case. I need you to take over for awhile. K?"

"Roger, ten-four, over . . ."

Chapter 56

I'm out of the station like a flash and into my cruiser. Lights and siren clear the way. In five minutes I pull into my driveway. Even before the last note dies, I'm assailing my back door. It appears that Dutch has barricaded himself and Ruth Ann in.

A call to his cell proves frustrating. "Dutch, it's your cousin. Open the back door. I need to talk to Ruth Ann."

"So *you* say. I was told to protect her and unless I have somethin' better than you sayin' so, I ain't budgin'."

"You hear the siren?"

"Yeah. Don't prove nothin'."

"Look out the parlor window and you'll see my cruiser."

"Yeah and someone will shoot me tru da glass. I'm not gonna fall for that."

"Put Ruth Ann on, K?"

"He's just following your instructions."

"Ruth Ann, I need to talk to you. Have Dutch open the door, please? He will if you ask."

Dutch comes on. "This better be you, cousin. If not, I'm gonna really hurt you."

After he slides back the deadbolt and unhooks the safety chain, I hear the scraping sound of my kitchen chair being moved. Probably had it wedged under the door knob. The door opens a crack. A pair on dark brown beady eyes peer out. "Lemme see yer badge."

I hold up my shield and cuz finally opens the door. I'd like to yell at him, but like Ruth Ann said, he was following instructions.

"Good to see you're careful, cuz."

"Nobody gets in here lessen I say so."

Ruth Ann is waiting for me and I suggest we feed Dutch while we talk. She gives me a sour look.

"You're really suggesting I make lunch for all three of us. Right, buster?"

"Just a suggestion, but since you volunteered . . ."

"Geeze. Who's the person in terrible agony? The one who's been suffering? The one who's . . ."

"All right. All right. I'll call for a pizza."

"Make it two extra large pepperonis. My protector's been telling me how hungry he is."

Twenty minutes later, I answer the door and pay for the meal.

Ruth Ann sits with a sly grin on her face until I get some plates and silverware. I'm thinking she's enjoying being waited on. Sure, she's been burned, attacked at least once, probably twice, but she could at least help. I chastise myself for even thinking like that. But a vision of a yellow bikini clad Heather, massaging a porterhouse flashes into my mind. Before she sees what has to be my reddening face, I hurry to the fridge for beers all around.

My cousin is busy with his pie. Two-thirds of it disappear as I take a moment to look at Ruth Ann.

"So what was it that got you so excited?"

"You remember Roy Fritz?"

I'm instantly on alert. Ruth Ann's features soften, a faint smile comes to her face, and her eyes drift towards the window. I'm sure she uttered a sigh. Now it's her turn to develop a crimson complexion.

"Now that you mention it . . ."

"Now that I mention it? You and he were Siamese twins our second year in high school."

"It wasn't that bad. We dated some."

"Some? Some? The two of you were at every dance. Every time I called, your mom said you and he were at the movies in Bemidji, or at the library, studying. Sure you were. I bet you were in the back seat of his car. That's what I think."

"Oh, Archie. That was years ago. I haven't dated anyone but you since. So what about Roy?"

My first reaction is I'm pissed how quickly she brushes off the relationship with him. True, I haven't seen him around before today, but then I haven't been watching her like a hawk. Maybe they've hooked up when she's been out of town.

Did I just see a pair of fluorescent green spots bounce off her white bandages? I take several deep breaths before calming down enough to tell her about Jackie running for mayor.

Ruth Ann's mouth drops and her face is now ashen.

"Are you okay?"

She nods and covers her mouth. "It's starting to came back, dear. I remember parts of that afternoon at Betty's."

I'm still worked up but let her take her time. I feel like telling her about what happened at Heather's, but I bite my tongue.

Chapter 57

Dutch's finished one of the pizzas and downs a good part of the second. The conversation with Ruth Ann has distracted both of us and I pause to finish my slice and let the tension between us ebb.

"Anyone want that last piece?"

Neither Ruth Ann nor I reply. Dutch's paw smothers it. Crust, cheese, and pepperoni meet their intended fate.

"What do you remember of that day?"

"I think I recall making some notes about something I heard. I believe I used a napkin 'cause I left my briefcase at the office. You know the one. Brown fake leather. Looks like alligator skin."

I nod. I want her to cut to the chase, but she needs to take her own sweet time.

Ruth Ann gets that dreamy look again and I wonder if her mind's floated back to Roy. She takes a sip of her Moose Drool beer.

"There was a guy sitting one stool away from me. A really big, fat guy."

"Bruce," I say.

"Bruce? How do you know his name?"

"There were two guys, Ruth Ann. Lenny was the other one. Not as fat as Bruce, but hardly a light-weight, either."

Now she has a puzzled look.

"Why do you know about these guys?"

"It's a long story. I'll tell you later. Back to your recollections."

She pauses, her mouth all twisted like she's working to bring back a memory. I'm thinking she probably thinking about the back seat of Roy's Ford convertible.

"The really fat guy, what was his name?"

"Bruce."

"Yeah. That one. He was coming on to me. Talking like he was some super important guy working on a pipeline. Did someone discover oil around here?"

"No. Tell you later." I take a swig of my Moose Drool.

"He said he knew 'bout real estate. Could make a fortune around here, if what he heard about West Clover Bottom was anywhere close to true."

That sets me back. Heather said the same thing. Said she was into the business down in Florida. Is there a connection here? I may have to talk to her again. Not an entirely bad idea.

"He say any more, or was that the reason for your note?"

"Note? What note?"

"Just something Betty said. You wrote down 'real estate' on a napkin. She thought it was important, as you wrote it in capitals and underlined it."

Ruth Ann screws up her face again. "Doesn't ring any bells."

Dutch gets another beer and looks around my fridge. He's probably still hungry. Only had two extra large pizzas.

"There's some ice cream in the freezer. Help yourself, cuz."

He grunts his happy grunt and proceeds to remove my half gallon of cherry chocolate chip. Finds a spoon and digs in. I make a mental note to add two gallons of ice cream to my grocery list.

Ruth Ann stretches, yawns, and drops a bombshell. "I'm really tired, Archie. Your guest bed is too hard. I'd like to go home to my own."

I'm speechless. She gets up from the table and heads to her bedroom. I can't move. A minute later she returns to the kitchen. With her suitcase.

"Ready, Dutch?"

The next thing I know is my back door closing and my house is empty. I still can't move. No thanks, no kiss, not even a peck on my cheek. Ruth Ann just walked out on me.

Chapter 58

Am I dreaming? Is this a nightmare? It must be. One where I'm stuck in thick gooey mud and can't move an inch. In this case, I'm a tree and my roots've fixed me forever in my kitchen. There's a chiming. The hall clock is sounding midnight. I saw off the roots and stumble to the guest bedroom. Ruth Ann must really be there. I think I can hear her snoring. I creep in, trying not to wake her. Her absence strikes me down. I realize there's no need to be quiet. Her bed and the room are as empty as my soul.

I pull out my cell phone and start to dial her number. I make it to the sixth digit and flip it closed. The grandfather clock confirms it's now Friday. The opener is a mere twenty-four hours away. I try to choke back my depression and go to my cold, empty bed.

An hour or so later, I leap up in a cold sweat. I dreamt Ruth Ann and I were on a Sunday drive in the country. We drive by hay fields, green and lush; by fields of oats, their viridescent heads waving in the breeze. A flock of birds parallels my car. Their songs sweet and melodious. Then we enter a ticket of trees. Their boles nearly touching each other. The sunny day turns chilly and dark. The road climbs a low hill. At the crest, it turns sharply to the left. The car won't obey my commands and we go right off the road.

Onto a narrow trail. Now the brakes decide to work and we stop. Before I know it, Ruth Ann gets out and the car descends down the path. A sign catches my eye: Lake Entrance.

There's a boat launching pad of concrete. I drive right for it. And enter the lake.

The water covers the wheels, the hood, enters my car. I'm under water. It's a light aqua color. I continue deeper and the water becomes dark and foreboding. I'm paralyzed. The water is way over me.

I wake up.

I fight off any thoughts of sleep as long as I can. Sometime in the wee hours of the morning I drift off. My alarm sounds six-thirty. To hell with fixing breakfast. I shower, skip shaving, and drive to Betty's. The last stool is open and I plop down. Betty tries to start a conversation to which I reply, "Usual."

"My, aren't you just a ray of sunshine, today."

A glower from me sends her on her way.

This is followed shortly by the thump of a coffee mug. The first sip of her recycled asphalt wakes me up. I try a smile when Betty brings me my blueberry pancakes, scrambled eggs and OJ.

"Problems, Archie?"

"Yeah."

Betty leans down, her elbows on the counter. She whispers. "I can tell it's girl problems, right?" She doesn't pause for my answer. "Everyone has a little spat. Ruth Ann loves ya. Don't forget that."

She gives me a pat on my shoulder and attends to another customer.

I'm fairly certain her 'pat' only cracked my collar bone and didn't shatter it. Today is going to be hell, what with the opener hours away. I hurry through my food and head to the station.

For the first time today, I take the time to glance up, trying to read the weather. I'm surprised to see that the sky is bright blue, not gray and filled with boiling, angry clouds. For some unfathomable reason, people on the street are happy looking, going about their business seemingly without a concern.

I crawl inside a shell and pretend I'm one of those happy people. My first task of the day is to swear in four temporary deputies. They'll spend their day directing traffic and helping *that* woman's Uncle George. Crowds of people will be getting last minute fishing licenses or checking they've paid for the privilege of fishing Clover Bottom Lake.

I'm greeted by Jerome and the about-to-be-deputies. All four had this duty for years. They're retired farmers from outside of town. Known by most citizens and the ninety percent of the returning fishermen. Down at the pier, they'll keep things moving well.

By ten, all the swearing in duties are accomplished and my temps are on duty. Alex will be in later so I have a some quiet time. I can't help but think about last night and the abrupt change in my life. As much as I want to believe Betty that Ruth Ann and I will patch things up, I can't bring myself to feel she knows what she's talking about.

A few cups of station coffee doesn't help my mood a bit so when my cell rings, I'm prepared for bear. Expecting, or better stated, hoping it's Ruth Ann I try to answer in a somewhat pleasant voice. I convey that with, "Yeah? Whatta ya want?"

"Is this the same Archie I've known for years? Sounds like some asshole."

"Oh. Roy. Sorry. I'm a little grumpy."

"A little? Could have fooled me."

I don't come up with a snappy retort so I keep quiet.

"Assuming you are in fact my friend for life, I'm calling about the little talk we had yesterday? The one about you requesting some computer hacking?"

Even though I'm convinced he's been secretly seeing my former *friend*, I stuff the feeling because I need his help pulling this off. I force myself to sound decent this time.

"Hey, Roy. Must be coming down with something. I feel like shit. So. Can you help me?"

"You bet I can. And will. One thing, though. I'm on my way to MSP. Got a flight back to New York at noon. I got called back to work. I didn't get a chance to see Heather. Can you take over that task?"

"Yeah. I'll see her today. Wish we had more time to catch up. Good seeing ya though, buddy. Thanks for the help and have a great trip back."

Hate to admit it, but it *was* good seeing him. Kinda glad he's leaving, though.

My defenses are down, but I better see Heather at work. Don't trust myself alone with her again.

Chapter 59

We've been through enough day-before-fishing-openers so that everything goes off like a well oiled machine. Like finely tuned Swiss clockworks. Like a hot knife through butter. Of course, you have to overlook the minor traffic jam that's driving Jerome up the wall. Or the fact that *her* Uncle George slipped off the wagon and is smashed to the gills, causing a huge backlog of boat launching, which in turn is causing the traffic jam. Or the dozen or so fights that break out because someone tried to cut ahead in the line at the dock. Or one of the new deputies that wrongly arrests the party of State government officials for jumping the opening gun. So, I feel comfortable enough to wander to the bank and strike up a friendly conversation with Heather.

I take a short cut through Gunner Olsen's Clover Bottom Hardware. This takes the better part of thirty minutes. Seems *her* Uncle George also forgot to order any minnows, leeches, and night crawlers. Looks like a few fishermen—in round numbers I'd say three hundred, give or take twenty dozen—gave up trying to get bait at the pier—are mobbing Gunner's for his supply.

I finally make it out the back door. I congratulate myself for saving the three whole minutes it would've taken me to walk all around the block to the bank. Gives me more time to explain the plan to Heather.

Surprisingly, the bank, too is jammed with people. A few, not more than fifty, I'm guessing, tell me there's no money in the ATM machine at the dock. Looks like *her* Uncle George forgot to make sure Dave, Heather's boss, restocked the stupid machine.

A few of the happier ones ask me, "How the #&$%!! are we supposed to pay the (*&*(^ stupid launching fees?"

I use my charm and quick thinking and answer with a shrug. I'm dumfounded when this doesn't solve the situation.

Heather spots me and waves me over. Her frantic arm motions stir the air, blowing off a few baseball hats. In no time at all, I've elbowed my way through the crowd. She puts her mouth to my ear and yells over the commotion, "Do something."

I effortlessly vault up on the counter, catch my balance before falling off the other side, and bellow out, "Bang! Bang!"

My imitation gun shots have everyone ducking for cover.

When order is restored, I calmly tell everyone to form a line and proceed to the bank's outside ATM.

There's nothing like an armed police officer giving clear, concise instructions to settle down a crowd.

I wish I was one.

Heather speaks up. Her voice sounds like a hundred fingernails scratching a blackboard. "Didn't you hear what he said? Now shut up, everyone."

Like I said: nothing like a high pitched woman's voice to assault your ear drums and restore order.

Following my clear, concise directions, the crowd dissipates in twenty minutes.

"Typical fishing opener evening, right?"

I give Heather one of my superior smirks. "I think it's way better than the last twenty years."

"Humph. Dream on, buster."

I brush off the compliment. " I need to talk to you about something. Have a few minutes?"

"For you, I've got all day. However, today's not the one. We're going through our annual audit. I can't spare the time. Maybe tomorrow night? Unless you're tied up with something. Like a date with Ruth Ann?"

Ouch. From the smirk on her face, she's already heard the news. "As a matter of fact, I am free. How about coming to my place? I'll fix the best pizza you ever tasted."

This gets a hearty chuckle. "Straight from the Clover Bottom Pizzeria. Right?"

"Kinda."

Before she can agree, her boss comes up and forces his way between us. I need to spend some time with this guy and educate him about proper Minnesota Biness Etiquette. Right after I teach him how to speak Minnesota Biness Talk.

"Miss Maple. We have to work late today and all day tomorrow. The auditors have some, ah-hem, questions."

Heather rolls her eyes and says, "No can do tomorrow, Archie. I do want to take you up on the dinner. I'll definitely be in touch."

With that, she hurries after Dave.

Chapter 60

By eleven-thirty, a half hour before the opener, calm and order is restored. I head over to City Hall and see that Jacky is standing by the air raid siren. Really. West Clover Bottom has a working World War II siren. Not that it got any use in the early '40's. Once a year exactly at midnight on fishing opener, it gets its golden pipes a workout. Jackie is standing by, her eye on her watch.

In the last ten years, half a dozen ham radio operators tune into a fascinating program run by a radio station out in Colorado some place. They send out a signal giving the exact, precise, to-the-millisecond time.

Jackie's watch has yet to hit twelve PM correctly. It varies several minutes. But, what's ten minutes over a five month season?

At almost the correct time she mashes the button and holds it for the prescribed thirty seconds, plus or minus a few. The opener has begun.

I drive to the pier to see the action. By the time I get there, all I see are the sterns of boats. Her uncle is standing, rather leaning, against a light standard. Coffee cup in hand.

"George. Everyone get off okay?"

Apparently he didn't hear me approach and my question startles him. So much that I have to grab his arm to prevent him from falling into the lake. The Fish and Wildlife people probably should give me a medal. The contents of his cup would've stunned all the fish within a twenty-foot circle.

"Startled me there, boy."

He's back to the 'boy' thing again.

I ask him once more if all the fisher people got off.

"Like clock work."

I see gears, springs, levers going every which way. No way I want to hear more. One thing is for sure, though; the whole fiasco was headed up by one big, drunken cuckoo.

I head for home.

My empty home.

My girl-friendless home.

When I arrive I don't feel like going to bed. Instead, I fix a Manhattan, not in a highball glass, but a twelve ounce tumbler. Fortified with a normal week's supply of booze, I grab a bag of chips and settle down in the library. Maggie tags along, licking her chops. Apparently she's finished off the last of her Friskies and wants a couple chips. Her dessert.

I stare at the shelves of books. Now that I'm free of the constraints of having a lady friend, there'll be plenty of time to catch up on my reading. Kent Krueger's latest has been unopened long enough. Then again, so has Greg Iles new issue, Lisa Gardner's, Grandfather John C's collection of Encyclopedia Britannica, volumes A through Z, plus ten years of supplements. To say nothing of Grandma Julia's extensive array of Readers Digest Condensed books.

Instead of catching up on my readings, my mind drifts back to Richard Stewart. The e-mails between him and Rupert were vicious. Threats and accusations dripped off each note. Did Rupert have any conversations with him? Maybe our now less-than stellar mayor said something he ended up regretting. I make a note to visit Stewart and talk face-to-face.

With that resoled, I polish off my drink. Unfortunately it's a quadruple Manhattan. I get five pages into Krueger, the booze hits me like a speeding truck, and I pass out.

The next morning, I think it's Saturday. My head wants to bury itself in the sand somewhere. Three aspirins, double strength coffee I eat with a folk, and I can feel my head is approximately where it belongs. Not tagging along behind me. After an ice cold shower, I dress, and head for Betty's. Two cups of her used road tar-like java will complete my transformation. I'll be like that old-time super hero, Flash Gordon. Ready to take on Ming. In my case I picture Ming as being a petite, auburn-haired woman with a pixie cut and her head swathed in gauze.

I shake the vision of Ruth Ann from my mind. A few minutes later, Betty's slinging hash alongside my usual blueberry 'cakes.

"This'll fix you ya up , buster. Nothin' better for a hangover than Betty's hash. Two bites of this stuff and you'll forget all about Ruth Ann, too."

Chapter 61

Bad news travels faster than a speeding bullet in good old West Clover Bottom. I'm sure everyone in town is aware that Ruth Ann walked out on me. I bet Aunt Bev's heart's broken. Here she was counting on Ruth Ann and me getting hitched; now her dreams of being able to lord it over Betty are dust in the wind.

After I finish, I decide to settle up with Betty and pay the two hundred twelve dollars and fifty-three cent tab. Another forty buck tip puts a smile on her face.

It's noon-time and the town seems deserted. Everyone's on the lake, I guess. As I wander to the station, I pull out my phone and start to dial what's-her-name. Four digits in, I snap it closed.

She-who-must-not-be-named left me. She wants to talk, fine. She can call me. Determined, with my head held high, I strut off.

Jerome and all four temp deputies are sitting around, drinking coffee as I enter. Their conversation stops. Two of the old-timers try to act as though one of them told a joke.

The laughter is fake. They jump up and say "Hi" as they scurry away. There's no doubt in my mind what the real topic was. Me and *her*. I nod to Jerome and the other two guys.

"Any more problems, guys?"

"Nope."

"Not a one."

"All taken care of."

"Good. Call me if you need me." I guess they answered, but paying attention is low on my list. So I leave for home. What an exciting thing to do.

On my way to my cruiser, I run into Al. He smiles and shakes my hand. Either he's the only person in the entire State of Minnesota who hasn't heard, or he doesn't give a damn. After all, he did try to poison *her*.

"Hey, Chief. Good to see ya."

"Al. How's tricks?"

"Great. I want to thank you again for looking out for me. I love the job. I'm really learnin' stuff. Dutch's taken me under his wing and showin' me all his techniques. He's some guy. He really your cousin?"

"Certainly is." I'm tempted to ask about *her*, but I don't.

"Gotta get back. Louie's busier than a three legged hound dog in a pickle factory. See ya."

Al's been around Dutch all right. Picking up his fractured metaphors. No one else stops me and I make it to my cruiser unscathed.

When I get home, I check my land line for messages. Kinda hoping Heather called and wants to get together. Or, *she* called and wants to make up.

No luck on either case.

Since tomorrow is the annual Schultz fishing derby, my gear needs checking out. 'Course, this year I'll only host myself. Ever since we were eleven, *she* and I'd go fishing on the second day of the season.

My boat sits on the trailer in the extra bay of my garage. Half heartedly, I dawdle away the rest of the day doing maintenance on the motor, oiling my reels, and organizing the tackle box. By dark, I manage to get my eighteen footer launched and tied up to my dock.

The night is warm and cloudless. There's little light pollution around WCB and the Milky Way is splashed across the heavens. I never get tired of seeing this fraction of the Universe. My mind wanders to years past when, on occasion, *she* and I'd be treated to a similar sight.

I tear away from the stars and look around. To make sure no one is around.

I can almost feel *her* cuddling me and tears fall unabashedly.

Chapter 62

Sunday morning and a few clouds have drifted in. The wind is light from the northwest. Enough to ruffle the surface. Last night's melancholy lingers and I answer to Maggie's culinary needs. She responds by hopping into my arms and purrs her little heart out as she rubs my cheeks.

I stuff some calories in my face and trudge to the boat. The lake is bustling with fellow fishermen, although none in my proximity. Fine with me.

To my left, north, the lake eventually shallows and is peppered with reeds and wild rice shoots. I know there's a place where, decades ago, a log raft sank on its way to the Schultz mill. Over the years, it silted over, providing great cover and making excellent spawning beds. This has always been one of my favorite spots early in the season. The blue-gills and sunnies are mating, making for a surefire catch. There'll be fresh fish for supper tonight.

The thought of fish frying in butter brushes away some of my dolefulness. Especially, remembrances of the butter running down my chin as I stuff my mouth. The beer chaser is an equally good memory. With a lighter heart, I crank my twenty-horse Merc and set out across the lake.

The wind whips my face, peeling layers of the remaining depression away like fall leaves before the wind. Apparently I'm one of the few people who know about this site. Or everyone's interested in walleyes or northerns, as I'm alone.

In minutes I've caught five sunnies, released four small ones and placed the fifth on the stringer.

I'm suddenly thirteen again. It's the third time Ruth Ann and I opened the season on the second day. We've been horsing around like teenagers do. I just caught a real nice-sized sunny and placing it on the stringer. My back is to her and I'm juggling fish and stringer when I feel my shirt being yanked open. A minnow slides down my back. Not expecting this, I yelp and jump around. Between screams, I hear her laughing. This inflames me more and next thing I know, I'm in the lake.

Apparently the sight of me floundering and sputtering is the most hilarious thing she's even seen. Fortunately, in those years, Clover Bottom's water level had fallen and I'm only up to my armpits. Ruth Ann's bent over, clutching her sides. She doesn't see me alongside. I grab one of her arms and yank. Seventy-five pounds of female joins me.

She's only an inch or two over five feet and the lake's over her head. My "That'll teach ya" victory turns to panic. In one smooth action, I grab her under her arms and heave her back into the boat. I'm not sure she was in the water long enough to even get wet.

Our teenage foolishness disappears faster than the flash from a lightening strike. I flip over the gunnel and hold her close.

"I'm really sorry, Ruth Ann."

"Me, too."

I know I wanted to kiss her, perhaps she wanted to kiss me, as well. Although neither one of us knew how. Or had the guts to try learning. We attempted to return to fishing, but she actually was in the lake long enough to get wet and we called it a day.

My reverie is ruined when my cell phone buzzes.

The screen tells me it's the office. "Archie, here."

"Ah, Chief, I hate to bother ya, what with it being your traditional opening day, and I really wouldn't ruin your trip. Hope you're killin' 'em. Like I said, you probably should know something. . . "

"What? What?" I'm speaking to empty air. Then I hear a muffled, "Let me talk."

"Archie, this is Alexia. We have a situation here. You better drop everything and come on in."

"Alex. What the hell's going on?"

"Not over the phone."

My phone clatters as I swivel around to start the outboard. Anticipating someday I might be called when on the lake, I've fitted my craft with a siren and a set of red and blue flashers. I slam the throttle forward, the siren begins its wail and my face is alternately red and blue.

I don't waste time going home but set my sights for the south shore and the town's dock. I'm forced to zig and zag several times to dodge a few slow responding folks. I'm pretty sure I only swamped three or four boats. At least now they know why no one is allowed on the lake without approved life vests.

George is waiting for me as I approach. I have to be a little cautious here as there's no law requiring drunk dock masters to wear a preserver. He looks a little tipsy, so I steer for a landing a few yards from the pier. I cut the motor as soon as I reach dock's end. My momentum carries me halfway onto shore.

George knows enough to drag my boat over to the dock and tie it up. At a dead run, I race to the station, a half block away.

Chapter 63

When I burst in, I first see Alex talking to my cousin Dutch. They're huddled together speaking softly. I think this is the first time I've ever heard my cousin speaking in subdued tones. Next, I take in Jerome, making up for the lower volume. He's talking to someone in the jail room.

"Sure you don't need me to guard ya?"

His hand is hovering over his holster. The butt of his pistol plainly visible. This really startles me. Whatever is going on has made him run home and find is .40 caliber. I wonder if he had time to find bullets.

He looks crestfallen as his question is answered,

"No, Deputy. I've got everything under control."

I recognize Doc Joyce's voice.

My panting and gasping alerts everyone: the Chief has entered the room. My colleagues gather around. Jerome begins his multi-page explanation, only to have me hold up my hands to stop his litany.

Alex takes the cue and explains. "Doc's in cell one working on someone who calls himself Blue Dog. Seems this bozo attempted to break into Ruth Ann's house, not knowing she's being watched over by your cousin."

I shake my head. The fool had no idea what he was in for. "So, how bad is he?"

"Not sure yet, but I think at least eight busted fingers."

Dutch smiles from ear to ear. "All ten, for sure, Ms. Alexia."

"Okay, cuz. What happened?"

"Tried to break in. Smashed a window and reached in, undid the lock and raised the sash. Guess he was boosting himself up. Ruth Ann's house gots those high off the ground windows? I shut it. Took five out right there. Closed the latch. Went outside. Had a gun in his left hand. I kinda squeezed it."

I know from experience, when you're squeezed by cuz Dutch, something's gonna break. "That took out the other five, right."

Dutch chuckles.

We plugged our ears and waited for the windows, and our teeth, to stop rattling.

"Yeah, I squeezed good and tight."

I shudder. I can almost hear Blue Dog's bones shatter, especially since he had a gun in hand. The grip's probably mangled and permanently bears the impressions of his fingerprints.

I didn't bother asking about *her*. There was no reason. I knew *she* was safe.

I take his arm and start leading him to the door. "Thanks, Dutch. You did good. We have everything under control now, if you want to leave . . ."

"Uh, yeah. I better. 'Case someone else gets any ideas."

After he closes the door, I check the windows for cracks.

"K, gang. I need to speak to James. Alex, check with LA. I bet there's a warrant out for this guy. Jerome, you listen in on Alex's call. See if you can help her."

In cell one, I see James is busy working on 'Dog. "How ya doing, doc?"

"His left hand's a mess. He'll need extensive surgery. Even then, I doubt either hand will function much. His days dealing cards are over. Won't be much good in any sport, either. Dutch did him over all right."

"Can't say I feel any sympathy. He was after the *person* Dutch was guarding."

"That *person* being Ruth Ann?"

I can't make myself say *her* name, so I nod.

Joyce looks at his handiwork. "Okay. I can only do so much here. What's next with you?"

"I'm gonna ship him back to LA where he belongs. They can worry about him."

Alex steps in. "He's wanted all right. The detective I talked to seemed a little ashamed we caught Homer."

"Homer?"

"Yeah. Homer Albion. His real name."

Since I'm not sure I want Jerome to be in charge of transporting a live body, I ask Alex to make arrangements to get this scum bag out of my sight as soon as Doc says he can travel.

"Day after tomorrow, Alex."

Doc inspects Homer's full arm casts. I suspect they're overdone, but I know he holds Homer's intended victim in high regard. Besides, it'll make Alex's job a lot safer. No way he'll be in any shape to try an escape. Nonetheless, he'll be shackled and trussed up like a Christmas turkey. Hope the plane runs into a lot of rough weather, to boot.

I ask. "We got Homer's pistol?"

Alex points to my desk. "Bagged and tagged, Chief."

A quick look and I call Jerome over. "First thing tomorrow. I mean first thing, take this Colt to the BCA. Be there when they open. I want El to work his magic. This's a Colt Woodsman. Maybe it's the gun used to kill Rupert, Helen, Fat, and Fatter. I'll call and let them know you'll be there with bells on. K?"

"Use my sireen?"

"You betcha. By the way, make sure the chain of custody is complete."

The problem of who's been after my former girl friend has been solved.

Might have two more mysteries cleared as well.

On my way out, I make a point to talk to 'Dog tomorrow about another matter. I leave the station in good hands, head back to the pier—where George moved my craft— retrieve my boat, and go home.

Chapter 64

I waste no time getting my boat back home. What with my mad dash across the lake, I forgot to pull in the stringer. Now it and my dinner are gone. Betty's tonight.

After tying up, I grab my pole and tackle box, drop everything on the kitchen floor and jump into my cruiser. I change my mind about talking to our prisoner tomorrow. Moments later, I'm back in the station.

Alex greets me with, "LA called. They're sending a plane to pick up Homer."

"Good. Saves us the expense. Say, Alex, do me a favor? Would you go over to the house where Dutch is? I imagine you weren't able to get 'Dog's prints. There should be plenty at the house."

"Sure, boss. Now?"

"Good a time as any."

Soon as she leaves, I wander back to cell 1. Homer's lying on the bunk. His arms straight up in the air. I suspect he's been sedated, but I open the door and sit by the bunk.

"Not a good day, was it, Homer?"

An eye lid flutters and a moan escapes. "Worst day my life, man."

"You should feel lucky. He takes it real personal if some-one tries to mess with her. Normally, we'd still be looking for pieces."

"Ruin my life, he did."

"From what I gather, it wasn't much to begin with. Hear your name was kinda down on the list for the Nobel Peace Prize."

'Dog's eyes close and he seems to drift away.

"You know anything about a couple fat guys who were killed in this very same cell?"

I'm not sure he's awake and hears me, so I ask again. After several counts, I'm about to leave and he mumbles. "Not me. My men. Two 'em."

Homer drifts off. His conversation may not be admissible in court, but I have a lot more now than yesterday. I'll try for Rupert and Helen later.

Before I leave, I drop off a note for Alex.

Got some info from Homer' bout Fat and Fatter.

Ask about Rupert and Helen when you feed him

Betty's crowded. Guess the out-of-towners are filling up before going south. Ninety percent of our visitors are from the Cities and environs. Don't want to be heading that way today. Bumper-to-bumper.

A stool clears and I take the spot. Fortunately, Betty and help are running ragged so I won't have endless questions about me and old what's-her-face. My mouth was set on a fresh fish supper, rather than eating Betty's breaded fish-part sticks. God only knows what parts they use for these delicacies. Instead, I order a hot turkey sandwich with her watery mashed potatoes and olive-drab green beans. As Rachael Ray would exclaim, "Yum-O."

I manage to pay my bill and slip out before Betty can descend on me.

The sun has just slipped below the horizon and I reach my car. The clouds are on fire. Orange, yellow, red hues take my breath away. The light has softened as though a blanket of the finest, softest fleece has been laid over the earth. All the day's sharp edges are smooth and rounded.

What a scene. Should be someone around to share it. *She* isn't and I drive home to Maggie.

Chapter 65

Monday morning arrives at the usual time, or should I say, Maggie arrives at the usual time. Five AM. I try to push her off my bed, which is as successful as attempts to put tooth-paste back in its tube.

I give up and feed her some dry food.

"Eat it or starve, cat."

I get a dirty look and she walks away, stiff legged.

"Tough."

I pad my way to the larder. I repeat Rachael's mantra. There's a loaf of bread with mold spots only the size of a dime. I cut them off and put four pieces in the toaster.

I argue that heat'll kill off any spores, so I'm good to go. My grape jelly's mold requires a spoon to get rid of the growth. But, what the hell, still tastes just as good as fresh, right?

It's only seven when I arrive at the jail. God, Homer snores. I spot a note in Alex's handwriting.

Claims he knows nothing about Rupert and Helen.

I believe him. He's a pretty sweet guy, actually.

Yeah, I bet all the gals said the same about Al Capone. After ensuring 'Dog's safe and sound, I fix my B-grade coffee. The aroma of Archie's Ambrosia is what probably wakes him as I hear some mumbling. I bring Mr. Sweetness a cup and find him trying to sit up. Pretty hard to do with a couple of white logs as arms. He eventually makes it and I recall Doc James left a bottle of pills for him. I take him a glass of water. After he's medicated, I fetch a mug of what will be the best coffee he's ever had.

I ignore him spitting it out. Probably likes his brew to be liquid, not fork ready. I dilute it with another glass of water and he drinks this swill. LA for ya.

"Care for some breakfast, Homer? We serve the finest pancakes you ever had. Add some sausage and eggs, you'll probably petition us for long term care."

In case a child reads this, I'll refrain from repeating his reply. I will say though, I have heard more complimentary words.

Nevertheless, I call a to-go order into Betty. I stop by and pick it up. After feeding our ward, I try to get more info from him concerning Fat and Fatter. I'm hoping the meds are working and his defenses are down.

That and the mention of Dutch still being mighty upset our guest attacked his favorite person. To say nothing about an imaginary phone call I got last night from Dutch wanting ten minutes alone. "My cousin says you've got a few bones he'd like to become better acquainted with."

Homer says, "Some woman contacted me."

"Got her name?"

"Nope. Said she knows this guy and he said to call me."

"You know this guy?"

"Kinda. We had some business dealings a few years back."

"Name?"

"Won't do ya any good."

"Why?"

"Got in front of AK when it was bein' tested by nudder gang. All I know he was from Florida years back. "

It takes a while, but it finally registers. I file it away.

The pills take over and 'Dog sinks into our famous adjustable mattress. Amazing the comfort two inches of foam offers.

I leave sleeping beauty and warm up my coffee.

Jerome reports in and adds three cups of water to the pot. "Good brew today, boss."

"Thought you were supposed to be in St. Paul with the pistol."

"No problem, Chief. They won't open till nine-thirty today. Some meeting or another. On my way now."

I know he's excited about the trip. Pedal to the metal with lights and si-reen. Mrs. Pederson will be calling in three minutes.

Two minutes and fifty seconds later, the phone is ringing. Better re-set my watch. After I explain we apprehended a ruthless, blood thirsty desperado, she purrs her approval.

"'Bout time you guys earned your pay."

Thirty minutes later, my phone rings. It's Regions Hospital. Can't be about Jerome, yet. When I answer, I hear Doc Hudson.

"You sitting down, Chief?"

Chapter 66

I drop the phone, fumble around and tell Hudson, "Sorry. Could you repeat that?"

"I said, the toxicology report came back on the Jackmans five minutes ago. There was a high level of alcohol, enough so you'd arrest them for DUI even if they were the mayor and his wife."

"I can't imagine they'd be drinking that much before their flight to Florida. Rupert always struck me as a light drinker. Maybe two beers at most. Never saw him loaded."

"There's more, Archie."

I hate to ask, but I do. "What?"

"They also had high levels of Rohypnol."

"The date rape drug? You've got to be kidding."

"Actually, it explains a lot. Remember when I said, based on the stippling, they were shot point blank ?"

"Kinda recall that."

"The reason it's called date rape is because people become very placid. If they *weren't* doped up, I would've expected to see some signs of a struggle. Like tissue under their fingernails. But there wasn't any."

"So he simply stuck the gun in their faces."

"If I were you, chief, I'd tread lightly on the assumption it was a *he*."

My steel-trap mind quickly absorbs the info and I rapidly see her logic.

"Why's that?"

"Rupert wouldn't be mistaken for Hulk Hogan and Helen wasn't Amazon Lady. Even so, neither of them would sit placidly while the other was being murdered, right?"

I had to agree.

"I can't see some macho guy admitting he couldn't handle both of them so there'd be some indication of a stru . . ."

I try to interrupt but the good doctor continues.

"On the other hand, a female shooter might be worried about being in a struggle and resorts to Rohypnol."

That steel-trap mind, minus some of the rust, swings into motion. Her information puts a slight dent in my thinking that Stewart might have acted out and popped our mayor and first lady.

While my Stewart contention has a serious hole, I need to put it to rest one way or another. I check my notebook and find his number. "Mr. Stewart, this is Chief Schultz. I need to speak to you about the murders we recently discussed. You have some time later this morning?"

He makes some flimsy excuse about being busy at work.

My reply changes his mind. "I can always get a warrant to haul you in. Funny thing about these warrants. The local press always seems to find out about them and sends a news van to cover the excitement. Or, we can meet at some nearby diner and have a nice lunch. Your choice."

Moments later, I'm blasting my way to St. Paul. We agreed to meet at the St. Clair Broiler.

I call him on my cell when I reach the outskirts of town. Ten minutes later, I pull up across the street from the Broiler. Stewart is waiting for me in a back booth.

"Richard."

"Chief. What do you want from me? I told you about Stormie blackmailing me and how that was resolved. Far as I can see this meeting is a waste of my time."

I debate for a moment about Minnesota Biness Etiquette, but figure it'd be a waste of *my* time. He's putting up a fence of denial. For his sake, I hope this *is* a waste of time. What I don't know is if the resolution to his problem was as simple as he suggests.

The waitress brings a pot of coffee and takes our orders. It'll be refreshing to have a decent cook prepare my burger and fries. I'm positive they use unadulterated beef, not like Betty and her sawdust helper version.

I was right about the food and after I feast on a second burger, I get down to work. "So, Dick, our mayor saw the light and acquiesced to your demands, right?"

"If you mean he got Stormie off my back, yeah, he buckled."

"Any other contact between you and the mayor?"

"Nope."

"How about Helen, ah, Stormie?"

Stewart hesitates a little too long before answering no.

I go out on a limb and using all my magical powers of interrogation, I respond, "Don't believe ya, Dick. I think you had words with her. Maybe threatened her if she didn't stop and desist. We have a beloved mayor and his wife lying in the morgue a few blocks from here. Folks in West Clover Bottom are pretty pissed. I'm under pressure to have the guilty party cooling his heels in our jail. The angry mob can be pretty demanding."

"Okay. I talked to Stormie two times after the ring thing was settled. She came after me for matching earrings. Told her no way. Look, check this out. I contacted a reporter at the Trib. He'll back up my story."

Dick's talking about the *Minneapolis Star and Tribune*. I get the reporter's name and call while we're still at the Broiler.

He backs up Dick. He was holding the story until Stewart gave him the go-ahead. The reporter went on to say he had looked into Stormie's background. She had a reputation of suggesting her customers might want to contribute to her retirement fund.

He says, "Funny how her marks were married men and her fund consisted of expensive jewelry. I take my hat off to Mr. Stewart for calling her bluff."

With that endorsement, the least I can do is pick up the tab and apologize to Stewart. He accepts graciously and I officially remove his name from my list.

As long as I'm here, I make a side-trip to Regions to see Doc Hudson and pick up her repot.

☆ ☆ ☆

I waste no time getting back to little old WCB. With the autopsy findings in hand, I make a bee-line upstairs to the mayor's, ah, ex-mayor's, office.

"Afternoon, Jackie."

She greets me and offers a cup of *her* coffee. I don't want to insult her, so I make it palatable with two heaping tablespoons of sugar. This time, I really use my conversational skills. We talk about the opener, the fish we caught, or in my case, didn't. I finally bring up the topic that brought me here in the first place.

"Anyone clear out Rupert's office yet?"

Her eyes immediately water and tears cascade down her cheek. "I haven't had the heart to. Why?"

"No special reason. Something's been nagging at me and I want to check it. K?"

I amble to his office, followed closely by Jackie. This disturbs me, but I ignore her and take my time looking through his files, desk, wastepaper basket. Hoping she gets more bored than I am, and leaves. I avoid his calendar, pretend I find what I'm looking for in his desk's middle drawer.

"Maybe if I knew what you're looking for I could help. He depended on me to keep track of just about everything."

I give her a winning Schultz smile. One that used to turn old what's-her-name's knees to Jell-O. I lower my voice to conspiratorial levels. "You know we caught a hoodlum from LA, right?"

She nods and leans closer. After all, this could be the juiciest bit of gossip that's hit WCB in a lifetime. "Maybe this good-for-nothin' bum might've had a hand in Rupert's death. I want to see if there's anything indicating he and Helen were threatened. That kind of stuff."

"You think the Mafia had a hand in all this?"

I don't remember talking about the Mafia, but if that's what Jackie wants to hear, so much the better.

I nod.

It has the effect I hoped for. She starts to move to the doorway. I know she wants to blab this all over town. Maybe she'll walk away with the Ladies Auxiliary prize for Best Gossip. Be quite a feather in her cap to snatch the cup away from last year's winner, my Aunt Bev. Come to think of it, Bev won the prize for the past ten years. This could easily eclipse my break-up with you-know-who.

Jackie apparently has hearing akin to an owl, makes an excuse about a phone ringing, and is away in a flash. I'm on Rupert's day reminder like white on egg. I looked it over a few days ago. Nothing registered at the time, but I didn't have the tox data then.

Our mayor had a habit of writing down everything, once told me it'd probably make the *Times* Best Seller list when he published his memoirs.

I'm sure people in New York were counting down the days until it hit the shelves.   It's buried under a stack of papers and I carefully slip it out. Not the least bit surprising Friday's page, the day before their trip, is missing. I remove Saturday's, then flip back in time. Not only did Rupert like the event listed, he also insisted on noting it a week before. Said to me, "Like to be prepared. You know, bone up on who'll be attending and little tid-bits of info about them. Never know when I might be called on for higher office."

Looks like he got called by a higher authority, all right. Probably not the invitation he planned on, though.

Friday, the week before is missing as well. I remove that Saturday and put the planner back under the papers. Making sure everything as it was.

I can't wait to get back to my office, but I putz around for several minutes in the file cabinet. I wave a goodbye kiss to Jackie. She's on the phone. Probably talking to Doc James about a phone-ectomy.

I'm not sure my feet touch the steps on the way down. One of the temp deputies is hanging and tries to talk. I brush by, mumbling about a potential break and slam my office door closed.

Wondering whomever wrote in Rupert's calendar, like it's a mystery, I rub Saturday, May 7th with a number two pencil.

Slowly, Friday's info comes through.

Chapter 67

Not satisfied, I do the same with the May 1 page. I can hardly believe it. In fact, I can't. The evidence is right in front of me, though. It turns ol' steel-trap into a useless hunk of rust. Needing a cup of decent coffee, I take the time to brew a pot my way, as Blue Eyes said about New York.

I'm on my way back to the pages from his calendar when my cell phone warbles. Caller ID says it's the bank. Got to be Heather.

"Chief Schultz, here."

"Hi, Archie." I immediately feel my brain coagulating. In my new-found soprano voice, I squeak out, "Hi."

"I wanted to tell you, the audit finished early and I have this evening open for pizza. If you're still offering it."

For some reason, I say, "Let me check my social calendar."

After a few poor attempts to sound like I have a social life anymore, I squish out, "Looks like I'm free tonight. Something got cancelled at the last minute. Seven okay?"

"I'll be there with bells on. By the way, I adore anchovies. Makes me, well. . . I love anchovies."

"K. Later."

I'm pretty sure her last sound was a wet kiss. In fact, I know it is as for some reason, my left ear's wet.

I can't get back to my office, as another deputy temp interrupts me with some cop stuff.

"George caught this guy with six northerns on his stringer." He pushes the world's greatest criminal towards the jail room.

"Don't put him in a cell close to Homer. Don't want our current guest learning any tricks."

"Thanks, boss. I never thought of that. Come along, buster."

For some unknown reason, *her* Uncle George thinks WCB PD's responsibilities include game wardening. No way I want this *criminal* cluttering up space. I wander back, tell him he can go after he pays a hundred buck fine.

He digs out a check book. "Payable to whom?"

"West Clover Bottom."

Moments later, a Mr. Christopher Smith hands me a check. I open the cell and another satisfied customer walks away. Actually, with his payment in hand, I have a good excuse to see Jackie. I head up to her office and explain what happened. She places his fine in a metal box stored in one of the five drawer files.

"Say, Jackie, did Rupert and Helen have a going away party?"

"A going away party?"

"Yeah. You know. Maybe he had some people over, like the Councilmen, to plan what golf course they'd be playing. Maybe some others, like yourself, to make sure the town's biness was carried out. That kind of thing."

"If there was, I sure wasn't invited. His wife and I never got along. Never been to Rupert's since he married *that* woman."

"I'm sure he felt he was leaving us in your fine hands."

"Is there something new in the case? You find some clue?"

"Not really. But, since we've cracked the other two murders, I can devote my time to this one, that's all."

Jackie's one good actor. She didn't blink an eye when I asked about the party. Unfortunately for her, I've got proof there was such an event. If I'm not mistaken, even though the words, *Party. 7-9:30,* are just pencil tracings, they sure look like her handwriting.

I'm leaving her office and stop. "One thing. Could you write out a receipt for Christopher? He asked for one. Maybe for his taxes. Who knows?"

"You betcha, Chief."

She hands me a slip of paper. I take it by the edge and wave it as though I'm saying good bye.

We have a top-of-the line copy machine in the station and I make a high resolution photocopy. Next, I copy the Saturday pages and call the BCA. I'm quickly connected to the handwriting analysis department and explain what I have. A Tommy Kamski agrees and I fax the copies to him.

I have no doubt about the outcome, but that's just one small step for WCB PD. The leap'll come when I can make an arrest. My stomach tells me it's time for lunch and I stroll down the street to Betty's. The Blue Plate special today is meat loaf. I've had her version before. I'll bet a month's pay, some place in her back room her stash of sawdust escaped the fire. Either that, or she spends a couple hours each week generating a new batch of select pine and old-growth oak hamburger extender.

Chapter 68

I polish off the special with a slice of her banana cream pie and two cups of asphalt coffee. This pot was made from fresh tar, not her usual recycled stuff. Guess no one's redoing a road in the area.

Betty hands me the check and I fish out my billfold when she leans over the counter. "Heard someone's having an operation tomorrow morning. Thought you'd like you know."

For a moment, I'm stunned. I mumble something about her injury and before I can put my foot further in my mouth—it's up to my knee already—Jerome bursts in. He's waving his arms to get my attention. Like his entrance went unnoticed. He follows his gyrations with a stage whisper that has people sticking their fingers in their ears. "Gotta see ya, Chief."

I put a ten on the counter and leave with my deputy. Outside I say, "What's up?"

"Not here. Too many people around."

A glance up and down the block shows a total of five people. "In the office?"

He insists on driving and I cover the siren switch before he can activate it. The trip takes ten seconds and he slides into the parking spot. I'm sure he's seen some old movies where the cop executes a one-eighty turn and he's been practicing the maneuver.

He races inside and heads to my office.

"Hurry up, Archie. This is hot, hot, hot."

I control my excitement and sit down. He's got both hands on my desk and leans over.

I grit my teeth, knowing a chapter-long preamble is about to begin.

"I saw Eldon and he test fired the pistol. You know, the one we recovered from the scum-bag back there?"

"I seem to recall something like that, Jerome. Was this the one we came across yesterday?"

"We find one yesterday? I don't remember . . ."

Satire is not his strong suit. "Never mind. Go on."

"Well, like I said, El test fired that 22. It's got 6R rifling all right."

I refrain from stating we already knew that.

Jerome straightens up, a skunk eating stuff grin on his face. "Guess what?"

Oh no, Twenty questions.

"What?"

"Has to do with the slugs from Rupert."

"Jerome, unless you want to spend the next month patrolling WCB's dump, spill it."

"The lead from Rupert and Helen were 22 shorts. The lead from Fat and Fatter was 22 long rifles."

"I thought he initially said the slugs from all four bodies were the same."

"He really apologized for that, Boss. Said things were really confused, seems they were getting some gument certification. He's been busier than a three legged dog in a pickle factory."

"He said that?"

"Not exactly. I kinda dressed it up. Sounds better than some old cat on a roof, right?"

The implication of his revelation is two different guns were used. My, how the plot thickens. I decide to stir the pot a little more and head back to cell one.

Homer's back's against the wall. His plaster-like logs are resting on his pulled up knees. "Afternoon, Homer. Ready for your flight back to LA?"

"Better than this hick town."

"You realize you'll be under our care for the next several hours."

"So?"

"So. I asked Dutch to come over and say good bye. He'll miss ya."

His face makes the white plaster casts look dingy. I start to leave, then as though I just thought of something, I wheel around.

"One other thing."

"Yeah?"

"Perhaps you remember my cousin squeezing your right hand? Recall how it felt as he pulverized the bones?"

Now his face is really colorless. I might need to put a tourniquet on his neck to save whatever blood is left in his head.

"Couple weeks ago, my cousin hugged me. Near broke my ribs. And he's my blood relation."

"So?"

"So, I can tell Dutch he only has a little time left to wish you good luck. Or I can forget calling him."

'Dog looks like he's hoping in the next five minutes NASA will announce they have a functioning moon base and need volunteers to man it. Especially West Coast folks. Anything would be preferable to spending another second in Dutch's embrace.

I give him another micro-second to think over my offer. "All I need is a couple little ol' names."

Sweat forms on his forehead. He'd probably like to wipe it away. If I were he, I'd end up with a concussion as my arm slammed into my skull.

"Who?"

"The two guys that came after Fat and Fatter."

"Only one left.'

My raised eyebrows ask the question.

"One was next to that guy that caught all the AK's slugs. Actually not all of them. Catch my drift?"

"Loud and clear. The other guy?"

Homer starts to laugh. "Man, you sure are one dumb cop, ain'tcha?"

"Hey. Better people than you have already noticed the same thing. So who's the other guy?"

He waves me closer with a nod of his head. After he tells me, I'm tempted to beat myself with one on his arms.

After I tear it off.

Chapter 69

What an ass I've been. Trying to be Mr. Goodypants. Showing the world how compassionate I am. Fool, more like
it. I passed off Ruth Ann's reaction to him as though she
didn't have the faintest idea of what was really going
on. Made me a little—hell, more that a little—pissed. She
should have realized I knew what I was doing. Sometimes
I could kick my ass for my superior, I-know-better-than-you
attitude.

I stuff my feeling and call Alex. "When's that plane from
LA arriving?"

"About eleven. They're flying into Bemidji. Their airport
can easily handle their jet. Why?"

"No reason. Just want to check the details. You're going
to accompany, 'Dog in Newberry's ambulance, right?"

"Right as rain, Chief. He'll be 'cuffed and shackled. Jerome's leading the way."

"Be sure you've got heavy duty ear protection."

Alex laughs as she hangs up. I'm on the phone to my buddy, the Chief of Duluth PD. Minutes later, he confirms what I suspected. No use tipping my hand until it's time.

I place the order for a partially-cooked pizza, then leave for our municipal liquor store for libations. Once home, I give the place a lick and a promise—I put my dirty clothes into the hamper. Maggie's fed, and I do the necessary paperwork for tomorrow.

One minute after seven, my front doorbell rings. This sends my attack cat upstairs so she can hide someplace. Where, I haven't the faintest idea. Heather's standing on the stoop, a six pack of beer in her hand.

"Hi, Archie." She holds the six-pack for me. Before I can take it, I'm enveloped in her arms. After breaking the lip-lock suction, I lead her to the kitchen.

As she looks around I say, "The pizza will take a few minutes to finish. Care for a beer?"

She nods and I fill two glasses.

"Can I get a tour of your place?"

"It's nothing like your house, but sure." We go from room to room, bypassing my office. Heather stops and tries to open the pocket doors.

"I keep that room locked. It's a long story. Let me show you my library." I can tell she wants the locked door story, but I ignore her inquisitive eyes and lead the way to the library.

"This is one grand room. Do you ever eat in here?"

"On occasion."

"What better place than here to have pizza? Would you build a fire and we can eat by its light."

Being a certified campfire constructor, a three flamer no less, I gather newspaper, kindling, and a few logs. After three failed attempts to start anything but paper, I resort to the certified constructors' closely guarded secret: I dose the kindling with charcoal starter. As soon as I remember to open the flue, most of the smoke flows up the chimney.

The oven timer buzzes and I stumble about getting the coffee table ready for our sumptuous one course supper. I'm figuring I can ply her with anchovies and beer to overcome her inhibitions as I explain the reason she's here.

Twenty minutes later, only a few crumbs of the pie are left and we're polishing off the last of the six-pack. We're also on the floor in front of the fire. Heather is on her right side playing some kind of game on my chest. Whatever it's named, the rules apparently call for her to unbutton my shirt and run her fingers through my chest hair. Hell, being unattached I decide to join in this marvelous past time.

I'm at a disadvantage though, Heather doesn't have any hair on her chest. Actually, it's a relief she doesn't. Because I enjoy what I'm playing with much more than winding threads of protein around my fingers. She, on the other hand, enjoys entangling her fingers. What a fortunate arrangement.

An hour later, I discover where Maggie goes to hide: under my bed.

Chapter 70

The following morning I awake to find my bed empty of female companionship, unless you count Maggie. She's staring me in the eye as though I've made a terrible mistake. Little does she know. I'm betting she's really upset over all the racket that occurred during the night. She's used to sleeping *on* my bed, not under it.

The sound of rattling pots and pans filters its way upstairs. I make a quick trip to the bathroom, splash some cold water on my face. It helps waken me; that and thoughts of what might follow. I slip on a T-shirt and a pair of shorts. On my way downstairs I resolve to tell Heather what I have up my sleeve. For some reason I never got around to explaining my plan last night.

"Mornin', Heather. My, you look alluring."

She's dressed in one of my shirts and a pair of socks. Maybe I should tell she forgot to button the shirt.

Nah.

She embraces me and whispers, "Breakfast, then a shower?"

Good thing she's holding me close or my rapidly dissolving legs would collapse. "Absolutely."

She squeezes me and returns to the pan of bacon and eggs.

The toaster spits out a set of nicely browned slices. As we sit down to eat, I figure I better tell her about the plan. Otherwise the morning will somehow slip away.

Between bites I start. "Heather, my dear, I've come up with a plan to get the councilmen back to town. Since it involves you . . ."

She stops eating. A fork halfway to her lovely mouth. Something flashes across her face, then she smiles. "Let me guess."

"You'll never come close. But go ahead. Try to decipher my subtle yet elegant plan."

"Archie, you're so transparent. I have a harder time seeing through that window than you."

"Hah. That's because it needs washing."

She looks at me like you might look at a kid who denies he's been playing in the mud. Even though he's covered from head to toe.

"I saw Roy Fritz in town the other day. He didn't recognize me and was asking if I knew Ruth Ann Boyer. I told him she wasn't around and he headed towards your office. It involves his *talent*, right?"

"Gotcha. It's hardly a talent, as you put it. He has a *skill*."

Even quicker than some super hero, my right hand streaks out to catch a chunk of jelly coated toast. A split second after it impales itself on my forehead.

Grinning, Heather asks for the details.

"Roy'll hack into the Sixth Bank of the Bahamas and transfer their money to Clover Bottom. There'll be a trail as wide as Second Street for them to follow. You will, of course, immediately transfer it to another account. They won't be able to find it and our erstwhile councilmen will come home after their stash."

I see Heather's digesting my plan. No doubt she sees how complex, urbane, and epicurean the twists and turns are.

"You know, someone could end up in jail."

I tap my knife on my plate. "Exactly. The councilmen, for starters."

"Let me think about this, Archie."

"Please do. I want this to be over in the next few days. Now, about that shower."

An hour later, Heather heads to the bank. I need to re-re-charge my batteries so I brew a pot of coffee, using the janitor's formula, and retire to my office. It takes me a minute or two to concentrate after this morning's romps. The key is not on the second row, first hook on the right. It's in the middle of the third row.

Just the other day I was saying to Heather how marvelous it'd be doing *it* with her. Now I'm not so sure. But, maybe I'm being overly suspicious. Maybe I missed the hook when I last hung up the key. Then, when I unlock the French doors, the picture of you-know-who I keep on my desk, gives me another pause. It's almost on the edge of the desk. I always keep it further in.

I stare at the image. Those green eyes, looking so intently at the camera, seem to be peering into me. I remind myself I shouldn't be feeling this way—dirty. I just took a very long hot shower. Two sips of coffee and I'm re-thinking the past several hours. Two more sips and it dawns on me. Something's wrong with my office. Saturday's paper, the issue I haven't taken the time to read because it's mostly about *her*, is lying face down, folded in half. I'd bet—well, I don't know what, but something dear to me—I left it there rolled up. As delivered.

Another thing, I can open the middle drawer. Funny about that. It's supposed to be locked. Adding to the mystery is one of Maggie's toy mice. Her favorite pink one. It's in the corner, close to the fireplace. How did it get in here? I didn't bring it. After all it's covered in dried cat spit.

My initial fears are confirmed when I dig out my leather bound notebook. The one where I keep my musings. Once again, something's amiss. A few pages back, I jotted down the sightings of strange nighttime activity across the lake. The activity that eventually led to the arrests and deaths of Fat and Fatter; it's got a small tear.

Now I know without a doubt. *I'm* the one who's been used. I fire up my computer and send a message to Roy.

'Immediately, repeat, immediately freeze accounts. Make access by subjects impossible. Then execute plan.'

Chapter 71

What an absolute idiot I've been. Ruth Ann dumps me and I can't wait to get into Heather's pants. I ask myself, "Are you so stupid to think she really wants you? You really think she carries a torch for you?"

Unfortunately, the answer is yes. I am that stupid. Then I compound my stupidity by giving away my plan to bring the councilmen to justice. Although I can't prove it, all the handwriting's on the wall. Fat and Fatter testing the soil in the park. Why? To determine the suitability for construction. Her own admission there'd be a fortune to be made if the town charter allowed housing developments. Then her interest in Florida housing. Homer's claim some guy from Florida called him to arrange the hit on Rupert and Helen. All her books on making it big in real estate. Add to the list, all the strange events in my home office.

Two hours before the plane arrives for 'Dog. Plenty of time. I dress in my uniform and head to town. On the way

I call Alex. "The plans have changed. Newbury can drive Homer by himself. You and I are making a short trip."

Once I pick her up, I explain the plan.

"Heather? Heather Maple? I can't believe it. Are you sure, boss?"

"If I was one hundred percent sure, she'd be in jail right now. I know the Bemidji office of the BCA office has tracking devices. We're going to borrow one."

Alex's voice rises. "You want the Bureau of Criminal Apprehension to loan us a device so we can . . .what?"

"I want to know if Heather's planning on making a quick trip out of the country. We can't follow her—not enough of us and she'd spot us in a minute. We're going to keep the responder with one of us twenty-four seven. She drives around, one of us will follow. She leaves town, we arrest her."

After I explain to the BCA superintendent, he loans us a unit. Neat, small, compact. All I have to do is attach the magnetic thingy to her car and we're in business. Since it took longer than I expected, Alex and I drive directly to the airport.

The reason it took longer is we had to have a cup of coffee and a Danish before we got down to biness—the folks at the BCA sure have Minnesota Biness Etiquette down pat—even I learned a point or two. I really like the sweet roll touch.

While waiting for the plane, I bone up on *The Use of Tracking Devices*. A fine pamphlet produced by the manufacturer. It contains such gems as:

Point One. Never attempt to attach the Acme unit to a plastic bumper.

This had to be prepared by a committee of idiots. Further down another item catches my eye. I'm sure glad I familiarized myself with this award winning piece of literature.

Point Ten. Install a NiCad,—nickel cadmium—battery prior to use.

I give up reading more when I'm reminded, *For best results, turn the unit on.*

We hear an approaching jet. Since there's a slight wind from the east, it's approaching from the west. How convenient, as LA is also west of here. When it descends over County 9, I see it's one of those small business jets. It flares and touches down. It taxies to the right hand side of the terminal and the engines wind down. I gather they aren't going to take a sightseeing tour of Lake Bemidji and the famous statue of Paul Bunyon and his Blue Ox, Babe.

Jerome and Newberry arrive. I grimace, as they left the sirens on until the last second. Most of the patrons inside the small terminal, to say nothing about the entire residents of town, spill out, trying to see what's going on.

A contingent of Bemidji cops are on hand. I'm betting the whole scene will become one great talking point for the better part of the year. Especially since three uniformed LA cops depart the plane and are greeted by four of Bemidji's finest.

Jerome looks to be all puffed up, leads Newberry and the gurney holding Homer. His encrusted arms straight up in the air, looking like some prone zombie, to the open chain-link fence gate.

I nod to Alex and she leaves to join the parade. She was the one who made all the LA contacts and should be the one who takes whatever credit will be handed out. I see handshakes all around and within ten minutes 'Dog's escorted into the plane. Moments later, the engines wind-up and the jet taxies to the end of the runway.

Soon it's a speck in the sky as it wends westward. One of our problems is now LA's headache.

I spend a few minutes with my crew after dismissing Newbury, explaining the tracker. The awesome responsibility of attaching it to Heather's car falls on me, since I've read the manual.

On the drive back to WCB, Alex asks me how I'm going to accomplish my task.

"Simple. After I get back to the station, you're going to wander into the bank, engage her in small talk—making sure she doesn't decide to check outside—while I slash a tire. I'll inform her she's got a flat tire. Being a close friend, I'll volunteer to fix it."

"So, how close are the two of you, now that *things* have changed?"

"I never kiss and tell, Alex."

"Even so, word gets around."

Just what I was hoping.

The plan goes like clockwork. I only have to wait twenty minutes, talking to the half of WCB's population, before I can clandestinely approach her car. I bend down to work a knife into a side wall when another guy comes up.

"Looks like Ms. Maple gots a flat, Chief."

I look closer at her left rear tire. "Looks fine to me," I respond.

"That's not her car. Her's two down. The Toyota. That's a Dodge. Her right front's flat."

I grin. I know for a fact neither side of her front is flat. I pass on making the correction. "There's a cigarette butt here. Can't have trash cluttering up the bank parking lot. Right?"

"We pay the Chief of Police to pick up trash? Guess we gots too many cops, then."

"In case you missed it, my dear fellow, our motto is 'To *Serve* and Protect'."

Having successfully maneuvered around that situation, I excuse myself and enter the bank. Heather spots me and smiles. Poor gal, she has no idea. When she finishes with her customer, I step up. She reaches across the granite top and squeezes my hand. Before I can tell her about my discovery, she says, "How about a repeat at your place tonight?"

Chapter 72

Heather's offer throws me. I may be crass, but not to the point where I'd go for a romp in the hay, then spy on her. Although, come to think of it, that's exactly what *she* did. Actually, it might make my job easier. She could hardly flee the country while she's working me over in bed. On the other hand, my well-tuned skepticism rises to the top; she may have a plan to slip *me* some Rohypnol and then leave, after she puts a round in my head.

"That sounds super, but right now, I've got some bad news for you. One of your tires is flat. I spotted it walking through the lot."

"I know. You're the third guy that mentioned it. Someone from Louie's is coming over to change it."

Just dandy. Probably Dutch. He'll be able to lift her car by hand. "The least I can do, sweets, is change it myself. Call them and cancel. K?"

"I'll have to pay you," a long pause, "in some fashion." She says this and licks her lips. Like last night. My resolve is fading faster than the air went out of her tire.

"Let me fix the tire, then I'll check my schedule. We've been pretty busy today."

"I heard about the event at Bemidji."

She better be referring to the airport scene, not what Alex and I did at the BCA. "Yeah. You had to be there. At least one of our problems solved. Now, we law enforcement types can concentrate on Rupert and Helen."

I take her keys and start to leave. She calls out, "Let me know about later."

With her car jacked up, I attach the magnet to the frame—thankfully it's not plastic—and change the tire. I'm lowering the car when Dutch arrives in Louie's wrecker. Al's in the cab with my cuz.

No time like the present. Before Al can close his door, I have him cuffed. Dutch's head is moving like he's some giant bobble head. He obviously hasn't a clue.

"Watcha doin', cousin?"

"I'm arresting Al for attempted murder." I spout his Miranda rights and toss Heather's keys to Dutch.

"Give these to Heather. I'm takin' Al to jail."

A huge shadow falls over me as Dutch steps in my way. "Mind tellin' me why?"

I don't appreciate being threatened, especially by Dutch. "Yes I do mind telling you. Now excuse me."

My cousin has never seen me like this and apparently decides he better back down. Cousin or not, he'd be in big trouble if he tried to stop me. Dutch may be short on 'book learnin', but he understands street smarts. I march Al to my cruiser and put him in the back seat. "I told you once, Al, never give me a reason to put you back here."

A crowd has gathered. Apparently they've never seen an arrest before.

I ignore the myriad questions and drive off. In the station, I leave the booking procedure to Alex and call Duluth. I figure they should have first crack at him as they've got a better case than WCB. I'll lay out the case against Al for Uncle Jerry and my city attorney cousin, Manny. Probably tomorrow.

I'm about to call my Duluth bud, when *she* walks in.

Chapter 73

"Good morning, Chief Schultz. I heard about the arrest and, as editor of the *Clover Bottom Clarion*, I'd like to get the details for the paper. In case you've forgotten, I'm Ruth Ann Boyer, editor and reporter."

"I thought you looked familiar. It is an on-going investigation, Ms ah, Boyer, is it?"

I'm fixed with a stare that curls my hair.

"I see you've done a lot of research via the cop shows on TV. Have you been practicing that line for some time now?"

I stare back at her. I'm sure mine is way more devastating.

"I believe the gentleman you just arrested committed a crime in Duluth recently. One against a helpless female patient. One who suffered a grievous injury. Yet he was turned loose on the public to continue his crime wave. I believe some cop from this area was the party who, allegedly, interfered with the course of criminal justice. Care to comment on that, boy?"

"Well, *girl*, if I believed the *Clarion* was good for something other than wrapping up fish guts, I'd love to comment. However, since the editorial staff has such a low believability ratio, I decline to answer."

Ms Boyer's face is taking on the color of her hair to the point it's hard to tell where her forehead stops and her hairline starts. Besides, the cap she's wearing clashes with her coloring. Never mind it's a Minnesota Viking hat. Purple and gold don't go well with her auburn hair. At least in my opinion.

"In that case, I'll just have to go with my story. You may find, if you can actually read, it may not paint a flattering picture of the WCB PD."

Damn! She's got me again. "Out of concern for your 'grievous' injury, I will condescend to look over your story and make the several corrections it no doubt needs."

She digs into her briefcase and flops a folder on my desk, spins an her heels, and stomps out of the station.

In bold type her article begins:

Arrest Made

Early Thursday afternoon, Mr. Aloysius Throckton, Jr. was apprehended in the Clover Bottom Bank parking lot. Initial indications are he will be charged with attempted murder.

Throckton was originally arrested in Duluth, Minnesota on the suspicion of the same charge. He allegedly tried to poison a female patient while she was being treated for burns. The patient was injured in a recent fire in downtown West Clover Bottom.

Throckton was released by the Duluth police into the custody of Chief Schultz.

At the time, it was believed Throckton had been coerced into the poisoning by a Los Angles gang.

(See side bar concerning the alleged leader of the gang and his arrest and subsequent deportation to LA.)

Initially, Throckton appeared to be on his way to a full rehab. Subsequent events proved this was an apparent error.

Another attack on the patient resulted in the arrest of the gang leader. Sources close to the investigation have stated Throckton was allegedly feeding information concerning the whereabouts of the intended victim. He was arrested and is waiting arraignment.

I see no errors in the story and, begrudgingly, think it's well written. I re-read her article and start to put it back in the folder when I spot a second, smaller sheet.

At first, I think it's blank. Then I flip it over. In Ruth Ann's fine script is a hand written addendum:

Dear Archie,

I'm an ass for leaving you. I accept it was a dumb, but mostly I became angry with you for bringing Throckton to town.

Can your forgive me?

If not, I never, ever want to speak to you again.

All my love,

Ruth Ann.

Ka-ching. Another dime.

Chapter 74

After reading Ruth Ann's article and apology, I'm feeling like a bum. I gave into Heather's wishes and was on the verge of having a repeat session. Now that Ruth Ann wants me back, I certainly can't go through with another pizza party. I call Heather and tell her something's come up in the case and I have to beg off.

"I hope this break, as you call it, is really important. Somehow I get the feeling you're actually brushing me off. After all, why buy the cow when the milk's free, huh? Gonna put another notch on your bedstead?"

She ends the conversation by slamming down the receiver. It takes a minute or two for the ringing in my left ear to subside.

Next, I call Ruth Ann.

"I have one correction to make in your article, Ms. Boyer. Care to discuss it over a pizza at my place?"

"Actually, Chief, I have other plans."

"Too bad. I guess I'll have to give my scoop to another reporter."

"Okay. Only if you promise it's worth my valuable time. I'll tell Brad Pitt I can't accept his invitation. He'll just have to return to LA."

An hour later, Ruth Ann's favorite—onion, sausage, pepperoni, olive—is finishing. The timer rings and we untangle on the library floor.

As soon as Ruth Ann showed up, in a sense of honesty, I told her about last night with Heather. I was about to explain my scoop but got distracted by her promise to erase any thoughts of the banker.

She was very convincing.

I grab two more beers, a fistful of napkins, and the pizza. We use a towel from the bathroom as a table cloth. For the next several minutes, we're too busy eating to speak. When we're done I take her hands and tell her how her real estate note got me thinking. I relay all the details about how her original clue concerning the councilman's deposit sparked the investigation.

It always pays to toss a few tidbits in the direction of the media. Like earlier, they do have the most welcome way of repaying the debt.

I finished with the tale of bugging Heather's car.

"So what you're telling me is that Heather is the brains behind all of this?"

"I don't think she's involved with Rupert and Helen's murders. I'll go into that later, but, as far as Fat and Fatter and the attacks on you, I'm as positive as I can be. Only one tiny, insignificant detail missing."

"And that might be?"

"Proof."

"Oh yeah, that's pretty minor all right. Going to use a rubber hose to get her to confess?"

"Actually, the way I see it is this. Roy's working on transferring the councilmen's money back here. Heather, because of my feeling a little sorry for myself, knows of the plan."

"What if she contacts them and tells them to move it?"

"If Roy was quick enough, it's frozen and they can't touch it."

"Archie, love. I'm confused. Maybe the pills are still affecting me, but what does she get out of this, anyway? Before you answer, how about a nice romantic fire?"

Strange request, but who am I to argue with a beautiful woman? In moments my campfire skills are in full display. This time I *start* by dosing the kindling with lighter fluid.

"In answer to your question, she gets the town's charter changed and starts a housing rush. And ends up with a bundle. The councilmen each get their million plus and everyone's happy."

"So where did the councilmen's money come from to start with?"

I notice how her voice is changing; getting lower and kind of panting. "There you go again. Looking for details."

Ruth Ann saddles up close and whispers in my ear. "Did I ever tell you that the combination of pizza and a nice fire have a strange effect on me?"

"First, I'm giving you this scoop that'll probably win you a Pulitzer, and then you tell me that pizza has some strange effect on you."

It is really hard to concentrate on anything when someone's nibbling your earlobe and running their hand up and down your leg. I put up with the distraction for several micro-seconds before I give in.

Chapter 75

A ringing, buzzing sound wakens me. Pulling the pillow over my head doesn't block the sound. Ruth Ann's elbow in my ribs followed by "Answer that" finally gets me moving. It can't be my phone, but the sound is demanding. Then it dawns on me. The tracking device. Heather's on the move.

"Gotta go, babes, Heather's in her car."

It only takes a second to get some clothes on. I'll tie my laces some other time. Still buttoning my shirt, I hop into my cruiser, set the receiver's display on the dash, and leave my warm bed and a warmer Ruth Ann behind.

The flashing dot indicator shows her progress out of town. She's about two miles away, driving at a reasonable speed. Once we leave WCB's city limits, I'm sure Heather's not going for a gallon of milk. I call Alex.

"Subject's on the move. Currently we're heading east on Highway 2. If she's got MSP airport on her mind, at this speed I expect we'll get there around 5."

"Need me to back you up?"

"Tell ya what. Call Northwest and see if she's got a reservation. She could be going anywhere. They should be able to search her name."

"What if she's not flying with them?"

"Have a cup of coffee and think about that, Alex."

I can imaging my deputy turning red.

"Oh. Right. Guess it's waking up in the middle of the night."

"Understand. If she has a reservation make them put a hold on it. Tell them there's a warrant out for her arrest."

"There is?"

"Will be."

I sign off and concentrate on driving. Wish I could ask Heather to pull in to the nearest all-night stop for a cup of coffee.

We reach the northern edge of Brainerd when my phone rings. I've got it mounted on the dash so I can drive and talk at the same time. Doing two things at once is a major accomplishment. I practiced this feat time and time again. Fortunately, I did it while driving in a farmer's pasture. The damage to his prize Holstein was fairy minor. The vet said her leg'd be good as gold in a month.

It's Alex. Her voice is still a little sleep slurred. "No Maple has a reservation. I called a couple other large airlines—American, Continental—no reservation for a Heather Maple either. Could be she used a different one."

"She'd need a fake ID as well. Let's hope she's not leaving the country. Thanks, Alex. Go back to bed."

I steer back from the left shoulder and continue following the bouncing ball.

Thank goodness the traffic's light. Heather and I are making a bee-line for the airport. She's not concerned about the speed limit and maintains a steady 70. The target's already in the parking lot when I arrive at MSP's main entrance. I spot her car on the first floor of the ramp and drive to the top level. Hopefully she won't cruise around and see my cruiser. Now I have to make a decision. Should I wander through the terminal to spot her, or wait here?

If she is using a fake ID, she could be checking in. Great! I'm sitting here and Ms Maple is on her way to some exotic land. What to do?

I gamble on entering. I'm not in uniform and have an old fishing hat in the trunk. I don it and pull the floppy brim down. I adopt a old-man shuffle and enter. A quick glance up and down the ticket counters and no one fitting her description is conducting business.

I make a slow halting circle around the upper level and head for a down escalator to the baggage claim. A nearby pillar shields me from the few people milling around. Leaning against the far wall is a long legged blonde. No doubt who it is, so I back away. I'm ninety-nine point nine percent sure who she's waiting for.

I shuffle my way upstairs. Once in the terminal, abandon all pretenses and sprint for my vehicle.

Twenty minutes later, the blip starts moving. A record time to get one's bags. Heather isn't scoping out the garage and drives directly to the exit. I wait a respectable time, five minutes, and leave as well. Back on the road heading north, I call poor Alex again and tell her to stake out Heather's place. I'm betting she and our three councilmen have taken the bait.

The first glimmers of dawn are breaking the eastern sky as we head home. We're an hour away from WCB when my cell rings.

"Hey, Archie. Just reporting in. I parked my cruiser a good half mile away from Heather's. I'm dressed in camo about a block away from her house, hiding in a nice patch of brush. I can watch her place with my bi-nocs. Say, what's that honking for?"

"Some idiot drifted across the lane. Nothing to worry about."

The rest of the trip is uneventful.

I make a stop at the office and quickly draw up an arrest warrant for Heather and the councilmen.

Before starting again, I call Alex. "They still in her house?"

"Far as I can tell."

"Good. Make your way back to your car and meet me in her driveway in ten. I gotta see my uncle and have him sign this warrant. They're going down."

Uncle Jerry was not the happiest person I've ever seen, but he signs. I dash off and meet up with Alex. We converge on Heather's. I tell Alex to cover the back. I march up to the front door. "Police! Open up!"

I hear people running around and moments later a single shot comes from the back. This is followed by Alex demanding, "On the ground."

Racing around her house, I see all four suspects flat on their faces. Alex has her ten-millimeter in a classic two fisted pose.

"Good work, deputy. Well, guys and gal. It's over. Alex, cuff two of them together while I cover."

Then I cuff Heather to Horace and we lead them to our cars. Minutes later, they're in separate cells. After reading them their rights, Alex begins booking.

Heather calls me to her cell and whispers she can really make it worth my while to let her go. "If you thought our evening was something, you ain't seen anything. I'll fuck your brains out and split a million with ya. Whatta ya say, stud muffin?"

"I always thought you, Horace Schmidt, Frank Klinestadt and Herb Van Pelter would look just lovely in orange jumpsuits."

She's spewing fake tears as I leave to call Jerome and tell him to make tracks for the station. He swaggers in, like the Barney we know and love, and nearly faints when he sees two-thirds of the cells occupied.

He finishes the booking process and Alex and I bogie to Heather's. We force the door and start searching the house. I'm betting the money Roy transferred back to Clover Bottom Bank is stashed somewhere. Heather was quicker than I figured in warning the colleagues about the sting. They had to have grabbed the first plane back to the States.

Alex and I put our heads together to guess where the money is stored. A million bucks, let alone three or four, are hard to put into a container the size of a bread box, no matter what size the denominations are.

It takes us the better part of two hours before I have an idea.

"Why not hide it in plain sight?"

My comical deputy opens a closet door and proclaims, "It's not hiding here."

"Ha, ha. Look at the living room pillows."

Bingo! Every one is carefully stuffed. We slit each one open and stack the bills on the kitchen table. When her pillows resemble flaccid Frisbees, we have a little over four mil. Alex retreats to the master bedroom, checks those pillows and hollers out, "Must be a million feathers here, Archie."

We use the pillow cases to load up the money. As I leave, I seal the front and rear doors.

Back in the station, I call Cousin Manny, the city attorney, and fill him in. It'll be in his hands now. Next, I call home and whisper sweet nothings to Ruth Ann.

"Come on down to the station and see what we caught."

"You really know how to get a gal excited, mister. See ya in five."

Tonight, I'll tell her my suspicions concerning Rupert and Helen.

Chapter 76

Ruth Ann bursts into the station like a newspaperwoman hot on a story. Which, of course, she is. She stays long enough to snap a few pics of the jail birds and hear the details of the arrest. I figure it's best not to mention Roy Fritz's involvement. I'm not sure his actions were legal, but then, neither were those of my prisoners. She gives me a kiss and dashes off to bring out a special edition. I'm guessing there'll be a steak diner in it for me. Providing I do the cooking.

Manny steps into my office and tells me all four will be arraigned first thing tomorrow. "No doubt they'll seek a change of venue, Archie. Jer is kinda sticky when it comes to things like a fair trial."

He's referring to Judge Jerry Schultz. There's no way an impartial jury can be found in West Clover Bottom.

"Okay with me. There is one little thing I should mention to you."

One thing none of my relatives likes is a surprise. I tell Manny about a hypothetical situation where a police officer arranges for a little computer hacking. He responds by saying he'll tell the judge about it when it seems appropriate. Say, in twenty years.

He leaves to take care of lawyer business and I bask in the glow of having solved the case of the missing councilmen. A tiny part of me is sorry Heather's involved, but I look on the bright side. Ruth Ann is back and well on her way to recovery. Best of all, she's been making noises about moving in. We'll cross that bridge later.

My revelry is interrupted by the ringing of the fax. Hoping it's from the BCA, I hurry out. The cover letter tells me it's a one pager.

My mood goes dark as I read it. It confirms what I suspected. It was bad enough to discover Heather's involvement, but this really depresses me. With the evidence in hand, there's no way I can wait till tonight to tell Ruth Ann about Jackie. I have to act now.

With a heavy heart, I climb the stairs.

Perhaps the look on my face telegraphs my mood. Jackie turns white. She lowers her head and starts crying.

I let her compose herself, then say, "I know all about it, Jackie."

Her crying turns into wretching sobs.

I hate this part of my job. It's one thing to pull over a speeder, but I've known Jackie all my life. I refuse to humiliate her any more. I take her arm and gently pull her up. The others in the office are dumbstruck as I guide her away from her desk and down the stairs. Once we're alone, I Merandize her and lead her to a cell.

My second call is to Manny this morning and I suggest he return to the station. Then a call to Ruth Ann to tell her I've made another arrest.

Meanwhile, I start booking Jackie. During the process she starts to explain. "I did everything for Rupert. Then when—"

"Stop, Jackie. Remember, anything you say can be used against you. Call a lawyer."

"I know my rights, but I have to speak. I did it, Archie."

"Please, Jackie. No more."

"No more what, cousin?"

Before I can answer, Jackie starts crying and tells Manny she killed both Rupert and, to use her words, "that bimbo, gold digging, slut wife of his."

To his credit, my uncle says he'll call a defense attorney in the Cities for her. "You need a lawyer, Jackie. Andy Flynn is a real good guy."

After I book her, I escort her back to her cell. "Care for some decent coffee?"

She nods and sits on the edge of the bunk, her head in her hands. I hurry out and brew a cup using the formula my hospital janitor friend gave me. I pour an extra large mug and take it back to her.

"Thanks, Archie." She takes two sips and immediately starts confessing again. I don't try to stop her; she needs to get it off her chest.

"After his wife died, I wished so hard he'd propose to me. After all, I was his wife in every aspect except in name. I mean in every aspect, Archie. He was so tender and loving. I was in heaven. I could have done so much more for him. I guess I didn't, or couldn't, see he was so vulnerable."

I sit beside her and she sets her cup down. She appears to be recalling memories. She has a wistful look on her face and her eyes are focused on the far wall. Perhaps she's seeing him in those tender moments.

Then abruptly, "A year after she died, he went to that mayors conference down in St. Paul. You know. The one the governor calls every year?"

I nod.

"He was a changed man after that week. He had me make reservations at a hotel nearly every weekend. He was seeing Miss Put-Out. How can a homely, nearly sixty year-old woman compete with a twenty-five year-old bimbo?"

I had no answer since I had a recent fling with a thirty-one year-old one myself.

"Then he started bringing her up here on weekends. He didn't want anyone to know, but I was the one who had to make all the travel arrangements for her. It near broke my heart."

I'm not the tough as nails cop I pretend to be, at least on occasion. Right now wasn't one of those times either. My heart goes out to her. Rupert used her in every which way and then dropped her like she was a tainted woman. Helen was eye-candy, no doubt. Yet Jackie's that comfortable pair of slippers. She's a warm fire in the middle of a winter storm. That marvelous novel you read on a quiet winter day. Someone obviously devoted to Rupert.

My impression of him as a man is lower then a bottom feeding carp.

"Could you warm this up, Archie?"

"Sure thing."

When I return she's still sitting on the edge of the bunk. Her eyes are closed. Her voice is strained as she says, "I slipped them that date rape drug stuff and used my pistol. I did it, Archie, and I'm not sorry one bit."

Jackie blows on her coffee, scratches her hair, and makes a coughing sound. She covers her mouth for a moment, then takes a long drink. She lays down, smoothes her jump suit, folds her hands across her chest and says, "I was the one who gave Ruth Ann the tip about the bank account. Now, it's time. Good bye, Archie."

Before I realize it, she stiffens and expels a long sigh. The mug falls to the floor and shatters. It takes me a moment to react. Then I realize when she scratched her scalp, she had reached for a hidden pill.

I touch her neck and then run out and make a call to Doc James.

His nurse answers and I say, "I need doc at the police station, immediately."

Chapter 77

It's hard to believe September is half over. Fishing's ended—since the town owns the lake, we control the season. An early end helps the *piscine* population recover.

A sunbeam bursts from behind a cloud and warms me. Across the lake, a patch of birch trees is showing fall colors. Their golden leaves glisten in another beam. They seem even more lustrous with a backdrop of verdant pines.

A contented sigh escapes and a smile crosses my face. Ruth Ann's also turned a leaf. The trauma of spring seems to have changed her from 'that snippy Ruth Ann Boyer' into a more serene, attentive woman. She's become so attentive, in fact, she's making even more noise about moving in. Already spending a lot of time here. I view this as good and bad. Good in that she's also becoming way more affectionate. Bad in that she wants to make a *few* changes in my décor.

My cell phone rings, disturbing the solitude of my lakeside dock. I put my iced tea down and answer. The ID tells me it's Gunner Olson, the new mayor of West Clover Bottom. He still operates his store and I can hear hardware noises in the background.

"Yes, Mayor, or am I talking to Gunner?"

"Funny, Archie. Just want to tell you the new council voted this morning to increase your budget. They feel you could use another deputy and improve some of your equipment. Gots ta thank Heather and the old council for the increase, I guess."

I know the town confiscated the four plus millions she and the former council took in bribes. I never expected the police department would share. "How much?"

"Half a mil."

"Thanks, Mayor."

I sign off and enjoy the thought of having three deputies. Means I get some time off. Not only that, I keep seeing travel brochures to Hawaii or the Caribbean Islands around the house. Now, with a larger staff, I won't have any excuses for not taking a winter vacation.

The scene before me is so inviting, I wish I could head over to my favorite spot and wet a line, but then I'd have to arrest myself for poaching. Instead, I let the September sun continue to warm me and think of poor Heather and boys sitting in a Minneapolis jail. Since federally regulated banks were used in their nefarious activities, the FBI took over the case. Rumor has it they're pushing for a minimum of twenty years in a federal prison. Probably get it. Heather may get life because of her involvement in the deaths of Bruce and Lenny.

That brings a smile to my face. The thought of people whom the town trusted, sitting in some penitentiary for twenty years or more, is justice served indeed. It also means I put to rest that nagging question of who started the fire at Betty's and why. The last day before Heather and her gang were hauled off to the Hennepin County jail in Minneapolis, I sweet talk her into explaining. I use the line that I knew who started the fire, just want to know why. At first she balks. I mentally cross my fingers and tell her a little white lie.

"I'm taking Dutch over to Duluth to have a heart-to-heart with Al. Then I'll use it against you at your trial. Or, I can say you were very cooperative."

A flight of blue-wing teal zip by going their usual five hundred miles an hour.

Heather breaks down and says, "Yeah, Al did it all right. I put him up to it. Believe it or not, Archie, I really care for you. I thought if Ruth Ann was disfigured, you'd drop her and I'd finally get my chance.

"The night you came over to see the bank records and I went into the bathroom? I called him to get going. Said you were here and would be 'busy.' He hid in Betty's back room. When she was at the other end of the counter, he flipped a lit match into the French fry oil. Then a glass of water."

Ah, I think, that was the hand Ruth Ann thought she saw.

Heather looked at me, pleading her case with those eyes of hers. For an instant, I almost felt sorry for her. A fleeting instant.

"I guess you know the rest. I figured little Ruth Ann'd be so startled, the grease would end up all over her face. Little did I know she could react so fast. I guess she ducked her head and it caught her hair on fire."

What with Ruth Ann's psychological effects still lingering, it'll be a long, long time before I can tell her the story.

My reverie is broken by the sound of a car door slamming. Ruth Ann's home. I hear her clipping down the stairs to the dock .

"I see you got Rupert's truck."

This brings another smile to my face. The last puzzle in all of this was the whereabouts of the mayor's '65 Chevy pickup.

I turn to Ruth Ann. "I couldn't figure out where his vehicle was. I knew from the start it was a waste of time to drag the lake, but it had to be done."

"So what led you to its discovery?"

"Jackie's death bed confession."

"She tell you?"

"Nope. Used my power of reasoning to figure it out."

"I don't follow."

"When she shot them, I couldn't see her carrying Rupert, so she had to get him to the truck by subterfuge. After she slipped them the Rohypnol, they were like lambs she could lead to the slaughter. I suspect, since she made all the arrangements, she convinced Rupert to drive her back to City Hall because she forgot their tickets."

"Why didn't he use his car?"

"She let the air out of a tire, so he had to take the pickup. He walks by the truck, and somehow, Jackie convinced him to rest on the tailgate he pops him with her derringer. She leads Helen outside and pops her. With Helen being so light, Jackie has no problem getting her into the truck."

"Now I get it. She drives them to the pier and deposits them in the lake."

I look down at Ruth Ann with my patented superior look. "Then she drives the pickup to her place and hides it in the old barn. Effectively hiding it in plain sight."

"How very clever of you."

"Apparently his kids thought so as well. They gave me first dibs on it."

"One thing I don't understand. How did Jackie get the poison? Didn't you search her after her arrest?"

"Kinda. When I escorted her to the jail, she took her purse. I swear if you women were caught in a fire and had to choose between getting dressed or taking your purse, the purse wins hands-down. I looked in it, of course, but I was looking for a weapon. All I saw was a ton of makeup stuff. She had to have the pill in one of the makeup thingies and hid it in her hair. At least that's what I think happened. "

"Poor Jackie. I feel sorry for her, regardless of what she did. In my book, Rupert was nothing more than a low-life scoundrel."

She slides closer, puts her arms around my neck, and nibbles on my right ear lobe. She obviously has licentious plans for me this afternoon.

"Say, mister crime-solver, let's go up to the house."

"Gee, honey. I've got a headache."

"Get off your lazy tush or I'll never speak to you again."

Ka-ching, another dime.

About the author

Paul gave up his chemistry set six years ago, to take up a computer and begin a career in writing. The switch from including all the minute details required in various reports to writing fiction took some time. His technical background helped enormously though. Asking "what if" he mixed this with that eventually led to nine patents. Now, "what if" leads the reader down the twisting paths of fiendish antagonists.

He's currently working on his next novel, a thriller involving, what else, a chemist and his startling discovery.

He and his wife live in suburban St. Louis with three obedient and extremely well behaved cats.

Visit his website at www.authorpaulschmit.com

E-mail Paul at authorpaulschmit@gmail.com

Follow his blog at www.aquestforpublication.blogspot.com